THEIR HAUNTED HEARTS

BOOKS BY D.K. HOOD

DETECTIVES KANE AND ALTON PREQUELS
Lose Your Breath
Don't Look Back

DETECTIVES KANE AND ALTON SERIES
Don't Tell a Soul
Bring Me Flowers
Follow Me Home
The Crying Season
Where Angels Fear
Whisper in the Night
Break the Silence
Her Broken Wings
Her Shallow Grave
Promises in the Dark
Be Mine Forever
Cross My Heart
Fallen Angel
Pray for Mercy
Kiss Her Goodnight
Her Bleeding Heart
Chase Her Shadow
Now You See Me
Their Wicked Games

Where Hidden Souls Lie
A Song for the Dead
Eyes Tight Shut
Their Frozen Bones
Tears on Her Grave
Fear for Her Life
Good Girls Don't Cry

DETECTIVE BETH KATZ SERIES
Wildflower Girls
Shadow Angels
Dark Hearts
Forgotten Girls

PSYCHOLOGICAL THRILLERS
The Liar I Married

D.K. HOOD
THEIR HAUNTED HEARTS

bookouture

Published by Bookouture in 2025

An imprint of Storyfire Ltd.
Carmelite House
50 Victoria Embankment
London EC4Y 0DZ

www.bookouture.com

The authorised representative in the EEA is Hachette Ireland
8 Castlecourt Centre
Dublin 15 D15 XTP3
Ireland
(email: info@hbgi.ie)

Copyright © D.K. Hood, 2025

D.K. Hood has asserted her right to be identified as the author of this work.

All rights reserved. No part of this publication may be reproduced, stored in any retrieval system, or transmitted, in any form or by any means, electronic, mechanical, photocopying, recording or otherwise, without the prior written permission of the publishers.

ISBN: 978-1-83618-744-8
eBook ISBN: 978-1-83618-743-1

This book is a work of fiction. Names, characters, businesses, organizations, places and events other than those clearly in the public domain, are either the product of the author's imagination or are used fictitiously. Any resemblance to actual persons, living or dead, events or locales is entirely coincidental.

To the members of the D.K. Hood Readers' Facebook Group, for your support and encouragement.

PROLOGUE

THE WEEK BEFORE HALLOWEEN

Sunday

Never trust a stranger. Darlene Travis' mom's voice echoed inside her head like a good fairy whispering in her ear. The Triple Z Roadhouse, with its tempting smell of hot coffee and fries, had lured her inside. After she'd ducked under a garland of grinning jack-o'-lanterns and sidestepped a laughing skeleton in a cowboy hat waving a toy pistol, she'd headed for the counter. Walking slap-bang into trouble in a busy diner was the last thing she'd imagined might happen. She stared at the man across the Formica-topped table, stained with fifty years of coffee rings, and tried to get comfortable on the sticky plastic-covered seats. When four rowdy ranch hands had grabbed at her, insisting she party with them, the Good Samaritan had stepped in to help her. She'd expected him to leave but he hadn't. Why was he being so nice to her? Could she trust him?

The size of the man had intimidated the cowboys, but it wasn't only that. His face held an expression of menace that would stop anyone in their tracks. Wearing a Stetson down over his eyes, and a leather jacket stretched over an impressively wide chest, his presence would be enough to make most troublemakers wary, but she'd glimpsed the gun in a shoulder holster he'd flashed at them. The men had backed down, laughing and holding up their hands in mock surrender. She'd sat where he indicated, grateful but fully aware of his intimidating presence. She glanced up at him. "So much for grabbing a quick snack. Is everyone in this town so nasty?"

"Nope." He loomed over her. "Most are good guys like me. I'll grab some food. I'm hungry. What can I get you?"

Swallowing the gnawing in her stomach, she shook her head. "Just coffee. I'm short of cash right now."

"I guessed as much." He strode away.

Stuck in a "do I go or do I stay?" situation, she stared out of the window at the approaching darkness and her stomach dropped in dismay. With nowhere to go and no cash in her pocket, staying the night in the diner had quickly become her only option.

"You look like a lost puppy." The stranger smiled and unloaded their meals from a tray and then slid into the booth opposite her. "Eat something. It will make you feel better. How come you're in Black Rock Falls with only a few dollars in your purse?"

Starving, Darlene bit back a groan at the tempting aroma of burgers and fries he pushed toward her. Her fingers trembled as she reached for a fry. "I have a job interview on Monday in Blackwater. I took the bus but ended up in the wrong place and used all my spare cash to get to Butte. After that, I got a ride with a trucker but he turned around here after dropping his deliveries, so he couldn't take me any farther."

"Where were you planning on staying? You can't stay here all night. It's not safe." His gaze searched her face as he pushed a cup of steaming coffee toward her.

That was her only plan. Darlene's cheeks grew hot. "I've added my name to the board. I'll grab a ride when someone stops on the way to Blackwater."

"Then what?" He nibbled on his fries. "You have the interview and you get the job—or not—then where do you intend to stay? You'll need to pay for a motel room and you have zip."

This had been a problem she'd considered. The temperature had dropped by the hour and she couldn't sleep outside. She looked at him. "I'll be okay. They won't throw me out of here. If I get the job or not, I'll find a shelter or someplace I can work for a bed. There are ranches all over and stables that need workers. I'll earn enough to get a place of my own eventually."

"What about your folks? Won't they be worried about you?" His large hands wrapped around his cup. "Maybe they will deposit some cash into your account to help you?"

Darlene tossed her hair over one shoulder, recalling the argument she'd had with her parents. Her dad had cut up her credit card for overspending. They'd threatened to throw her out and she'd pushed a few things into a backpack and gone to a local diner. There she'd found the server job in the newspaper, called and made an appointment. Within the hour she'd been on the bus to nowhere. "That's not an option, I'm afraid. I'm on my own."

"I have a place a few miles away." He indicated over one shoulder with his thumb. "You're welcome to use my spare room. Have a good night's sleep, take a shower, and I'll drive you to Blackwater in the morning."

Darlene stared at him, the burger halfway to her mouth. *Here it comes.* This man wanted her body as payment for his help. Buying her a burger was one thing, but going with him was something completely different and she wasn't stupid. "You've been very kind but I don't know you."

"Ha! That's a great answer. If I had a daughter, I'd expect

her to say that. Your parents taught you well." He placed his hands on the table and stood. "I'll leave you to it then. I was only offering a place to stay for your own safety. I didn't want anything in return. I live with my two sisters and they'd have watched over you." He indicated to the four cowboys making loud comments to the female server. "Just watch out for those guys."

Swallowing hard, Darlene glanced at the men and then back at the Good Samaritan. He was dressed well in good clothes, and when he dropped the stern expression, he had a very nice smile. "Maybe you should stay and finish your burger. They might leave soon."

"Guys like them will be back and forth all night." He sat slowly and smiled at her. "I'm the lesser of two evils. I promise, cross my heart, I won't disturb your sleep." He crossed his chest.

Her mother's voice was screaming in her ear. *Don't trust him.* Her concern must have registered on her face. He smiled again, pulled a Glock 22 from a shoulder holster and placed it on the table. Suddenly afraid, she went to rise but he made a calming gesture with his hand.

"I'm not threatening you." He chuckled. "I assume you know how to use one of these? Just point and squeeze—no safety. Eat your meal and let's get out of here. Take the gun. You can keep it all night but there's a lock on the bedroom door." He held up both hands. "Look, I don't have an ulterior motive. I don't like seeing people in trouble and you remind me of my little sister. I'd hate to see her like this. Make me feel better by helping you."

Darlene chewed the burger and then sipped her coffee. She shuddered at the taste. "Why is roadhouse coffee so bad?"

"I'll brew you a pot for breakfast and my older sister makes great pancakes." He checked his watch. "I gotta go. You coming or planning on sitting here all night?" He pulled his hat down over his eyes and headed for the door.

Pushing away the screaming voice in her mind, Darlene stood, pulled her hoodie over her head, pushed in her hair, and picked up the weapon. It was heavy in her hand but still warm from his body heat. She hesitated for a few seconds, swallowed down the coffee, and then followed him out to his truck. When he opened the door for her, she thanked him and slid inside, dropping her backpack into the floor well between her feet. The inside was immaculate and had a hint of masculine cologne. "I appreciate your help."

"The pleasure is all mine." He started the engine. "It's not far."

They drove along the highway saying nothing. Thick forest surrounded all sides of her. After traveling for about twenty minutes along the highway, her heart pounded when he took a dirt road. "You live down here? It's pitch black."

"Uh-huh." He swung her a gaze. "Most ranches are down roads like this. This is Black Rock Falls. It's not a city. Are you a city girl, Darlene?"

Nodding, although she could hardly see him inside the dark cab, she turned to him. "Yeah." She yawned as exhaustion gripped her with ferocity and she fought to keep her eyes open. Her lids closed and she became too tired to open them. When her head banged against the window, she didn't have the strength to lift it away. Her limbs grew heavy and the Glock slid from her fingers. She forced her eyes open a slit. Beside her, the man moved in and out of focus. Something was terribly wrong. He'd drugged her coffee. Fear gripped her and she forced her mouth to form words. "What's happening to me?"

"This is the easy way, Darlene." He flashed her a grin, his white teeth showing in the moonlight. "You should thank me. In the morning you'll be free."

Her tongue stuck to the roof of her mouth and her head lolled back and forth. "Free? What do you mean?"

"They all say that. I know you came a long way to find me."

The man chuckled as the truck bumped along the uneven road. "The thing is, Darlene, I know exactly what you are. I see you're surprised. Don't be. I've been hunting down your kind for a very long time. This time, the game is going to be played my way, and before the sun sets tomorrow, you're going to die."

ONE

Monday

Bang! Bang! Bang!

The sound of glass shattering, feet running, and people's terrified screams greeted Sheriff Jenna Alton as she followed her deputy and husband, Dave Kane, from the sheriff's department. She tightened the straps on her liquid Kevlar vest, reached for her weapon, and hurried after him. Chaos greeted her and she reached for her phone to call Chief Deputy Zac Rio. "Rio, shots fired on Main. We're going in. Number of shooters unknown at this time. Where are you?"

"We're approximately seven minutes from town." The engine of Rio's department SUV roared as he accelerated. Sirens blared. *"We're coming in hot."*

Jenna searched the sidewalk ahead as Kane vanished into the shadows between an array of Halloween displays. As an ex-Special Forces sniper, he could move around practically unseen, which for a six-five, one-hundred-and-seventy-pound fighting machine was remarkable. "I want you both geared up. We need you both here, yesterday."

"*Yes, ma'am.*" Rio disconnected.

On Main, gunshots ricocheted from buildings, shattering the windows of vehicles angle-parked nose-in alongside the storefronts, setting off a cacophony of car alarms. Macabre motion-activated Halloween automatons lining the sidewalk cackled and moaned, adding to the noise. Vehicles frantically reversed or drove into side streets in an effort to get away from the madness. Jenna glimpsed a man dressed all in black waving a Glock 22 and wondered why one of the usually armed townsfolk hadn't put a bullet in him already. The man, his long greasy hair flowing past his shoulders, wore a long coat hanging open to display two shoulder holsters. He meandered along the center of the blacktop, weaving slightly and taking potshots at random. He held his weapon in one hand and dangled a bottle loosely in the other. His disjointed ramblings and hysterical laughter set Jenna's nerves on edge. She pressed her com. "Dave, can you see him?"

"*Oh, yeah.*" Kane's voice came over the noise of a car alarm close by. "*Take cover. I can handle him.*"

Knowing what Kane was capable of doing to someone firing down on him, she sucked in a breath. "He's drunk by the look of things. He might be having a midlife crisis or something."

"*Why don't you just tell me not to kill him, Jenna?*" Kane chuckled. "*I take orders real well. He's raving on about ghouls and vampires. Maybe Halloween triggered a PTSD episode or maybe he's just batshit crazy. Either way, we're gonna find out. Take cover. I don't want to turn around and find my wife bleeding out.*"

An uneasy feeling made Jenna's breakfast form into a solid lump. Watching Kane risk his life was never easy, and if he died here today, she would have never told him she'd discovered his real and very secret name. The implications of knowing it held a great risk and one she understood would mean her beloved husband would be whisked away never to be seen again. She'd wanted to know his name for years, and overhearing a conversation Kane had with her baby son had thrown her into a quandary. Should she tell him or take the secret to her grave? At the time, she'd chosen to keep the secret and now, fifteen months later, the temptation still lingered. The problem was that Kane would never risk her and the children's lives to an assassin who would use them to get to him and collect the massive bounty on his head. He'd tell Wolfe, who was his handler and also Black Rock Falls' medical examiner. When that happened, the government would swallow them up and relocate them. She'd not only lose Kane, she'd lose Wolfe and his entire family. Even Wolfe didn't know Kane's real name but would go with him to wherever in the world they'd be safe. She'd be left behind, relocated, and need to start again, alone with two young boys. She shook her head. *Concentrate. Don't even think about it. Stay focused.*

The breeze brushed her face, bringing with it the smell of gunpowder mingled with the fresh aroma of coffee and baking from Aunt Betty's Café. Jenna slid into an alleyway and peered around the solid redbrick wall just as Kane stepped out into the middle of the road. Her heart raced as she watched him, moving easily, hands relaxed at his sides as if he confronted a drunken gunman every day. He had no fear of dying and that scared the life out of her. She held her M18 pistol in two hands and aimed. All she could do was have his back.

Sheer terror rushed over her when the shooter finished the dregs in the bottle and then dropped it to the blacktop to draw a second gun. Without a care in the world, he fired haphazardly in all directions and then noticed Kane walking toward him along the centerline. Wearing a Kevlar vest with SHERIFF emblazoned across the front in iridescent yellow, Kane was hard to miss, but the man kept shooting and bullets slammed into parked vehicles and pinged off buildings.

"You're lucky I'm in a good mood." Kane kept walking

toward him. "Sheriff's department. Why don't you put your weapons down and I'll go easy on you?"

"You need to keep them away from town." The man waved his guns toward the Halloween displays. "All that attracts them and makes it easy for them to hide in plain sight. No one can see them until it's too late."

"Who are you talking about?" Kane stopped walking and stared at the man. "Who is hiding in plain sight?"

"It's Halloween, man. You all believe it's just a joke but it's not. The gates of hell open and ghosts come back for revenge." He wiped one arm across his mouth and then aimed his guns at Kane. "You must be one of them. They look like you and me in the daylight but at night they change and will try and kill us. I've seen them."

"Put down your weapons. Now!" Kane's eyes narrowed. "Trust me. If you lived here in town, you'd know not to mess with me. Do as I say or I'll hurt you."

The man squeezed the triggers. Bullets whizzed past Kane, and Jenna held her breath. In a split second, Kane had drawn his pistol. Two shots rang out and the man howled like a wounded dog, dropped his weapons, and fell to his knees. Jenna ran along the sidewalk, reaching Kane as he kicked away the pistols, rolled the man on his face, and secured his wrists with zip ties. She stared down at the holes in the man's coat just below the shoulder on each arm. Blood oozed over the material but it wasn't gushing. "That was close."

"Nah." Kane smiled at her. "He might have fluked it and hit my vest, but the chances of a headshot were minimal. He's just an idiot swimming in cheap bourbon. He's not hurt bad; I just nicked him, is all." He dragged the man to his feet. "What's your name?"

"Ow, that hurts. You shot me!" The man pulled a sad face. "Ask anyone. I was protecting you all from the night creatures."

"It's just a scratch and a Band-Aid will fix it." Kane glared at him. "Name?"

"The Prince of Darkness." The man gave him a yellow-stained grin and the smell of alcohol filled the air. "Take me to your leader."

"She's right here." Kane spun him around to face her. "Meet Sheriff Alton. She doesn't like people shooting up her town."

"I'm pressing charges." The man turned bleary red eyes toward her. "This Neanderthal shot me."

Jenna raised both eyebrows. "Oh, there will be charges. I'm throwing the book at you." She looked around just as Rio came to a screeching stop right behind them. "Great timing. Read the Prince of Darkness his rights and throw him in a cell to sober up." She considered calling a doctor and then decided on the medical examiner. As a member of the law enforcement team, Dr. Shane Wolfe, a badge-holding deputy, was highly trained in forensic science. She nodded to herself. "I'll need Wolfe to take a look at him. We'll leave him for the night and question him in the morning." She turned toward Deputy Jake Rowley, Rio's partner. "Call Wolfe and ask him to drop by. It's only flesh wounds, as far as I can see, and one of you will need to stay overnight to watch him."

"I'll do it." Rio sighed. "I've got a ton of paperwork to do."

Jenna nodded. "Okay, head home at noon and get some sleep if possible. Rowley, take over at six in the morning."

She watched as they loaded the prisoner into the SUV and then turned to Kane. "Good job. I guess we'd better spread the word for anyone with damages to get a report from us for their insurance." She scanned the street. "There's a ton of damage. If you sort out the traffic, I'll make sure no one is injured and then I'll take photographs of the damage to the parked vehicles."

"Another action-packed Halloween on the way. It seems to erupt the week before and around the time the decorations go up." Kane rubbed his chin. "People just want to have fun, trick-or-treat, and look at the displays with their kids. Someone always spoils it. Why can't we have a normal one like every other town?" He waved his hand to get the traffic moving.

As Jenna searched the sidewalk for anyone in trouble but found no one in need of a medic, people poured out of the stores looking bewildered and angry at the bullet holes in their vehicles. She pulled out her phone to snap license plates and damage, and shook her head. "I've come to the conclusion that's impossible in Black Rock Falls. Beautiful one day, total chaos the next." She sighed. "Let's keep walking, we'd better make sure everyone's okay."

Boots crunching over broken glass, Jenna and Kane made their way along the sidewalk, stopping to take images of damage and to take down names. Townsfolk moved around, some cleaning the debris away or talking in small groups. They'd gone all out with the Halloween decorations this year and there'd be more to come. She noticed the usual orange-and-black bunting, along with strings of pumpkin-shaped lights, but the new displays popping up this year intrigued her. One of the old stores was in the process of being changed into a haunted house. Spiderwebs had replaced the curtains and one or two vampires hung out of windows, laughing when people went by. In the alleyway beside the haunted house sat an old wagon piled high with hay bales. Two cowboy skeletons with flashing red eyes sat up front brandishing rifles like in the Old West. The display of carved pumpkins on the hay bales had been blasted into pieces and squashy green and yellow lumps littered the sidewalk.

As she headed toward the couple cleaning up the mess, two women ran toward her, eyes wide and faces sheet-white. She grabbed Kane's arm to get his attention. "Something's happened."

"You've gotta see this." One of the women, wearing a thick fleece jacket, pointed wildly behind her.

"That maniac shot up part of a display outside Aunt Betty's." The second woman wiped a trembling hand down her face. "It's the coffin that opens up—and there's a vampire inside.

TWO

Jenna laid a hand on the woman's arm. "Take a deep breath and tell me what's happened. Are you sure it's a body?"

"Yeah, it's real." The first woman looked over her shoulder, her eyes wild. "It's not a mannequin; I can see her teeth where a bullet damaged her face."

"I'll need your names and contact details." Kane pulled out his notebook. "We'll need to talk to you when we're done here. I want you to go into the grocery store and wait for us there."

"Okay. I'm Christine McEntire." The first woman moved closer to Kane. "This is my friend, Terry Bauman." They both gave their details.

Jenna looked at them. "I know this has been a shock but we'll need your statements. You should grab a cup of coffee and something from the deli. It might be a while before we get back to you."

"Does this mean we have another serial killer in town?" Christine McEntire searched Jenna's face. "That vampire had a stake in her chest."

"Give us time to look at it, okay?" Kane pushed his notebook back inside his pocket. "People go to crazy extents to make things look real. Don't worry until we know for sure." He turned to Jenna. "Ready, Sheriff?"

Nodding, Jenna stepped around a pile of shot-up pumpkins and picked her way along the sidewalk to Aunt Betty's Café. A crowd had gathered around the shot-up coffin. A figure of a young woman with long black hair and dressed in a white nightgown hung from the door, head down and arms hanging loose. A garden stake protruded from the chest and two red puncture marks stood out on the pure white neck. The odor of death drifted toward her on the breeze. She reached for her phone and called Wolfe. "Are you at my office?"

"*Guilty as charged.*" Wolfe chuckled. "*Your prisoner is fine. He's sleeping right now.*"

Jenna stared at the coffin. "Just a minute, I need to look at something."

Pushing a hand through her hair, Jenna took a few steps closer. She had no doubt by the discoloration of the skin and the ruby stud earrings that this was a person. She moved away to preserve the evidence and looked at Kane's stony expression. "Create a perimeter around the body." She lifted her phone to speak to Wolfe as Kane ordered the onlookers away. "We have a homicide. Outside Aunt Betty's. A female in a coffin."

"*On my way.*" Wolfe disconnected.

A sheriff's department vehicle stopped outside Aunt Betty's and Jenna turned as Deputy Johnny Raven slid out to greet her. His K-9, Ben, hung out of the window, his mouth open in a doggy smile, tail wagging. "Raven, you have great timing."

"Rio called me." Raven scanned the scene. "He mentioned the gunman but that smells like a corpse to me."

Jenna nodded. "Yeah, I figure it is too. Wolfe is on the way but you take a look." As a medical doctor, Raven flew a medivac helicopter in the service. After being wounded, he retired to a cabin in the forest to train K-9s and personal protection dogs. When he'd stepped in to help them with a case, Jenna had talked him into becoming a part-time deputy.

"No one in the crowd saw anyone dumping her here." Kane stepped closer to Jenna. "I've contacted Bobby Kalo. He'll search the CCTV cameras in town and see if he can find anything suspicious."

Jenna nodded. "It's great to have an FBI computer whiz kid on hand when we need him, isn't it? Then again, Agent Beth Katz out of Rattlesnake Creek is good too."

"Kalo is always in the office." Kane shrugged. "I really don't like to drag Beth from a case to do us a favor when she's not involved."

A white van drew up at the curb and Wolfe jumped out along with his daughter and new medical examiner, Emily, along with Colt Webber, Wolfe's assistant and badge-holding deputy. He looked at Jenna.

"What have we got?" Wolfe's eyes narrowed as he scanned the crime scene. "Is the shooter responsible for this?"

Shrugging, Jenna looked at him. "Right now, I have no idea. He shot up the coffin. Who put her in there is another matter."

"White female, eighteen to twenty. She has sharp force trauma to her neck and a wooden stake through her chest pinning her to the coffin." Raven pulled off examination gloves with a snap. "Good luck working out this one, Shane."

Everyone stood back as Wolfe moved around the coffin. He examined the body and then turned to his team.

"Webber, record the crime scene. I'll need to take her back to the lab in situ." Wolfe looked from Kane to Raven. "When Webber has recorded the scene, if y'all give me a hand to get her and the coffin into my van, I'll do the preliminary examination at the morgue." He leaned toward Jenna. "She's been dead for at least twelve or more hours by the state of rigor." He looked at Emily. "Do you concur?"

"Yeah." Emily frowned. "The marks on her neck, are they supposed to resemble a vampire bite? That's pushing the Halloween theme a little far, don't you agree?"

Nodding, Jenna glanced at her watch. "Nothing surprises me any longer." She turned to Wolfe. "When will you do the autopsy?"

"Two o'clock suit you?" Wolfe frowned. "Or do you need to be home for the boys?"

Jenna smiled. "No, they're fine. Jackson is okay with us leaving him with Nanny Raya. He's a big boy now, fifteen months, walking and talking. Tauri dotes on him." She sighed. "I know you haven't seen him for a month or so. We've just been so busy. I had no idea the extent of the catch-up we needed after taking a year away from the office."

"I've been busy myself." Wolfe smiled at her. "Getting the medical examiner registration documents in order for Emily to work with me and organizing an office for her has kept us busy too."

Surprised Wolfe didn't have his new wife and forensic anthropologist, Norrell, with him, Jenna frowned. "How is Norrell? Is she well?"

"She's great." Wolfe smiled. "She has a case. A couple renovating an old house in Helena discovered a mummified body inside a wall. She's working on identifying it, is all."

After Wolfe loaded the coffin and body into his van, Jenna turned to Kane and Raven. "I'll go and speak to the women who discovered the body. As we're short-staffed, I'll take them back to the office to interview them and get their statements. If you can go talk to everyone and ask if they've seen anyone hanging around and then follow up on the damage, it will save time. When we're done, Raven, you take lunch. I'll be heading out to the autopsy with Dave." She looked at Raven. "Unless you want to come too? We can eat later."

"Wouldn't miss it." Raven indicated to the damage to the town and shook his head. "Another day in paradise, huh?"

Jenna grimaced. "Yeah. Paradise lost." She headed for the grocery store.

THREE

After speaking to Christine McEntire and Terry Bauman, Jenna left them with the receptionist, Maggie, to sign their statements. She called the mayor to give him a report of the incident and arrange for a crew to come out and clean the mess on the sidewalk and road. She went back downstairs to speak to Rowley. He had been with her since she first joined the sheriff's department and she'd trained him. Rowley was married with boisterous twins, and his wife, Sandy, had given birth to a baby girl a few months after Jackson was born. "How's the prisoner?"

"Sleeping." Rowley stood from behind his desk opposite the cells. "We took his prints. I'm running them through the database now. He wouldn't give his name and has no identification on him. He had his weapons and a bunch of keys, is all."

Jenna frowned. That was unusual. "We'll let him sleep." She leaned against the wall. "How are Sandy and the kids?"

"They're fine." Rowley smiled and pulled up a photograph on his phone. "The kids are growing like weeds, and Mia is walking and talking up a storm already."

Jenna peered at the image. "Mia is so like Sandy." She tapped her bottom lip. "You're going to be stuck here for a while. We discovered a body in town just before. Wolfe is conducting an autopsy at two. You'll need to order takeout for lunch and grab sandwiches for the prisoner. He'll wake up hungry."

"Body?" Rowley raised both eyebrows. "Where? Is it a homicide or did the drunk guy shoot them?"

She nodded. "I think homicide, but he did shoot her in the cheek but she was already dead. Wolfe believes she died hours ago." She straightened from the wall. "The victim was found in a coffin outside Aunt Betty's. The guy in the cells shot it up and two women noticed it wasn't a mannequin. It was starting to stink, so it would have been discovered before long." She sighed. "It has two marks on its neck and a stake through its heart. I figure we have another Halloween lunatic running around. It's going to be hard to keep this murder under wraps, half the townsfolk have seen the body."

"So, you don't figure the shooter and the corpse are connected?" Rowley rubbed his chin.

Jenna checked her watch. "Right now, I don't have a clue." She sighed. "As Dave and Raven aren't back yet, I'll walk into town and see what's delaying them." She headed for the door.

On the way she collected their bloodhound, Duke, from under Maggie's desk and headed back along Main. She moved through people trying to put things straight on their displays. One older man sat on a pile of hay bales carving a pumpkin and around him he'd scattered corn husks. A line of pumpkins at his feet grinned at her. After the disturbance everything was returning to normal. She found no sign of Kane or Raven on Main, but Raven's truck was still parked where he'd left it. When she reached Aunt Betty's Café, Duke did a happy dance and ran around her legs. As a patrol dog he was allowed inside and the manager spoiled him. She pushed open the door and swept her gaze over the room. Kane and Raven sat at their reserved table drinking coffee.

"There you are. I figured you'd show sooner or later. We're starving and couldn't wait." Kane stood and pulled out a chair for her. "You need to eat too. Do you want the special? Pulled pork sandwiches and apple pie. I'll go and order."

Jenna nodded. "Yeah, that's fine and something for Duke." She looked at Raven. "Is Ben allowed to have something to eat?"

"Sure." Raven smiled at her. "He eats anything."

"Okay, three specials and two dog meals." Kane headed for the counter.

Needing to know what they'd discovered, Jenna looked at Raven. "Did you find anything interesting?"

"Nope." Raven leaned forward. His hands loosely gripped the table. "No one saw anything. We spoke to the assistant manager, Wendy, and the coffin has been there since Friday last. It's an automaton, with motion sensors. The door opens to display a vampire with red glowing eyes. She didn't notice anything unusual until about half an hour before the shooting started. She figures she smelled something bad."

Jenna pushed her hair from her eyes and retied it at the nape of her neck. "Most of the displays remain outside all night. They're too heavy for one person to move. I can't imagine someone carrying a body along the sidewalk, removing the mannequin, and replacing it with a corpse without being seen."

"They might have been seen." Kane dropped into the chair beside her. "The thing is, no one would pay much attention to someone setting up a display. I saw someone carrying a headless body just before and went to check it out but no one was taking any notice. It's Halloween and people are setting up their displays. We all know they do this the week before. In this town the Halloween festival lasts about ten days."

"Yeah, they like to make it last." Raven chuckled. "Although, I can't buy enough of the pumpkin pies from the bake-off. I'm first in line every year."

Jenna smiled at Wendy when she delivered the meals. "This looks great. Thanks."

"If I'd come in the front door when I arrived this morning, I'd have noticed something was wrong with the display." Wendy's brow creased into a frown. "I wonder how long she's been there. It gives me the shivers knowing that poor woman has been there all morning." She looked at Kane. "I've checked the CCTV footage for last night right through until nine this morning. I see shadows moving, is all." She pulled a thumb drive from her pocket and handed it to Kane. "I saved it for you just in case you can get anything from it."

"Thanks." Kane slid the drive into his jacket pocket.

When Wendy headed back to the counter, Jenna turned to Kane and Raven. "We need to check the displays and make sure there are no other surprises."

"Already done." Kane bit into a sandwich and moaned. "Aw, man, this is amazing. Mine has a honey glaze sauce with apples in it."

"Mine too." Raven chewed slowly. "I could become addicted to this."

Looking from one to the other, Jenna laughed. "You two will be moving in here soon."

"Nah." Kane grinned. "I'm addicted to you."

FOUR

He watched in amazement as chaos erupted in town. Standing in the crowd of onlookers and seeing the ruined corpse angered him. He wanted to make a statement, send a warning, and now it had become a sideshow. Almost as bad as the so-called amusing ghouls and other blood-soaked atrocities the townsfolk wheeled out each year. It didn't matter in which town he spent Halloween, the people ignored everything as if the vampires had used their glamor on them and bent them to their will.

All this weird exhibitionism—the costume-wearing and the need to outdo the graphic brutality each year—was the result of the vampires. They waited patiently for this night and snatched people from the streets. Once bitten, they become slaves, willing to do anything their masters tell them. It wasn't like the movies. Vampires moved through time and they don't catch fire in the sunlight. He'd seen them and understood what it was like to have the woman he loved seduced by one and taken from him.

He could read the signs. They snuck into town at night, always wore dark clothes and had pale skin. Many faked a problem. They'd lost their money, were hungry and homeless, or escaping from abuse. If these terrible things had really happened to them, rather than being wary, they were the opposite. He'd found them easy to talk to because they believed they could manipulate him. Luckily, he understood their glamor—the way they mesmerized people with their eyes to make them believe their lies. They figured they had their target in sight and would follow him home. He understood their intention to strike the moment he shut his eyes, but luckily, they never made it that far.

He'd destroy them before they rose on the second night to wreak havoc in Black Rock Falls. If the vampires were left to run free, many innocent people would be taken—and no one would know until it was too late. It needed to stop. Not a soul would listen to him—and nobody could stop him. He would deal with the problem by sliding into the role of a vampire slayer to take them down before they infected everyone in the town. He smiled to himself. Each one was a thrill. The discovery, the chase—and the execution.

FIVE

That afternoon, Jenna stepped into the brightly lit corridor leading to the examination rooms in the medical examiner's building. Behind her, she could hear Kane's and Raven's boots clattering on the tile floor. The air had a strange aroma of vanilla and formaldehyde as she led the way to an alcove where they changed into scrubs and PPE. Once ready, they moved to the door with the red light glowing above it and Jenna swiped her identification card across the scanner. The door slid open in a whoosh and the faint smell of decomposition oozed through her face mask. Cold immediately seeped through her clothes, raising goose bumps and instilling a feeling of unease. Autopsies were a necessity, but she hated attending them, sometimes unable to push the sight of a murder victim from her mind. She guessed being here made her more determined to catch the killer.

Trying to breathe as shallowly as possible, she blinked into the brightness of the overhead surgical lights, reflecting in the stainless-steel surfaces, over the neat rows of instruments and the array of screens. Wolfe stood beside an instrument tray, his white-blond hair partly covered by a surgical cap, his face masked and covered with a plastic shield. He nodded to Jenna and turned to greet them.

"There y'all are and Raven too." Wolfe's gray eyes twinkled. "Almost ready. Emily will be along soon." He removed the tops from specimen jars filled with liquid and lined them up.

Jenna moved to stand under the air-conditioning unit. The constant flow of fresh air made being in the autopsy suite a little more palatable. She leaned her back against the counter. "Have you completed a preliminary examination?"

"I've taken the body temperature, swabbed the exterior for any hairs or trace evidence, and taken a good set of prints. I figure she died around eight to twelve hours before her body was discovered." Wolfe sighed. "Emily is running a DNA sample in the sequencer, but unless she or any of her relatives are in the database, it will be no use until she shows on a missing person's file and we can test a relative."

The door whooshed open and Emily Wolfe, the new medical examiner, came through the door in a squeak of shoes. She dumped an armful of specimen jars on the counter and turned to look at them.

"Hello, everyone." She arranged the jars within reach. "Hi, Raven. It's good to see you again."

"I couldn't miss watching you work." Raven gave her hand a squeeze. "It's been a long road for you but it's finally happening. Your dad must be so proud of you." He glanced at Wolfe.

"I'm just about bursting." Wolfe's eyes crinkled at the corners as he smiled behind the mask. "But it makes me feel terribly old. It seems only yesterday I was bringing her home from the hospital." He looked at Emily. "Okay, we'd better get to work." He walked over to a bank of drawers, slid out a body on an autopsy table and then pushed it under the lights.

"I have everything we need." Beside him, Emily pulled down the microphone and positioned it in front of her father.

Jenna pressed her face mask tighter over her nose as the

distinct smell of bodily fluids wafted from the corpse. When Wolfe removed the sheet, the acrid sweet smell of decomposition became overpowering. The victim was sheet-white, and the tips of her toes and fingers had turned blue. A bullet hole in her cheek showed white teeth. "What have you got, Shane?"

"The victim is a healthy white female between the ages of eighteen and twenty-two. Five feet, six inches and approximately one hundred pounds." He examined her mouth. "The gunshot wounds to face and right upper torso, I assume, came from this morning's shooter. The bullet went straight through and was collected along with others at the scene. I've checked them and they match the shooter's weapon. I don't believe the gunshots contributed to this person's death." He went back to the mouth. "We'll concentrate on the victim and cause of death. She has a full set of porcelain veneers, blue eyes, and ear piercings but is without any other distinguishing features." He glanced up at Jenna. "I already checked for any signs of sexual abuse or activity and found nothing significant. The finger- and toenails are clean."

Jenna had attended many autopsies in her time as sheriff and understood the process. "I don't see any defensive wounds on her anywhere. Have you completed a tox screen?"

"Yeah, we've taken a number of samples and they're being run as we speak." Wolfe turned back to the body. "As you can see, there are two small sharp forced injuries directly above her carotid artery approximately two inches apart. I will examine the marks under the microscope to determine what made them. Although from prior knowledge, they are not made by an animal."

"There would be some distinct tearing if an animal had bitten her neck." Emily turned to look at Jenna. "There would also be scratching or other indications of animal interaction. We would also find fur or saliva and we found neither of these."

"Did she bleed out?" Kane had moved closer to the gurney and was watching with interest.

"Yeah, I believe so. The pale waxy skin tone and lack of livor mortis would indicate exsanguination." Wolfe glanced over his shoulder. "I believe the body was drained of blood prior to death via the carotid artery. Likely using a wide catheter inserted directly. It is clean and she has no bruising or abrasions around the neck to suggest her killer restrained her. There is no doubt that she was unconscious at the time."

"The stake wound appears to be postmortem." Raven moved closer to Jenna and leaned his back against the counter. "It's on a strange angle. Do you figure he hammered that through while she was standing up inside the coffin?"

"Yeah, that was my determination as well when I removed it to get her out of the coffin. The lack of tissue damage, as in no bruising, would indicate a postmortem injury." Wolfe waved him forward. "The stake was plunged in with considerable force, although he used the interior wedges that suspended the original mannequin to support the body. Unless this is a powerful man, he must have used a mallet of some kind."

"What type of wood is it?" Kane peered at the body.

"Treated pine as used in garden stakes." Wolfe looked at Jenna over the top of his face mask. "They sell them all over town." He looked at Emily. "Crack her open."

Jenna looked away as Emily went to work. When Emily had cut through the rib cage to expose the internal organs, she gathered herself and lifted her gaze. "What else do you see?"

"There is an absence of blood in the major vessels and organs, which would confirm exsanguination as the primary cause of death." Wolfe stopped recording and turned back to Jenna. "The marks on the neck and the stake could indicate the killer's obsession with vampires. The positioning of the stake indicates a ritualistic mindset." He glanced at Kane. "Don't you agree?"

"I do." Kane lifted his gaze to Jenna. "I hope this doesn't cause panic with people believing we have vampires in town. You know what the townsfolk are like over the week before Halloween. The mist rolls in and everyone starts seeing things."

"Do you figure it's the man you caught shooting up the town?" Wolfe stepped away from the autopsy table, leaving Emily to remove the organs and weigh them.

Recalling the slight figure waving a gun, Jenna shrugged. "It could be, but I doubt it. The shooter was intoxicated and has a small frame. Someone dismantled the display, ripped out the mannequin, and installed a heavy body and then staked it. If the shooter did it, he had help." She straightened. "Do you mind if we leave you to finish up here? I want to get back to the office and search for missing persons so we can identify this poor woman."

"Not a problem." Wolfe nodded sagely. "I'll upload the reports to the server as soon as I've finished them. The DNA and toxicology screen will take some time but I've tested specifically for a date-rape drug and a few narcotics. The rest will take longer."

"Thanks." Kane followed Jenna to the door.

Jenna stood in the alcove and ripped off the scrubs. She lifted her gaze to Kane and Raven. "That's all we need. A killer who has a fascination with vampires."

"I'd keep a lookout for any large bats." Raven grinned at her. "Since I've lived here, it seems nothing is impossible."

SIX

Jenna and Kane spent the rest of the afternoon hunting down missing persons from every county in Montana. They sent out the description of the victim to all the law enforcement offices throughout the state. She collected the names and descriptions of a few people but none of them seemed to fit the person she'd seen on the autopsy table. After writing a media release, something that she usually gave to Rio to complete, she contacted Bret Housing at the local media outlet. She discovered the media were already buzzing with information from the public. The rumor about a vampire being found in town was rife among the locals. Many people had called the local TV station to get information. A small segment had been on the news about a body being found on Main but nothing had appeared online yet.

She had little choice but to give a statement and rolled her eyes at Kane, sitting at the desk across the room. "Yes, a deceased woman was discovered on Main this morning after the shooting. We do not consider her to be a victim of the shooter, who is currently in custody. The investigation into the woman's death is ongoing and we will keep you updated when necessary."

"There are many people calling in and giving eyewitness accounts of seeing what appeared to be a newly bitten vampire killed with a stake. They are saying they could see marks on her neck. You can't deny she had a stake through her chest because we have photographs taken at the scene." The reporter sounded excited, as if this was the story of a lifetime.

Jenna's eyes went to Kane, who shook his head in disgust. She cleared her throat. "I would request most strongly not to publish those photographs. This poor woman has a family, who has no idea she has died. Can you imagine the shock at seeing your murdered loved one splashed all over the news? You must wait until we identify the victim and notify the next of kin. I'll need the names of the people supplying you with images and warn them not to post them on social media."

"I can't do that and there's no law that compels me to reveal my sources, but I will make the request, as you have issued a statement." Bret Housing tapped away at a keyboard. *"One thing: do you believe that this is a sick Halloween joke or something more sinister?"*

Jenna pushed both hands through her hair. "Honestly, we haven't gotten all the facts together. The autopsy report is pending. I'll give you more information as it comes to hand. There's no need to panic the townsfolk. I can assure you the poor woman we discovered is not a vampire."

"Have you considered she might have been stolen from a grave?" Bret Housing paused a beat as if waiting for a reaction. *"Body snatchers or someone stealing from a medical facility?"*

Considering that line of investigation might be a good idea, Jenna shook her head. "Right now, I can't give you an answer. It's under investigation. I'll call you with another media release when we have more information." She disconnected and blew out a long sigh. "This is going to blow sky-high."

"I've read about people who are abnormally fixated on vampires." Kane stood and went to the counter. He filled two cups with coffee and handed one to Jenna before dropping into a chair in front of her desk. "They fall into different categories. There are those who are fixated on horror movies, so this might not be one person. It could be a cult of likeminded people. Then there are those who dress like them, have their teeth filed into points and such like but are generally harmless, and others who descend into ritualistic meetings where they drink blood." He sipped his coffee. "That would tie in with a stolen-body theory."

A chill skittered down Jenna's spine. "Okay, so I'll make sure the graveyard and the hospital are checked for any missing cadavers. What's the other kind? I know there's something much worse. I can see it in your eyes."

"Yeah, I'm afraid so." Kane rubbed his chin and his dark blue gaze moved across her face. "We don't need to be dealing with a twisted vampirophile. I guess we'll know if this is a one-off, it's likely a cult or a disgusting prank."

Unsettled, Jenna swallowed hard. "Define vampirophile."

"The last type is more sinister and caught my interest when I read about a case way back eighty years ago about a serial killer who believed they were ridding the world of creatures disguised as humans." Kane eyed her over the rim of his cup and then sighed. "This guy convinced himself that if people had very pale skin or moved around at night, they'd turn into a vampire or other mythical creature at Halloween. So, he'd hunt them down, drain the blood, and then stake the heart to ensure the victim wouldn't rise the following night."

Horrified, Jenna blinked a few times. "From the things you've read, I wonder how you can sleep at night." She shook her head. "That's not how a vampire is born, is it? If we're considering the folklore of a vampire, isn't it a vampire that does the draining of the blood? They bite their victims and turn them, and then the next night they rise as vampires?"

"That's what I've been led to believe in fiction." Kane shrugged, stood, and gathered the cups. He took them to the counter, rinsed them, and set them to dry. "In the case I mentioned, we are talking about a serial killer. What they choose to believe depends on how deeply they're involved in their delusion."

Stretching and biting back a yawn, Jenna leaned back in her chair and stared at the ceiling, thinking. "So, if we have another murder, we can assume this is a serial killer who is triggered by the Halloween displays?"

"Yeah, and they're an out-of-towner or we would have seen his activity before now." Kane headed for his own desk. "This murder looks clean to me. It wasn't rushed and it was well planned. So, from our past cases, I can only imagine that this killer is living in a fantasy world at the moment. He is surrounded by his obsession and the only way he can get through another day is to prevent the monsters from overrunning the town on Halloween night. If this is correct, more things will happen this week we don't expect. He might have started with a vampire but there are other mythological ghouls that could be in his wheelhouse as well."

Concerned for the safety of her townsfolk, Jenna frowned. "So, if it's worst-case scenario, it's likely he'll escalate fast over the next few days?"

"I believe so." Kane twirled a pen in his fingertips. "The other problem I can envisage, is that he could be targeting people of different sex and ages. Anyone who appears unusual to him would become a threat."

Horrified, Jenna stared out of the window. The wind had blown the fall leaves from the forest and they littered the sidewalk and blacktop. The decorations bounced in the wind, and the smiling jack-o'-lanterns gave the town a festive feeling.

Their adopted son, Tauri, had been talking nonstop about Halloween. Being a Native American, with solid ties to his people, he had both sides to the story but really enjoyed the costumes and trick-or-treating. This year they'd planned on allowing their fifteen-month-old, Jackson, a peek at some of the nonviolent displays. Kane had already purchased a few pumpkins to carve and now someone was going to spoil it. She turned back to Kane. "We've got five days to catch whoever did this. We start with hunting down any missing corpses. I'll take the hospital and undertakers; you check out the graveyards."

SEVEN

It was five after four when the receptionist, Maggie, called Jenna to inform her that two women were waiting at the front desk with information about the murder. She headed downstairs with Kane on her heels and led the women into the interview room. They introduced themselves as Claudia Klipr and Kayla LeBlanc. "Please take a seat. Can I get you anything? Water, coffee?" When the women both shook their heads, Jenna sat down with Kane beside her. "I'll record our interview, just in case I forget something important." She turned on the camera and recorder. "Okay, Maggie said you both saw a vehicle outside Aunt Betty's Café this morning."

"We both work at the bakery and arrive around four each morning." Ms. Klipr glanced at her friend. "I rarely see any vehicles alongside the road at that time of the morning. Sometimes a few are passing through, is all."

Jenna nodded. "Can you describe the make and model of the vehicle?"

"It was a pickup, blue or silver maybe." Ms. LaBlanc leaned forward in her chair. "I saw a man in the shadows, tall and broad-shouldered near the display."

"I saw the same truck and someone bending down near Aunt Betty's front door." Ms. Klipr frowned. "I figure it was blue or silver too. I saw someone hunched over. It was only for a few seconds as I drove past. I didn't stop to take a better look. I assumed it was a delivery. We got to talking, after hearing about the body found outside the café, and figured we should come in and tell you what we saw."

"You did the right thing." Kane smiled at them and held up his phone with images of popular trucks. "Do you recognize the truck from any of these images?" He looked from one to the other. "Why don't you close your eyes and try and picture the truck in your head. How was it parked?"

"It was parked at an angle with the back into the curb." Ms. LaBlanc opened her eyes. "Can I see the pictures again?" She took Kane's phone, scrolled through the images. "I think it was this one." She pointed to a logo on the front of the truck. "This looks the same but I only got a glimpse."

Jenna smiled at them. Information like this was gold. "Is there anything else at all you can remember?"

When the women shook their heads, Jenna turned off the recording and stood. She handed them her card. "Thank you so much for coming in. If you think of anything else, please give me a call. We may be in touch later if we find the truck in question to see if you can identify it." She waited for Kane to open the door and waved them outside.

As they headed through the glass doors, Jenna turned to Kane. "I wasn't expecting to get a sighting of the killer. Now we know it's a tall man with broad shoulders driving a pickup—one person and not our shooter."

"The problem is that description and vehicle cover about forty percent of the men in town." Kane raised both eyebrows. "Maybe Kalo will have more luck with the CCTV footage? He hasn't called yet, so I assume he's still searching." He checked his watch. "It's a little after five. We couldn't find any missing women, so we might just as well head home. There's nothing else we can do here now."

Nodding in agreement, Jenna headed up the stairs to her office. "That sounds like a plan. I'll grab my coat. Where's Duke?"

"Raven took him for a walk with Ben." Kane stretched. "He figured he could canvas the stores and ask if anyone has seen anything unusual in the last twenty-four hours. He should be back soon."

By the time Jenna had tidied her desk, Raven walked in the door with the dogs. She glanced up at him. "Did you discover anything interesting?"

"Most people I spoke to said the only thing they saw were people putting up displays." Raven shrugged. "Everything seemed perfectly normal until that guy started shooting up the place. That and finding the body, which people seem to believe is a vampire, is just about all the talk in town at the moment." He looked from one to the other. "Are you heading home now?"

Jenna picked up her things. "That's the plan. Will you be able to come in tomorrow? I need you to assist us with this case. I'm going to be tied up with the shooting perp first up, and Rio will be heading home to get some sleep after pulling an all-nighter."

"Sure." Raven handed Kane Duke's leash. "I'll check the server later and see if any information has been uploaded." He turned to Kane. "I did what you suggested and called Emily to ask her to the Halloween Ball. She accepted." He grinned.

"I figured she might." Kane slapped him on the back. "You did the right thing waiting until she became a certified medical examiner."

"I hope so." Raven gave Jenna a wave and headed down the stairs.

Jenna raised one eyebrow and stared at Kane's grin. "So, you've become his romance advisor now?"

"Why not?" Kane headed for the door. "I know Emily better than anyone, I figure. She comes to me all the time for advice. She figures Raven is overprotective and is wasting his time working with dogs. I told her he is a great asset to the team and uses all his skills. I also mentioned being happy is more important than anything."

Surprised, Jenna bit back a smile. "And what did she say?"

"That you're happy and I'm overprotective, so maybe that's a good thing." Kane turned to her on the stairs. "I told her it's what we do for people we love." He took her hand. "Let's go home. I want to see my boys."

Jenna walked beside him. Happiness *was* everything. "Me too."

EIGHT

Exhausted, with blistered feet and aching muscles after cleaning the filth left by the patrons of the Triple Z Bar, Bunny Watkins grabbed a handful of beef jerky, a few packets of chips, and emptied the tips from her jar into her pocket. She shrugged into her coat, pulled on her gloves, and turned around to scan the room before extinguishing the lights. It was a thankless job. She cleared tables and cleaned for twelve hours a day, seven days a week, but was glad to have a job. She'd arrived on the bus penniless after escaping an abusive relationship and had made it this far and stayed. She'd spent her first couple of nights in the motel out back of the bar and regretted it. Now she had a room in the Black Rock Falls Motel, only three miles from the bar. It wasn't much better but it was an escape from the patrons. It would do until she could get a room at the Stanton Forest Bed and Breakfast. It had opened only recently, along with many old renovated ranch houses in the area, to cater to visitors passing through who wanted something better than a motel room. She'd been very happy to discover the flyer on the noticeboard not long after she'd arrived and left her details for the moment a room became available.

She'd been in Black Rock Falls for two months and had planned to find a better job, but as the regular patrons, mostly men—truckers, ranch hands, and bikers—had gotten used to her now and given up trying to give her money for sex, she'd decided to stay. The sexual harassment was something that both the day and night managers conveniently ignored, as if treating someone like that was normal, but she'd soon discovered ignoring the annoying men worked just fine. She did her job well and avoided talking to almost anyone. Sometimes a lonesome guy would be crying into his beer and she'd listen to him, but most times, she ignored them and kept busy.

Stepping outside, she scanned the parking lot, looking for anyone hanging around in the shadows. Eighteen-wheelers stood in rows of military precision under the dimly lit flickering street light, casting long shadows across the empty blacktop. Silence surrounded her, broken only by the occasional rumble of a vehicle's engine as it left the local roadhouse. It had been raining and a gust of damp air tousled her hair. Mist rose in coils of white from the forest like ghosts walking out to seek souls. She shivered and pulled her coat tighter around her, remembering how close it was to Halloween. The walk to the motel seemed like one hundred miles away as she stared into the forest. She hated walking opposite the moaning, swaying wall of black. Anyone or thing could be waiting in there ready to pounce.

Gathering her courage and lifting her chin, Bunny made her way across the parking lot. As she approached the highway, the new neon sign buzzed like a swarm of angry bees, its reflection in the puddles making strange colored lights in the many potholes. With each step, her boots crunched on the wet gravel, but as she listened, the steps became different. Not one set of footsteps—two. Panic gripped her. Someone was heading straight toward her. She spun around and every hair on her body stood to attention. From the shadows near the eighteen-wheelers, a man emerged. If he planned to hurt her, she had nowhere to run, no place to seek help and no phone. Her only choice would be to fight. Bunny pushed her hand inside her coat pocket and her fingers closed around the handle of a small penknife. She turned away to open it and kept it concealed before turning back again. "Are you following me?"

"Nope, but I'd like a word, if that's okay?" The man looked strange as the colored lights flickered across his face. "We spoke earlier. You told me about staying at the motel, remember?"

Heart racing like a freight train, Bunny stood her ground. Her hand gripped the small knife so tightly the handle cut into her palm. "I remember—why?"

Bunny did recall the plainly but well-dressed soft-spoken man. He'd sat alone in a dark corner and ordered a bowl of chili and she'd filled his Thermos with fresh coffee. He hadn't been rude or aggressive and seemed to be nonthreatening. They'd chatted as she cleaned tables. As she waited for a response, a streak of lightning lit up the sky and thunder rolled over the mountains.

"I came out before and noticed you leaving right behind me." He held out a hand to catch the increasing raindrops. "It's raining and from that thunder there's more to come. I saw you heading for the highway. I'm guessing you're planning on walking? I figured that you might appreciate a ride as I'm heading into town."

Instinct telling her to turn and run, Bunny shook her head. "Thanks but no thanks. I'll walk."

"Are you sure?" He indicated to a pickup parked in the shadows. "You'll be soaked through by the time you get to your room and the bears are hunting. I've seen the signs of them all along the edge of the forest." He sighed. "It's not safe to be walking alongside the highway at this time of night. I have coffee and I'll share it with you along the way."

The rain increased, bringing with it the smell of diesel and damp leaves. Legs heavy and back aching with exhaustion, Bunny glanced at him. Every part of her screamed a warning but the road ahead was dark, wet, and cold. Hot coffee sounded good. She looked at him, trying to assess the threat. "I know it's not safe but getting into your truck isn't safe either."

The man stared into the forest but said nothing. Needing to leave, but unable to risk turning her back on him, Bunny moved her attention to the forest and then back at him. Bone weary, she needed to get going before becoming too exhausted to walk the long three miles. Her stomach cramped when a shadow moved along the perimeter, rustling the fallen leaves. Trees moved and twigs snapped like gunshot. It could be anything, an elk or a bear. Right now, she didn't want to find out. "Okay, thanks."

"You'll be safe with me, Bunny." He opened the door for her. "I'm not like those rough men in the bar who give you a hard time." He slid behind the wheel and offered her the Thermos. "I'm one of the good guys. Help yourself to the coffee. I'll have you home by the time you've finished."

Noticing how clean and nice smelling he kept the inside of his truck, Bunny poured a small cup and offered it to him. "You got this for yourself. I'll be fine."

"I've had enough for a while." He smiled at her. "I'll keep the rest for the other half of my journey. It's going to be some time before I go to bed tonight."

As they turned onto the highway, rain pelted the windshield and the wipers flashed back and forth. Bunny sipped the coffee. The brew at the Triple Z Bar was nicer than most and she usually took a to-go cup with her, but she'd given him the last in the pot. Heat rose from the vents in the dashboard, at first welcome and then almost too hot. So tired, she fought to keep her eyes open. Sleep overwhelmed her, she couldn't fight it a second longer. Bunny dozed and snapped awake a few seconds later—but how long was it really? It was as if time had stopped and the next second started again, but something was terribly wrong. The heat had gone, and under her, cold seeped into her flesh. She forced open her eyes, but the lids closed again refusing to obey. She couldn't move, as if all her energy had drained away. What was happening to her? Her neck ached and she wanted to touch it, but her arms refused to move. Finally cranking her eyes open, she peered into a dimly lit area, maybe a barn. A light came from a lamp on a table beside her and then a shadow came closer. She tried to force words from between her lips but only a moan escaped.

"Oh, look, you're awake. My first turned vampire. Surprise." The man from the bar was smiling at her. He had a long stake in his hands and waved it in front of her. "Enjoy your time on the dark side because it will only last another second or two."

Bunny wanted to scream, tell him he'd made a mistake, but it was too late.

NINE

Tuesday

"Mommy, Mommy."

The sound of Jackson's voice woke Jenna with a start. She stared down at the grinning face, cheeks bright red from teething and the wet bib around his neck. He was Kane's clone, solid build, black hair, and dark blue eyes, but Jackson had a dimple in his chin and she wondered if Kane had had his removed during his facial reconstruction, but she'd never ask. "Good morning, handsome." She swung him onto the bed. "You're up early."

"Yeah, he came out with me to do my chores this morning." Kane came into the room with a cup of coffee and set it on the bedside table. "I'm running a bit behind." He ruffled Jackson's hair. "He's a handful now he's walking. He refused to sit in his highchair, so I haven't been able to fix breakfast or wake Tauri."

Jenna pressed kisses all over Jackson's face, making big smacking sounds, and the baby giggled. "You should have woken me. I can't expect you to do everything." She smiled at him. "We work together, right?" She frowned as Jackson worried his gums with his fist. "I'll settle him and then get Tauri ready for school before I take a shower." She slid out of bed and carried the toddler to the kitchen. She took a frozen teething ring from the freezer, wrapped the handle in a bib, and handed it to Jackson, guiding it to his mouth. "Yes, that helps doesn't it. Poor boy, don't worry, it's almost through." She slid him into the highchair and grabbed the cup Kane handed her. "He should be fine for a while. Give me five and I'll come back and feed him."

Footsteps came along the hallway and Tauri burst into the kitchen. Jenna bent and gave him a hug. "Look at you, up and dressed. You are such a good boy."

"I'll get Jackson some toys." Tauri gathered a few things from the toy box in the corner and dropped them on the tray of the highchair. He smiled at Jenna. "He likes toys in his highchair now. Nanny Raya says it's okay."

Putting the shower on the back burner for now, Jenna took the scrambled eggs Kane had just prepared and slid some onto a small plate. She buttered small fingers of toast. Jackson was starting to feed himself and, although messy, was getting better by the day. She would feed him the eggs and eat her own at the same time. The toast he could negotiate himself as well as a sippy cup. After breakfast, she checked the time, bathed Jackson, and had him dressed by the time Nanny Raya came through the connecting door from her apartment. She smiled at her. "I'm afraid I'm running late. The boys are ready. Jackson's tooth is almost through. He's been up since before dawn."

"He'll sleep later, don't worry." Raya held out her arms to Jackson who gave her a toothy grin. "Come on, we'll take your brother to school and then we'll go and visit your friends. Grab your bag, Tauri." She headed back through the door with Tauri on her heels.

Separation anxiety gripped Jenna but Jackson had no worries at all. Their careful handling of easing back into the workforce had prepared the toddler for his parents' long absences. She'd discovered not making a big thing out of leaving and having Raya as a constant person in both the boys' lives meant her sons remained contented. She turned and looked at Kane. "I still hate leaving them."

"Me too." Kane held out his arms to her. "If we stayed home with Jackson, he wouldn't get the social skills he gets when Raya takes him to playgroups. We spend as much time with them as possible. Allowing Rio to run the office, we've been part-time law enforcement officers for the last four months. It's a compromise most parents don't have. Jackson and Tauri are well adjusted. Now we have a homicide case, we need to spend the time at work. Once we catch this guy, we can spend more time with the boys. They'll cope with the extra hours with Raya just fine. It's all good." He turned her around. "Go and get ready. I'll clear the table."

Loving the growing excitement of Halloween, Jenna peered out of the window as Kane drove the Beast, his tricked-out black truck, along Main. The displays and decorations set up outside the stores had reached a new level this year. She couldn't remember seeing so many automated displays. The black and orange theme continued along the entire length of Main. "Slow down so we can look. Oh, that one is remarkable." She pointed to a pair of gunslinger vampires, jumping from coffins to have a showdown, with stakes instead of guns.

"I don't know where they come up with these ideas." Kane buzzed down his window. "Can you hear them, Jenna? He's saying, 'Why are you coming at me with that stake?'" He grinned at her and crawled along the blacktop. "I figure the haunted house is going to be a hit with the locals."

Jenna waved at a couple of townsfolk tying skeletons to the light posts. "I agree, they've been working on it for a long time.

I've only heard gossip about it so far, but apparently, they completely gutted that old house so you can go in one door and move through rooms and have different terrifying experiences. I'd say it will be real spooky when it's finished. It's going to be a tourist attraction for sure. I heard it's going to be open for all the festivals and the theme will change. I figured it would just be basically a haunted house."

"I heard they're going to be using the pumpkin patch beside the old graveyard for something this year." Kane left Main and took the side street to the back of the sheriff's office. "We'll park here. I figure it's going to rain again today."

Jenna looked at him. "What about the pumpkin patch? Don't leave me hanging here."

"I'm not sure." Kane smiled at her. "They're having some stalls there selling stuff and apple-bobbing and other Halloweeny things, I guess."

Snorting, Jenna climbed from the truck and waited for Kane to unclip Duke from his seatbelt. "Halloweeny things?" She slipped her arm through his. "I can't wait to find out what they are."

"You know, spooky things." Kane leaned into the retinal scanner and the door clicked open.

The moment Jenna reached the counter, Rowley came over. "Morning."

"I have good news." Rowley held up a sheet of paper. "This just came in from Helena. The Jane Doe, we believe is Darlene Travis. Her parents caught the news report and called their local cops. They had a few things with her prints on and the local guys are running them against the set we took from her."

So happy for a break in the case, Jenna smiled. "How long ago did they call?"

"Maybe ten minutes or so." Rowley moved around the counter as Maggie, the receptionist, came through the front door. "I've just checked the server and Kalo uploaded a few video files. Do you want me to take a look?"

"Yeah, we'll check it out as well." She turned to go. "Let me know the moment Helena gets back to you." She waved to Maggie and then headed up the stairs to her office.

The smell of freshly brewing coffee wafted toward her as she dropped into a chair behind her desk, turned on her computer, and looked at Kane. "We have an unconfirmed ID on the Jane Doe, and Kalo has sent some of the video files he collected from around Aunt Betty's before and after the body was found. I hope he found something on the killer."

"We need suspects." Kane poured two cups of coffee and moved a chair beside her. "We have a body, with no idea where this poor woman came from or how she met her killer. For all we know, he could have brought her body here from anywhere and dumped it in town and then left."

Jenna lifted her gaze to him. "Really? Since when have exhibitionists like this guy not hung around to watch the reaction to their kills? It is part of their thrill; they love terrifying people. Look at the response already. People are starting to believe in vampires."

"I suppose, as many of them already believe in ghosts, it's not a stretch of the imagination." Kane made a whirling gesture with his fingers. "Okay, let's see this footage. Did he send any notes?"

Opening the accompanying file, Jenna scanned the page. "Yeah, he mentions the same figure and vehicle in each of the examples. He has tried to clear up the images and has included them in a separate file. He estimates the figure is approximately six-three and two hundred and forty pounds." She glanced at Kane. "What do you want to see first?"

"The footage." Kane leaned forward on the desk. "Often, I can get a good idea of physical fitness by the way they walk or carry themselves."

They sat in silence and watched the five video clips that Kalo had sent them. The street lighting cast deep shadows across the frames and the footage was grainy and jumped around. Jenna paused the footage and turned to Kane. "He knows about the camera. See how he walks keeping his chin down. He has the drop-off planned to the second, as if he made the automaton himself. One mannequin out and the body installed in minutes." She watched for a few more frames. "He discarded the mannequin in the dumpster in the alleyway." She shot a glance at Kane. "How come we didn't find it?"

"They're emptied at six. We missed it." Kane rubbed the back of his neck. "It will be buried by now in the landfill."

Next, she opened the enhanced images. "He's wearing a balaclava, gloves, and a heavy winter jacket, all dark colors. Apart from his size, there's not much here to go on."

"I can't see a weapon bulge." Kane moved closer and used his fingers to enlarge the image on the touch screen. "See, the coat goes straight down, but when he lifts the body from the back of his truck, the jacket rises. There's no holster belt and it would be clear from the back. That doesn't discount the fact that he could have a shoulder holster."

Searching the screen, Jenna moved her gaze over the man and then the vehicle. "No bumper stickers and the plate is unidentifiable. It's difficult to know what make and model it is."

"From what the witnesses told us, I figure we can narrow it down to one or two models." He stared at the screen. "There's something else. He's not wearing boots. This time of year, I rarely see anyone not wearing leather boots of some description. Most in town wear cowboy boots, the miners wear steel-toe boots, the hikers have insulated hiking boots, and the forestry workers wear logger boots. I'm not seeing any of these here, I'm seeing sneakers. That's unusual, so I figure he's not from around these parts."

A knock on the door signaled the arrival of Rowley. Jenna waved him inside. "What have you got for me, Jake?"

"It seems as if the Helena detectives followed up." Rowley leaned against the doorframe. "Darlene Travis is the daughter of Malcolm Travis, a lawyer in Helena. She has been a wild child since leaving high school. She refused to go to college, deciding to take a few years of study to find herself. She had an argument with her parents as she maxed out her credit card and this was becoming a bad habit. Her dad cut up her credit card and grounded her, which at twenty she didn't take too kindly. She packed her bags and left in the dead of night but forgot her phone. They said she was complaining about having no money, so we must assume she used everything she had on the bus tickets. They discovered she'd made an appointment for an interview for a job in Blackwater. She had also made inquiries about bus timetables. They assumed she was heading to Blackwater for an appointment on Monday." He blew out a long sigh. "I checked the passengers on the bus from Helena and her name wasn't there. I did find a bus that went to Butte and there she was on the list. I figure she took the wrong bus and likely got a ride in a truck."

"We need to check out the Triple Z Roadhouse." Kane pushed to his feet. "What time did the bus get to Butte?"

"A little after ten." Rowley scratched his chin. "So, she must have made it to the roadhouse by midnight if she picked up a ride right away. A woman alone, nicely dressed. I have the description of what she was wearing. I'll send it to your phone. She'd be noticed for sure."

Standing, Jenna walked around her desk to grab her jacket. "We must assume that the killer scoped out Aunt Betty's Café sometime in the week prior to dumping the body." She stared at Rowley. "Rio can handle the office. Head down to the diner and check out their CCTV footage for inside the café. We're looking for someone who wears sneakers." She gave him the general description they'd discussed. "If you find anyone that matches, ask Susie Hartwig, the manager, to give you a copy. Take a thumb drive with you."

"Yes, ma'am." Rowley headed downstairs, his boots clattering on the steps.

"Come on, Duke." Kane whistled and Duke's eyes opened. He stood in his basket, shook from head to tail, and then did his happy dance. Kane bent to attach the dog's leash. "Walkies."

TEN

Deciding to get an early start on the finishing touches of the Halloween house display on Main, Deb Meyer and Mary Milbourne took the alleyway to the back door. Mary pulled the key from her purse, but to her surprise, she found the door unlocked. She looked at Deb. "I can't believe they left this place unlocked. I hope no one got in last night and damaged any of the displays."

They stepped inside and went to the kitchen, where the boxes of bunting and other odds and ends had been left. Nothing had been touched. They removed their coats and collected a few items. "The workers were in here until late. They should have finished the heavy work. We just need to add a few things to make sure it looks okay. We'll start from the first room along the hallway and work our way around." Mary handed Deb a box of cobwebs. "Unless you want to work alone?"

"Nope, it's creepy in here with all the mannequins." Deb cracked open the door and peered into the gloom. "I'll turn on the lights. The owner said by today there would be two switches, one to light up the entire house and another to control the automatons." She indicated to the kitchen wall. "There they are." She went and pulled down the switch.

Immediately, the house filled with blue light. Mary frowned. "I'm guessing the individual room lights still function. I'll turn them on as we go, then it won't be so spooky."

"Wait for me." Deb followed close behind.

The moment Mary stepped into the hallway the smell of decay crawled up her nostrils. She ducked thick sticky strands of fake cobwebs hanging all around the doorways and stared at the peeling wallpaper and rotting wood. Large brown water stains were everywhere, and where the wallpaper remained, gouges covered the walls as if something had clawed them. She swallowed the unease crawling up her spine as she turned into the first room. She found the light switch but the bulb hanging from a long cord in the middle of the ceiling offered little light. Long shadows cloaked the corners of the dust covered room. Decaying furniture sat around a fireplace. In the two cobweb-covered chairs were two skeletons. As Mary walked inside, the walls moved in and out as if breathing, and in the portraits of people from long ago, the eyes followed them. The next second, maniacal laughter filled the room, the fireplace burst into flames, and the skeletons turned their heads to look at them, red eyes pulsating. Startled, Mary stepped back, bumping into Deb. "Oh, my goodness. I know it's not real but it still scares me."

"Oh, don't be silly." Deb chuckled and then sobered. "The thing is, this shouldn't be happening. I didn't switch on the displays, just the lights. Maybe they're triggered by pressure plates or something?" She stared around the room as the sounds turned from laughter to moans. "Look at this. The walls look as if they're actually breathing." She went and touched the surface as it moved in and out. "Yuck, it feels like damp clammy skin." She added a few cobwebs to the mantel and stepped back to admire her work.

Mary added a handful of plastic spiders and turned to go.

As she stepped out into the hallway the floorboards creaked and a closet door swung open. She shrieked as a witch jumped out, barring their way. Loud cackling echoed through the house and she shrank back to avoid the groping hands. "I can't work in here like this. Leave the boxes. We'll need to go back and make sure the automatons are switched off."

As the witch slid back inside the closet Mary took a deep breath and headed back to the kitchen, but before she reached the hallway, the door slammed and everything went black. Underfoot the floor shifted and soft whispers whirled around them as if someone was close by. Terrified, Mary grabbed Deb's arm. "Now what?"

"Do you have your phone? I left mine in my purse in the kitchen." Deb's voice was just above a whisper.

Mary shook her head as darkness closed in around her. "Same. We need to get out of here and call the owner. Something has gone wrong."

"We'll go to the front door." Deb led the way. "Stay close." She stopped abruptly. "I just walked into a wall. It wasn't there before." She shoved Mary in front of her. "You go first."

A carnival tune played softly and then louder as they moved along the hallway searching for the front door. The house plan had changed and Mary didn't know which way to go. She ran her hands along the wall and found a door. The doorknob turned and the door creaked open. Cobwebs hit her in the face and her feet stuck to something sticky underfoot. Her imagination was running wild imagining pools of blood, and heart pounding, she took small steps, one hand outstretched. The door slammed behind them and the temperature dropped as if they'd just stepped inside a freezer. "Go back. I don't like it in here."

"The door won't open." Deb let out a yelp. "Did you just touch me?"

Mary hadn't moved. "No. It wasn't me."

"I can't see a thing but we must keep moving forward." Deb grabbed the back of Mary's sweater. "That's me. There must be another doorway."

A light over a mirror flickered and came on and Mary made out another door across the room. "I see it." Behind her, Deb gasped. She stopped walking and pulled on Mary's sweater. "What?"

"Look! There are three people in the mirror." Deb pointed with a shaking hand and then turned slowly to look behind them. "There's nobody there."

Fear had Mary by the throat. She moved fast across the room and grasped the doorknob. The door opened into pitch black. "Which way?"

"Left." Deb was right behind her, breathing heavily. "There was only one hallway in this house when we first came here. I don't know where this one leads."

A child sung nursery rhymes in a disturbing loop as they shuffled along. Unknown things brushed their hair. Hands reached out to grab them. The floor suddenly dipped and Mary almost fell through a gap into another open space. Behind her, Deb slid down the slope and landed at her feet. The next moment, candles burst into flames around an altar-like table covered with a long white cloth. On the table, laid out was the mannequin of a young woman dressed in white. Her skin was the color of white porcelain, her lips blue, and a stake protruded from her chest. Dark hair cascaded down one side of the table, and then the smell of death crept toward them.

Horrified, Mary gripped Deb's arm. "Can you smell that? That looks real. You don't think—"

"We need to look closer." Deb took hesitant steps toward the body and reached out a trembling hand. "Oh... no it's real." The room went black and she let out an ear-piercing scream.

Frozen to the spot with fear, Mary screamed. The next second, wood splintered and the door across the room burst open. Bright light spilled inside, blinding her. Someone large and menacing filled the doorway. She gaped, needing to be anywhere but here.

"Sheriff's department." A dog barked and a deputy stepped inside. "What's happening here?"

Mary dashed across the room to him. She'd never been so happy to see anyone in her life. "Help us." Heart pounding, Mary stared into the concerned face of Deputy Raven and sighed with relief. "Oh, am I glad to see you."

"Come outside." The deputy ushered them both to a bench. "You're safe now. Sit down, take a few deep breaths, and tell me what happened."

ELEVEN

Raven stared at the trembling women. After hearing screams, he hadn't wasted any time breaking down the door. He looked over his shoulder at the broken lock and shattered doorframe. "Did the displays frighten you? Why were you inside? It hasn't opened yet."

"Forget about the displays. There is a dead body in there." One of the women pointed a shaking finger to the door. "It smells of death. We went inside to add some extra decorations and everything went to hell. The automatons turned themselves on and we were trapped inside. I guess it's been made that way to frighten people but we couldn't get out. We were stuck in there and then suddenly all these candles lit up around this body. At first, we thought it was part of the display but then we could smell it and took a closer look. The next thing, all the lights went out, we screamed, and you came through the door."

Raven took their names and details. He called the office and gave the information to Rio. "I'm going to take a look inside."

"We have a killer on the loose in town." Rio's boots tapped on the tile inside the sheriff's office. *"I'll be there in five. Don't enter the building without backup."*

Raven blew out a sigh. He was used to doing things alone and now as a deputy he needed to follow rules. "Copy that." He turned to the women. "So, what do you do in the scheme of things?"

"The company that built this haunted house employed us to add a few fine touches to the displays." Mary's pale face and wide eyes concerned him. "We are expected to be here anytime the house is open for tourists or festivals, to ensure it always looks its best. Things like adding cobwebs or spiders. We hadn't expected the electronics to suddenly activate and scare us half to death or to find a dead body."

"It's another vampire." Deb nodded slowly. "Same as the other one. Someone believes they are stopping them from invading Black Rock Falls."

Raven stopped writing notes and stared at them with his pen hovering above his notebook. He had been hearing similar conversations from the local townsfolk during his patrol. Many of them stopping him to ask him about the recent vampire discovered in the coffin outside Aunt Betty's Café. "I figure you're allowing your imagination to run away with you." He glanced from one to the other. "Common sense would tell you that vampires are fictional characters. They don't exist. Whoever is doing this is a stone-cold killer and not a heroic vampire slayer."

"The thing is that many myths are being proven to be true of late." Deb pushed a trembling hand through her hair. "What I saw inside that place fits the description. Maybe it's time for everyone to take a closer look. If there are vampires in our town, we all need to take precautions."

Trying very hard to smother a smile, Raven recalled the few townsfolk he'd seen wearing strings of garlic around their necks. He figured they were already taking precautions. "Well, I guess you do what you feel is best, but I can assure you the dead can't hurt anyone, unless they're infected with disease."

The *whoop whoop* of a siren signaled the arrival of Rio. His vehicle pulled up nose-in to the haunted house. Raven turned to the women. "I want you to stay here. We'll need to take statements as you are first on scene at a possible homicide. My dog will guard you." He gave Ben a signal and the dog dropped down in front of the women.

"Okay, let's take a look inside." Rio tossed him a flashlight. "They've probably seen a very real-looking dummy. Some of them could fool anyone, especially when you've been spooked." He glanced at the door. "We'll need to call someone to fix the damage and contact the owner." He swung a look at the two women. "Don't let anyone inside. I'll tell you when it's safe." He nodded to Raven. "After you."

Raven found it interesting how different members of the sheriff's department worked a scene. Kane was the military professional, putting his life on the line and always out in front. Jenna delegated everyone a job and they all moved together as a team. Rio spat out orders but never took the lead. He figured this attitude came from a man who'd never been injured in the line of duty. Being shot wasn't nice, but once it happened, a person knew what to expect and acted accordingly. First up, he didn't imagine that the killer was still on the scene—if indeed this was a homicide—but he could easily be someplace watching what was happening. Raven stepped inside the door, drawing his weapon. He swept the room with his flashlight and immediately moved across to a long white table with the body the women described. "Sheriff's department. Come out with your hands on your head."

No sound came from inside the house and only traffic noises came from behind them. He turned as Rio stepped in the door. "There's no one in this room. I'll check for life signs if you want to clear the house."

"Not alone I don't." Rio moved his flashlight around the room. "From what I know about the plans for this place, it has changing hallways and shifting floors. If the automation has been turned on, we could trigger it just walking through. As it's not finished yet it could be dangerous. I'll wait for you to examine the supposed body."

Raven walked across the room, his boots sticking to the floor. He played the light across the sticky puddle under his feet. It resembled blood. He turned to look over his shoulder at Rio. "I've contaminated the crime scene. Stick to the outside walls. There's a patch of what could be blood over here."

He went toward the body. He didn't need to check for vital signs. The wooden stake pierced the chest and would have destroyed the heart. He pulled out his phone and called Jenna. He gave her a quick update of the situation.

"We've just arrived at the Triple Z Roadhouse to hunt down a lead on the first victim." Jenna's boots crunched on gravel and the wind buffeted the phone. *"We'll get there ASAP. I'll call Wolfe. Wait for him and send Rio back to the office with the witnesses. He can take down their statements and let them go. I'll follow up later if necessary."* She paused. *"Tell Rio to charge the drunk in the cells with damage to properties and vehicles. He isn't our killer. He was locked up all night."*

Raven nodded. "Copy that." He had his phone on speaker and swung his gaze to Rio. "Did you get that?"

"Yeah." Rio scratched his cheek. "The person responsible sure knows how to make his victims look like vampires. The one thing missing is the fangs."

Picking his way carefully to the door on the opposite side of the room, Raven glanced at him. "This guy is infatuated by vampires. Part of him believes that he's killing them before they turn, so the teeth wouldn't be an issue."

The door the women said was locked opened smoothly and they stepped onto a ramp that led to a narrow hallway. They moved slowly throughout the house, checking each display and every closet they could open. A few automatons startled Raven but none of them became active. Everything seemed in order. "We've walked all over this house and nothing has sprung into life. The women were terrified when I found them and said everything suddenly came to life. We'll need to tell the owner to check out the control panel. It's not safe if it's going to switch on without notice. Someone could get hurt."

"I figure the controls will be in the kitchen." Rio followed close behind him. "From what I've read, entry will be from the alleyway. The ticket booth will be created beside the back door and the patrons start in the passageway beside the kitchen. The staff will be supervising by CCTV cameras in the kitchen. I haven't seen any cameras, so I guess that hasn't been set up yet."

As they reached the kitchen, Rio let out a long breath behind him and Raven turned to look at him, surprised to see his tightly guarded expression. "I figured you'd be more experienced in crime scenes."

"I'm very experienced in crime scenes." Rio holstered his weapon. "I was a gold shield detective in LA before I came to work here. What makes you believe I'm not experienced in crime scenes?"

Raven could understand if Rio's coldness toward him was because he'd stepped in as a rival for Emily's affections after their breakup, but on a professional level, he'd witnessed Rio's instant dislike for him. The man had a retentive memory and maybe that's why he had a little trouble letting go. Or maybe it was his instant close friendship with Kane? He and Agents Carter and Styles, along with Wolfe, had a bond that only those who'd served in the military enjoyed. Because of this bond, he'd slipped into the team with ease and spent a good deal of his downtime with the others building motorcycles. He gave Rio a long considering stare. "Maybe because this place freaks you out. You know it's not real—well apart from the dead body laid out on an altar in the family room—but I could almost feel your fear."

"My problem is I don't forget things." Rio rubbed his chin. "The patch of blood gave me a flashback to a case that I was involved in some time ago. I woke up covered in blood after investigating a dead body in a similar situation to this. I was the prime suspect for a time and the problem was I couldn't remember what had happened. For someone like me, forgetting never happens and it kind of freaked me out."

Nodding slowly, Raven slapped him on the back. "Yeah, I've been there. It gets better."

"I doubt it." Rio sighed. "Not being able to forget is a curse more than a gift."

Raven noticed the purses on the kitchen table. He pulled out his phone and took a picture of them. "I'll take these out to the witnesses. They'll need them. I'll get the details of the owner from them and call him. If you want to go, I'll wait here for Wolfe." He waved toward the back door. "Maybe we should go out this way."

"Sure." Rio pulled open the door and stepped outside into the alleyway. "I'll get someone out to fix the door. Will you be okay to wait here until it's repaired?"

Checking his watch, Raven shrugged. "I'll need Rowley to relieve me within the hour."

"I'll send him along." Rio strode away along the alleyway.

Raven scratched his head. He wondered why Jenna had made Rio chief deputy. When she'd been away on maternity leave, the position had sure gone to his head. Right now, he figured Rio would run in the elections against her the following year. Not that he could win. The townsfolk loved and respected Jenna and Kane. They knew they would keep them safe. The people he'd spoken to during her absence had been reassured knowing if a serial killer came into town, she'd be there defending them, even with a new baby. Luckily, the town and Jenna had been given a respite. Apart from a few local robberies and a small gang of kids from Blackwater stealing vehicles, it had been the quietest fifteen months in the past seven years.

He went back to the witnesses and called the owner, who was on his way with a crew. He explained the place was a crime scene and until the medical examiner had finished, no one would be entering the building. The door, however, could be repaired. The owner had a carpenter on his crew and would take care of it. He watched the women climb into Rio's truck and waved away the few inquisitive onlookers before sitting on the bench. His part-time job had expanded from the odd day to three days a week and, like now, maybe seven days a week until the perp was caught. Luckily, training dogs as K-9s or for protection wasn't precise. His dogs were super smart and could pick up their training when he had time. The people waiting for a protection dog understood a dog took as long as it takes. Having Atohi Blackhawk as a partner, meant he didn't need to be at home to feed them. When he worked, Blackhawk stayed in his own cabin on his land. They had a great working relationship. He leaned back, rubbed Ben's silky ears and sighed. He didn't mind sitting back for a time, watching the townsfolk prepare for Halloween, and he might get lucky and Emily would arrive with her dad.

TWELVE

The first thing that Jenna needed to do when she entered the Triple Z Roadhouse was to look on the board just inside the door where the truckers listed their destinations and offered rides to people. If Darlene had been trying to get a ride to Blackwater but never made it, there would be a chance her name could still be on the board. She went down the list and found four or more drivers heading for Blackwater in the next twelve hours. Darlene's name was listed against the one due to leave at six that morning and someone had written "no-show" beside it. "That's her. Look, his check-in time was ten last night. He must have had a sleepover."

"It's unusual for them to leave a name on the board." Kane indicated to the scrubbed-out areas against the time slots. "Maybe he left it there to tell her he'd left. Most of them are on a tight schedule and wouldn't have time to wait around."

Considering what Kane had said, Jenna went into the restaurant. The smell of dirty cooking oil and onions greeted her, mixed with a weak aroma of coffee. She made her way through the tables, feeling rather than seeing the eyes turn toward her. Conversations halted and the sound of silverware ceased for a moment before starting again as if everyone had taken a breath and waited to see if she planned to arrest anyone. She approached the counter to speak to the server. "Is it normal for the drivers to leave the entry on the board if the passenger didn't show?"

"Yeah, but it doesn't happen often. Most people are waiting for the drivers to come in for their meals before they leave. None of the drivers waste time waiting for someone to show." She smiled at Jenna. "Is there anything I can get for you, Sheriff?"

"Two donuts and two to-go coffees, thank you." Kane leaned around Jenna. "Do you know who was serving last night? We're looking for a young woman by the name of Darlene. She wrote her name on the board looking for a ride into Blackwater. It says she was a no-show. We need to know if she was speaking to anyone last night."

"Yeah, Alice took an extra shift last night. One of our girls called in sick." The server smiled. "She's on a break. I'll get her for you." She handed over the coffee and donuts.

Jenna smiled. "Thanks."

"That's fortunate." Kane dropped bills on the counter and added the fixings to the cups. "Do you want a donut?"

Jenna shook her head. "Nope, I don't want to become a stereotype. They're all yours."

When Alice came out from the back carrying a cup of coffee and a sandwich, Jenna led her to a quiet booth and they sat down facing each other. "We're looking for a young woman around twenty with long dark hair. She was dropped here by a driver from Butte and wrote her name on the list for a ride to Blackwater. She never made it, so we need to find out who she was in contact with while she was here. Do you recall seeing her?"

"Yeah, I remember her." Alice took a bite of her sandwich and chewed slowly before washing it down with a sip of coffee.

"She drew the attention of some of the cowboys and they were giving her a hard time. Then some guy came over and told them to back off. He purchased burgers and fries for both of them and sat over there in the booth. I figured he was just being kind because he was a lot older than she was, but not old enough to be her father."

Glad to get a lead, Jenna nodded. "Can you describe him?"

"I really didn't take that much notice." She sighed. "I was busy and very tired. He was tall and broad. He wore a dark coat and his hat was pulled down over his eyes. I saw him walking away from the counter and he moved easy, so not old. I'm not sure but I believe his hair was dark."

"Did they leave together?" Kane leaned forward, donuts forgotten.

"I can't say." Alice shrugged. "I carried a pile of dirty dishes out to the kitchen and when I returned, they'd gone. I'm sure I've seen that guy in here before. He comes in late for a burger and fries. I figure he's a driver. Maybe she got a ride with him?"

Jenna glanced at Kane. "Did you happen to notice his shoes?"

"No." Alice laughed. "If he comes by again, I'll be sure to look for you."

"So, you can't describe him, but you'd know him if he came by again?" Kane raised an eyebrow. "That seems a little strange."

"I'm attracted to tall, broad men, so he caught my eye." Alice smiled coyly. "I didn't get close enough to get a good look at him. Next time I will."

"Well, maybe you shouldn't get too close, if he comes by again." Kane's mouth turned down. "We found the young woman dead this morning."

"Oh, that's not good." Alice stared at Jenna. "Do you figure he'll come back to hunt down more girls? Am I in danger?"

Jenna handed her a card. "Not unless you get into his vehicle. Be sure to call me, day or night, if he comes in again. We'll be here right away."

"Not a problem." Alice slipped the card into the top pocket of her uniform. "Sorry I couldn't be more help." She reached for her sandwich.

Jenna stood and led the way back to the Beast. "Hmm, not much to go on but it's something."

"It's a start. He's in town if he killed the victim in the haunted house." Kane slid behind the wheel and patted Duke on the head. "I wasn't expecting another murder so soon. This guy is escalating fast. It seems to me the moment we stepped back into the office, the murder and mayhem starts again. I'm starting to wonder if we attract these monsters."

Jenna shook her head. "No, it's a coincidence. They had a rash of murders in Helena while we were away. Carter told me they were working there most of the year. It's just our turn again, is all." She cleared her throat. "They come out of the woodwork at Halloween. This must be a perfect setting for their murders and beating us is their ultimate fantasy—I blame the books. They believe now they can anticipate our every move."

"Maybe." Kane flicked her a glance. "That won't stop us. We have a great team. We'll catch him."

A shiver slid down Jenna's spine. "Or die trying."

THIRTEEN

As they drove to the haunted house, Jenna called Raya to check on the boys. Tauri would be at school and he loved being there, but she missed being home with Jackson and needed to connect each day. Her baby was still a little boy and knowing all was well and he was happy was important. She disconnected and squeezed Kane's leg. "He's fine as usual. I'm surprised he is so calm." She smiled at him. "He takes after you."

Taking a deep breath, she gathered her courage. "The Beast is a safe place for us to talk, isn't it, and our phones and electronics are safe too, right?"

"What's wrong, Jenna? You know you can ask me anything?" Kane flicked her a glance. "Yeah, it's very safe. Ask away."

A secret was gnawing at her and she couldn't live with it any longer. The night she'd overheard Kane speaking to Jackson and telling him information she should never know. Keeping it from Kane for so long was eating her up. She hated not being truthful with him. "You know you can trust me, right? You should know that even if I was tortured, I'd never give you up."

"Where is this leading, Jenna?" Kane pulled the truck off

the road and turned in his seat to stare at her. "It's not about you being tortured. I know you could endure that if necessary. You've been trained to withstand it but that's not how my enemies act. They'd hurt the kids until you broke. That's what these people do." He ran a hand down his face and his eyes seemed to bore into her soul. "What have you done?"

Frightened, she took in his anguished expression. "I haven't *done* anything but I need to tell you something. I can't keep it to myself any longer. I've been deceiving you."

"That's impossible." Kane shook his head.

Jenna swallowed hard. This wasn't going to be easy. "I have and I'm sorry, but you need to know."

Kane stared at her, his face like granite. "I never thought I'd hear a word like *deceive* come from your lips, Jenna."

This was the closest she'd ever seen Kane get to becoming angry with her and she swallowed the lump in her throat. "I overheard you talking to Jackson when he was a newborn. You told him your name and the name of your father and grandfather. I've been afraid to tell you in case you told Wolfe and he took you away from us. I know your true name, Dave. I'm so sorry."

"You do, huh?" Kane shook his head.

When Kane pulled out his phone, Jenna panicked. "Please don't call Wolfe. I won't tell anyone, I promise."

"Look." Kane held the phone in front of her nose. "There are approximately two hundred and seventy-three thousand males with the name Jackson in the USA alone, so finding me would be difficult. Okay, so it's my first name and you need to forget it, but you don't know my last name, do you? It's not Daniel, and my middle name isn't Daniel. I suggested the name Jackson in honor of my favorite uncle. In the military I was identified by my rank, initial, and last name. In the field by a code name." He leaned over and kissed her. "I'm glad you told me. Next time, don't wait so long. It's all good, but remember,

I'm Dave now. I've never responded to Jackson—it was always Junior—but keep that information away from Raven or he'll get suspicious."

Heart pounding, she blew out a long breath. "So, we're good?"

"Yeah, but you had me worried there for a time." Kane pulled the truck back onto the highway. "I can't believe it took you fifteen months to get the courage to tell me." He smiled at her. "Am I such an ogre?"

Jenna shook her head. "No, but I understand the implications and couldn't stand the thought of losing you. I know you'd leave to protect me and the boys. I'm sorry."

"I wouldn't leave you and the boys. I'd rather tear out my soul." Kane squeezed her hand. "We'd relocate, is all. Maybe find an island and spend the rest of our lives on the beach. Come what may, you're stuck with me." He shook his head slowly. "You pick the darndest times to confess. We're on our way to a crime scene. What made you tell me this now?"

Relieved, Jenna leaned back in her seat. Her heart still pounded from his reaction. "It's hard to get you alone, and in bed at night isn't the place. I figured you'd get mad, pack your bags and leave, and I'd never see you again. You said that once, remember?"

"I do. If it were just the two of us, they'd split us up and we'd go through what we did before." He glanced at her and then moved his gaze back to the highway. "Not having me near you would keep you safe. As a couple, you'd be the liability they'd exploit to get to me. That's not my opinion; that's a fact." He shook his head. "It would be tough but we'd be alive and we wouldn't really have a choice. The thing is, now we're a family unit we'd be harder to relocate. We could move overseas but I'd be inclined to stand my ground and fight it out. Think about it. We take on serial killers all the time. We have a specialist team and a fortified home. The team wouldn't need to know who the threat is... as in wanting me for the bounty, they'd just see a threat. We'd take them down and a cleanup crew would be all over it. There would be no one to report back."

Pushing both hands through her hair, Jenna looked at him. "Someone would have sent them here. None of them work alone."

"That's what a cleanup crew is for, Jenna." He sighed. "They have their ways. Maybe they use the assassin's phone to message his boss, saying the sighting here wasn't me but he's tracked me to another town miles from here. Then his body shows in a different town. Things like that." He cleared his throat. "Please stop worrying about this. If there had been any suspicious movements, I'd know. Right now, I need you to focus on the case. This killer is nasty and the team is relying on you."

Shaking the disturbing scenarios from her mind, Jenna nodded. "I'll be fine. I hope Wolfe is there by now." She looked at him. "We'll process the scene, and when we're done, I'm taking a break. I figure Raven will be needing one too. We can discuss our findings over lunch."

"That sounds like a plan." Kane pulled the Beast's nose in to the curb outside the haunted house. "It looks like the gang's all here."

FOURTEEN

Leaves blew around Jenna's legs as she climbed from the truck and a dust devil danced along the sidewalk as if playing with the decorations and making the skeletons hanging to the light posts dance. Rowley stood outside the shattered open door to the haunted house and she made out movement inside. As she stepped onto the sidewalk, Raven, with Ben bounding beside him, pushed through the gathering crowd and met Kane. She walked up to Rowley. "What's it like inside?"

"I haven't been in yet." Rowley pushed back his Stetson and shuffled his feet. "Wolfe wanted us all outside. If you're going in, he left booties and gloves here for you." He indicated to the bench. "He wasn't happy that Raven walked all through a puddle of blood."

Sighing, Jenna sat on the bench and pulled on booties and gloved up. She looked up when Kane sat beside her. She handed him the protective gear and looked up at Raven. "You were first on scene?"

"Yeah." He indicated to the door. "I heard screaming and kicked in the door. Someone is on their way to repair it. I didn't see anyone, no vehicles apart from what you see here now. Rio took the witnesses back to the office to get their statements." He took Duke's leash from Kane. "I'll take the dogs to the park. I'll be back before you miss me." He headed across the road.

Jenna smiled. "He looks happy."

"Emily is working the case." Kane snapped on gloves. "He likes her and she's finished her studies but he's taking it slow." He chuckled. "He reminds me of me... without the baggage."

Jenna stood and stared after Raven. "That's good. Maybe he won't keep her waiting for four long years." She chuckled, headed for the door and peered inside. "Can we come in?"

"There y'all are." Wolfe came toward them. "The blood patch on the floor isn't blood. It's a synthetic blood used in movies. The victim is female around the same age as the first one, and I'm seeing complete exsanguination. I couldn't get a sample of her blood and took one from the liver. Same stake through the heart. The tip is buried in the table, so I'd say he used a mallet to push it through."

"Does she have marks on her neck as well?" Kane peered behind Wolfe.

"Exactly the same as the first victim." Wolfe looked from one to the other. "This is without doubt the same killer." He stepped back to allow them inside. "We did a sweep for trace evidence and fingerprints and the place is covered with so many different prints, they'll be impossible to match. However, we'll send them to Kalo, along with the victim's and see if he can speed up the process."

Wrinkling her nose at the smell, Jenna swept her gaze over the room. The scene had been staged—the body laid out, hair draped over the table, and the victim's long nightgown hanging down one side. That was it, no clothes. The body was naked under the thin muslin nightgown. "Seems to me this guy wanted her to remain in the display. He wanted people to see his work."

"Take a walk-through, and when you're done, I'll remove

the body." Wolfe shook his head. "If this is another out-of-towner, this guy is hitting on high-risk women. Catching him will be a nightmare. I'll send a message to Helena to ask if this has been happening anywhere else in the state."

"Yeah, this guy is slick. He's been around the block a few times." Kane went to examine the body. "I'm assuming there was a mannequin here before?"

"That I don't know, but the owner is on his way." Wolfe indicated to the way they'd come in. "He needed to grab supplies to fix the door." He looked at Jenna. "You'll likely get a bill."

Jenna stared at the victim's sheet-white face and took in the two puncture marks on her neck and then turned to the stake plunged into her heart. The lack of blood surprised her. She'd seen so many bloody crime scenes this one appeared to be almost peaceful. "There's no signs of a struggle." She looked at Wolfe. "We've checked all the places a person could have obtained a body and found none missing."

A man poked his head inside the door and Jenna held up a hand. "Don't come inside. This is a crime scene."

"I'm Pastor John Dimock." His gaze moved over the prone body and he pressed his hand over his nose. "May I come in and say a prayer for her?"

"Absolutely not." Kane stepped in front of him. "Why are you here?"

"I watched the news about the other young woman. They said she was last seen at the roadhouse on Sunday night." He turned the Stetson in his hands with his fingers. "I was there and I did notice a young woman. So I figured I'd come and tell you. I was on my way to your office and spotted you here."

"Go on." Kane remained in the doorway.

"She was sitting with a man, and when he left, she followed him outside." The pastor looked at Kane. "I figured you should know."

"Okay. Wait here." Kane glanced over his shoulder. "Jenna."

An eyewitness was just what they needed. Jenna waved him to the door. "I heard. I'll speak to you outside." She glanced at Kane. "Do a walk-through and I'll speak to the pastor."

Kane held her gaze for a long second and then nodded, but before he turned away, Emily moved to Jenna's side.

"We're just about done here." Emily snapped off her gloves and balled them up before tossing them into the medical examiner's trash bag. She pulled on another pair. "I'd like to take a better look around, if you don't mind?" She looked from Jenna to Kane and raised an eyebrow. "Can you spare Raven?"

"Yeah, he's back. I can hear him talking to Rowley." Kane stuck his head outside the door. "Raven, I need you to do a walk-through with Emily."

"Sure." Raven peered inside. "I'll grab some booties."

"No need." Emily met his gaze. "We've processed the scene, the mark on the floor isn't blood. I want to take a better look around. I figure there's false doors or built-in spaces where a killer might hide."

As they walked away, Jenna went to the man waiting outside. She pulled out her notebook. "First, I'll need your details."

"I'm Pastor John Dimock." The tall man opened his arms wide. His face held a pleasant expression as his wide set eyes moved over her face. "I'm working with Father Derry at the shelter."

Jenna made a few notes as Kane moved to her side. "So, what took you to the Triple Z Roadhouse?"

"I do rounds, usually late in the evening. I go to the Triple Z Bar, the roadhouse, and the bus stations." He gave a sympathetic smile. "I look for those needing assistance. You'd be surprised how many people arrive here and have nowhere to go. They believe this town can offer them a new life. I usually direct them to the shelter or buy them a meal. Father Derry makes sure they get back on their feet."

Biting back the need to laugh hysterically at the idea of anyone willingly deciding to move to Serial Killer Central, she exchanged a meaningful look with Kane and then lifted her chin. "That's very noble of you, Pastor. Now can you tell me what you witnessed on Sunday evening?"

"I'd been to the Triple Z Bar. Many young women end up there trying to make a few bucks. They're desperate. I went from there to the roadhouse. I noticed the young woman being hassled by some men, and I was going to help her when a man stepped in and took her to a booth. She didn't complain. I figured she knew him. I spoke to the men. They'd been drinking. I offered to give them a ride home but they refused."

"What do you mean by hassled?" Kane stared at him. "What did they actually say?"

"They wanted her to join them." The pastor frowned. "They offered her money to go to the motel with them." His neck flushed and filled his cheeks. "They wanted to party with her. Their words, not mine." He cleared his throat. "I sat with them for a time and made sure they consumed a few cups of coffee. I don't believe they were bad men. They believed the woman was a sex worker." He scratched his cheek.

Noticing his rough hands, Jenna wondered if coming to Black Rock Falls was a pilgrimage or similar to prove his faith. He resembled the many penniless pastors she'd encountered in this part of the state. "Did you see where the woman went when she left?"

"No, but the men left soon after." The pastor nodded slowly. "I didn't see where they went and when I left, they'd gone."

"What can you tell me about them?" Kane moved closer. "Did you hear any names?"

"No, I'm afraid not." The pastor smiled. "I do recall the

man with the woman. I'm sure I've met him at the Triple Z Bar. He's my size and coloring. I didn't catch his name."

"Did you hear any of the men using names at all?" Kane rested his hand on the butt of his weapon. He stared into space.

"Let me see, one of them called the other Joker." He looked at Jenna. "You don't believe they were involved in her murder, do you?"

Straightening, Jenna stared at him. "I didn't say she was murdered."

"Really? I'm sorry." The pastor shook his head. "The entire town is talking about vampires. The women who found her have told everyone who will listen what they found." He moved dark eyes to Jenna's face. "Fang marks in the neck and a stake through the heart. I figure that means someone murdered her."

Wondering why Rio hadn't cautioned the witnesses to keep the murder to themselves until they'd identified the victim, Jenna cleared her throat. "That's for the medical examiner to decide. I'm not qualified to make that decision." She handed him a card. "Please head down to my office and ask Chief Deputy Rio to take your statement. You've been a great help. Thanks for coming forward. If you do recall anything else about that evening or see the man who was with the victim, call me."

"No trouble at all." The pastor smiled at Jenna. "I'm glad to be of assistance." He took the card and headed toward a pickup.

Jenna turned to Kane. "I'm glad he came forward. His information ties in with what we know so far."

"It looks like we'll need to look for suspects who frequent anywhere high-risk people hang out." Kane stared at the crowd gathered around the entrance. "This guy must blend in with the locals or someone would have spotted him. The townsfolk are more aware than most after all the murders we've had here. If they spot a stranger or someone who doesn't fit, they usually come forward."

Jenna nodded. "I agree. Let's wrap it up here and then grab

Raven and Rowley and head to Aunt Betty's for a bite to eat. We can organize the team to hunt down suspects."

"Ah, that looks like the owner with the carpenter." Kane indicated to a truck parking alongside the Beast. "I guess we clear the crowd and then wait until he's finished. Wolfe will need to give him the all-clear before they can continue working on the exhibit." He glanced behind him. "They're bringing the body out now." He looked at Jenna. "I'll go and speak to the owner."

Jenna sat down on the bench as Rowley pushed his way through the onlookers. She smiled at him. "There you are. We're almost done here. We'll need to wait for Wolfe, and Raven is doing a walk-through with Emily. I just need to make some notes and then we'll head to Aunt Betty's and I'll bring you all up to date. This case is moving faster than I imagined and we have work to do."

FIFTEEN

Emily handed Raven a pair of examination gloves. "I've read about this haunted house attraction. It is high-tech with moving walls and floors. I figure when it's finished it will be a terrifying experience." She smiled at him. "Although, I'm not too sure about walking through it in daylight either. From what Dad said about the terrible experience the women who work here went through, there's something wrong with the electronics."

"I won't allow anything to happen to you, Em." Raven gave her a lopsided smile, his white teeth flashing in the gloom. "It's safe. Your dad assured Kane everything was quiet when he and Webber walked through taking samples." He gave her a long look. "What is it you hope to achieve going through the house again?"

Emily shrugged and walked out of the front door. She nodded to Jenna and Rowley and stepped into the alleyway. "I'm not sure, but I'm starting from the hallway outside the kitchen. That's where the public will start the tour. I figure, there might be hidden places where a killer could hide. It's a perfect place to kill someone—don't you agree?"

"Not exactly." Raven walked beside her. "He didn't murder

that woman here. There's no blood, but why am I telling you? You're a medical examiner."

Loving hearing her new title, Emily glanced at him. "Oh, I know, but I got to thinking. If a killer hid here, he could drag off an unsuspecting woman and kill her. People scream in these exhibits; there's blood and things that don't make sense. He could make himself part of the show and murder people and just walk out. If he was covered in blood, no one would take a second glance—not at Halloween. That night, people wear costumes. He'd just walk free."

"That's just crazy enough to work." Raven followed her into the kitchen and turned to the control panel. "Your dad has finished, so do you want everything turned on and to see what happens? I have a Maglite and we both have phones to record anything weird. Wanna risk it?"

Not usually afraid, Emily's skin prickled as goose bumps rose on her skin, but he'd never know. "Sure. That's what I'm here for. Let's go." Raven flicked the switches, and she headed into the dark hallway.

As she stepped into the weird blue light, the sound of a slow heartbeat grew faster. Long tendrils of sticky spiderwebs brushed her face and caught in her hair. Behind her she could hear Raven batting them away. A door creaked open on her left. The heartbeat stopped and maniacal laughter came from inside the room along with the tinkling sound of a musical box. Emily stepped inside the room, glad to have Raven behind her. Inside a fireplace burst into flames and two skeletons sitting in front of the fire turned to look at her. "*This* is what scared those women?" She giggled. "I figure it's kind of funny."

The sound of deep breathing came so loud it almost deafened her. She turned slowly as a mist rose from the floors. The walls moved in and out in time to each breath and she went closer to touch them. Beside her Raven was doing the same.

"This is amazing." Raven grinned at her. "The sound effects

are a little disturbing, but it's all part of the show." He indicated to another door. "I guess we go through there."

Emily pulled open the door and stepped into the narrow hallway. Before she'd taken a few steps, the laughter started again and behind her a door opened. Startled, she turned to look just as a clown sitting in a wheelchair with an ax protruding from its head came hurtling toward her. Horrified, she turned to run. Over the noise she heard Raven calling her name, but the next second, the floor gave way and she slid through a trapdoor that shut behind her leaving her alone in the dark. "I'm down here Raven. I fell through a trapdoor."

Nothing.

A small child was singing and a candle burst into flames just ahead of her. Stuck inside a small, cramped space, fear had her by the throat. This wasn't funny any longer. She scrambled to her feet, and resting one hand against the wall headed toward the candle. Heart pounding, she tried to convince herself this wasn't real, but the looping disjointed singing was driving her crazy. A door swung open just as she reached it. Hesitating, she moved into another space. Hands grabbed out to touch her, and as she pushed through walls of cobwebs, cold air blasted her.

Lights went on and mirrors surrounded her. She peered into the distorted images and turned slowly. Fragments of someone else moved and panic gripped her. She edged her way forward through the maze. Dead ends greeted her at every turn and when she turned back passageways closed behind her and others opened. She caught a glimpse of a fragmented image, someone taller than her. Fear caught in her throat. The killer? She stopped walking and a wall slid away from beside her. The figure moved. "Raven, is that you?"

"Yeah." Raven appeared from nowhere. He held out his hand. "This way. I found the door." He pulled her through and into the room where the body had been discovered. Light poured in and workmen moved back and forth. "The front door is over there. Are you okay?"

Shaken, with her heart still racing, she gripped Raven's warm hand. Terror still shuddered through her. The place had frightened her more than she'd admit. "Yeah, fine. That was an experience. I'm glad we found the exit. I figured I'd be lost in there all day." As the sound of hammering filled the room, normality slid back into place.

"It was a multidimensional adventure. I'd say it gives everyone a different experience. What happened to you?" He looked down at her. "I was accosted by a witch and lost sight of you. Then I slid down a chute and into another room filled with ghouls and blood-soaked corpses. I found a door and ended up in the mirrors. That place is claustrophobic. I hope they've got someone to haul people out of there if they can't handle it."

Wanting to get outside and far away from the spooky house, Emily headed for the door. "I was chased by a clown in a wheelchair with an ax in his head." Trembling as the hideous clown face blasted into her mind, she looked at him. "I hate clowns and the sound effects were driving me crazy. I need a cup of coffee and something to eat." She could hear her father talking to Kane above the noise of the workmen. "I'll go and speak to Dad. He's probably waiting for me."

"Jenna and Kane are heading over to Aunt Betty's soon. We'll go with them and I'll give you a ride back to the morgue when we're done." Raven squeezed her hand. "I figure you're not returning here anytime soon?"

Reluctantly dropping his hand, she smiled at him. "Thanks, that would be neat." She turned back to glance at the haunted house. "No, I'm not coming back. Once is enough for me." She shuddered. "Clowns give me nightmares."

SIXTEEN

As she finished her meal, Jenna looked at her deputies. "The autopsy of the second victim is at ten tomorrow." She glanced at Raven. "Do you want to be in on this one too?"

"I wouldn't miss it." Raven pushed around a salt cellar on the table. "This case is very interesting. Emily was saying she took prints and Wolfe has already uploaded them into the database. If the victims are on file, we'll be able to identify them."

"There's one thing I noticed over the smell of decomposition: I could smell stale beer." Emily looked up from her plate at Jenna. "As she wasn't wearing anything, I'm assuming the smell came from her hair." She shrugged. "Maybe she works behind a bar."

"There is only one around here that really stinks and that's the Triple Z Bar." Kane dug into his bowl of chili, chewed, and swallowed. "The Cattleman's Hotel smells good and so does Antlers. If she worked local, it must be the Triple Z."

"Yeah, that would be the place." Rowley nodded in agreement. "I don't figure she's a sex worker. They do drop by there on occasion." He raised both eyebrows and looked at Jenna.

Not understanding how he could possibly know that, Jenna moved her attention to him. "What makes you say that?"

"Her nails for one." Rowley shrugged. "The sex workers I've seen usually have nice nails and the victim bites hers. The other thing is, she's not wearing makeup. They usually try to make themselves look attractive."

"Not necessarily, I've seen plenty who bite their nails and have track marks up each arm. Maybe the autopsy will tell us more. I don't figure we run to judgment about her just yet." Kane leaned back in his chair. "We should take a photograph of her and show it to the bartender out at the Triple Z Bar and see what he says."

Jenna nodded. "Yeah, that sounds like a plan. If she worked there, we might get some leads on who was talking to her last night. With two murders this week, I need suspects and right now all we have are shadows. To make things worse, the witnesses are talking and the news is already out that we've found another victim. Some people really believe the bodies are vampires. It's crazy, like mass hysteria, and people are getting spooked."

"What amuses me is, if they read the books, when vampires are staked they burst into flames." Kane chuckled. "We'd be finding piles of ash not dead bodies."

"I figure whoever is doing this believes he's catching them before they turn." Raven sipped his coffee. "Or he would have added fangs. You do know there are people out there who actually believe in all this woo-woo stuff? For them it's real. They're like kids who never grew out of Santa Claus."

"Unfortunately, I do." Kane grimaced. "We've had many cases influenced by the occult."

"I've seen many strange things in my life too. Things that don't quite fit into normality." Emily looked from Raven to Jenna. "I absolutely don't believe in vampires but I like to keep an open mind. I have a scientist's angle on most subjects but there are other things I find intriguing and can see the possibilities, for instance, the mythological gods. How does every civilization have the same story about visitations from people who gave them knowledge? Was there an ancient civilization with knowledge equal or above ours?"

"I find those things very interesting because even Santa Claus was based on fact." Raven placed his cup on the table and nodded sagely. "When we get time, we should talk. I have some theories to discuss with you."

"Now you two have found common ground." Kane grinned. "Jenna wants to allocate what needs to be done."

Amused by the turn of conversation, Jenna raised both eyebrows. "Yeah, I do. Raven and Rowley, there are images of the last victim on the server. Get one and crop it to make it less graphic and take it to the Cattleman's Hotel and Antlers. Show it to anyone who may have come in contact with the victim. We're going to the Triple Z Bar and will swing by the Black Rock Falls Motel and do the same." She looked around the table. "I'll call Rio and ask him to put out a media statement. I'll also ask the townsfolk to remain calm and not to be swept up in the Halloween hype. It might work but I doubt it. With eyewitnesses to the corpses, panic will be hard to stem." She pushed her cup back and stood. "Let's get at it."

Walking out to the Beast, Jenna watched Raven open the door of his truck for Emily and smiled. "I see Raven is old-school. I like that about him."

"Should I be jealous?" Kane lifted Duke into the back seat and then climbed behind the wheel.

Tossing back her hair, Jenna snorted. "No, he only has eyes for Emily."

The drive to the Triple Z Bar was glorious. Seeing the beauty of Stanton Forest dressed in its fall gown, with the many colors and wildflowers lifted Jenna's spirits. The sun had dropped and cast zebra stripes across the highway, between the flashes of sunlight, she caught sight of deer grazing just inside the perimeter of the forest on patches of emerald-green grass filled with sunshine. Tauri loved the forest and the horseback rides they'd taken lately. He'd talked nonstop about Native American folklore. She'd always encouraged him to learn about both of his cultures and welcomed Raya's assistance and, of course, their close friend Atohi Blackhawk's visits. His time with Tauri and their visits to the res ensured Tauri kept a close relationship with his people. She sighed as they bumped over the rutted entrance to the Triple Z Bar. It was close to the Triple Z Roadhouse. "If we'd had this information earlier, we could have saved time."

"It's all part of the job. We're making progress. It's all good." Kane pulled up outside the bar entrance and swung out. "Stay, Duke. We won't be long." He pushed through the old saloon-type double doors and disappeared into the gloom.

The smell of stale beer leaked out before Jenna stepped inside. Apprehension gripped her as she stood for a few moments to allow her eyes to adjust to the dim interior. She scanned the room. The amount of people who congregated here on a daily basis never ceased to amaze her. Bikers crowded around a few tables pushed together, ranch hands in cowboy hats and boots shared a jug of beer, and other men sitting alone bent over bowls of food. Conversation in the room dropped to a small buzz as the patrons noticed them. Law enforcement wasn't welcomed there. Many times, Kane and a team had found themselves in the midst of a brawl. Everyone in the room carried a weapon, and as they walked toward the bar, people behind them were leaving. Most times, for the criminal element, this place was a safe haven where they could get a good bowl of chili and cold beer at a reasonable price. From the condition of the place, it was obvious that the owner didn't pay for any maintenance.

The bartender didn't approach until Kane slapped his palm

on the bar. Jenna moved to his side and pulled out her notebook. She looked at Kane. "Take the lead. He might talk to you."

All eyes looked at them and Jenna could cut the resentment in the room with a knife. She slid onto a barstool and pulled a pen from her pocket.

"Have you seen this woman?" Kane held up his phone.

"I'm not sure." The barkeeper paled and his Adam's apple bobbed up and down. "Maybe."

"Try to remember." Kane enlarged the image. "Does she work here?"

"Is she dead?" The man's eyes widened. "Is she that vampire you found this morning?"

Annoyed, Jenna blew out a sigh. "Yes, she's dead and I can assure you she isn't a vampire. She's someone's daughter and we need to identify her."

"Just a minute." The bartender walked away and returned a few moments later with another man.

"I'm the manager, David Johnstone. How can I help you, Sheriff?"

"Have you seen this woman?" Kane pushed his phone across the top of the bar toward him. "Does she work here?"

"Yeah, she has worked here for a couple of weeks. Her name is Bunny Watkins." Johnstone stared at the image. "Is she dead?"

Jenna nodded. "I'll need everything you have on her."

"Yes, not a problem. I'll print out her information for you. I have it in the office." Johnstone's gaze never left the phone. "How did she die? I know she walks to the motel each night. Was she hit by a vehicle?"

"She walks from here to the motel?" Kane shook his head in disbelief. "What time did her shift finish?"

"Midnight." Johnstone looked up at Jenna confused. "Oh, not a bear?"

Jenna made a few notes and then lifted her chin. "The

cause of death is undetermined at this time. What we need is to speak to the bartenders who worked her shifts. They might recall who spoke to her or who was taking an interest in her at any time. Do you have a list?"

"I'll go and get what you need." Johnstone hurried away.

"I figured that was Bunny." The bartender moved closer, his hands pausing from drying a glass. "Although she looks different. She usually ties her hair back and she has rosy cheeks. She is... I mean *was* an attractive woman, and yeah, she did attract attention." He glanced up at the tables closest to the bar and lowered his voice. "I've seen men hitting on her but I'm not squealing on anyone. Customers who come here don't take too kindly to people who speak to the cops and I've got a family to support."

"I could arrest you for withholding evidence in a murder investigation." Kane's voice was just above a whisper. "Go out back, write the names down on a coaster. I'll order a beer and take the coaster with me if you're afraid of someone seeing you. Just the men who you recall having a conversation, not the catcalls or brief exchanges. We need to know if she mentioned anything about where she was going after work. Understand?"

"Yeah, sure." The bartender turned away. "There were a few men who held her up. It's my job to keep her moving but I don't mind her being nice to the customers. It's good for business, so yeah, I notice who she spends time chatting with. I know most of the locals, so I can give you names if you keep my name out of it."

"They don't need to know who we spoke to." Kane leaned into Jenna as if speaking to her. "We use general terms when questioning people."

Keeping her voice low, Jenna met the barman's gaze. "However, I will expect you down at my office to give a statement within twenty-four hours. Unless you want me to haul you out of here in handcuffs."

The bartender hurried away and the owner came back and handed her a sheet of paper. She left the document on the bar. "I want the bartender's full name and address."

"Okay." Johnstone took a pen from his inside pocket and made notes. "There you go."

A few moments later, the bartender came back, took a bottle of beer from the fridge, and placed it on a coaster in front of Kane.

"Thanks." Kane slid the beer toward him and the coaster disappeared into his pocket. He dropped a few bills on the counter and nodded to Jenna. "Is that all you need, Sheriff?"

Jenna folded her notebook and pushed it inside her pocket. She collected the sheet of paper, looked over it and smiled at the manager. "That seems to be in order. Thank you." She glanced at Kane as they stepped out into the fresh air. "I so feel like taking a shower and washing my hair. The smell of male sweat and stale beer is like death. It clings."

"Add gunpowder and it smells like war." Kane grimaced and climbed into the Beast.

SEVENTEEN

Cold wind with an icy chill filled the cab before Kane closed the door. Outside, leaves rose high into the air, swirling in the gusts of wind rolling down the mountain. It would snow soon; he could smell it in the air. Already the higher slopes of the mountain shone white through the trees. Before starting the engine, Kane pulled the coaster from his pocket and handed it to Jenna. "I'm surprised he gave us a list of names."

"It's better than the information from the manager." Jenna frowned at the coaster, turning it this way and that. "Her name was Bunny Watkins. No previous experience and she didn't work behind the bar. She bussed tables and cleaned. We have her Social Security number, and her address is listed as the Black Rock Falls Motel, room sixteen." She looked at the coaster. "This is almost too helpful. Why is he offering this information? They never help us in the Triple Z."

Kane started the engine, glad of the blast of hot air from the heater. "Know anyone on the list?"

"Nope." Jenna shook her head. "We have Dale Cash. He has added 'ranch hand.' Now that's even more helpful." She narrowed her gaze as if trying to make out the names. "Bryce

Withers, horse breeder; Daniel McCulloch, hospital maintenance; and Sly Goldman, cleaner, Triple Z. Hmm, we'll look at them back at the office. I need to follow up on the victim first."

Kane swung the truck around in reverse and they bumped over the uneven ground. He waited for an eighteen-wheeler to thunder into the parking lot and slow in a squeal and puff of airbrakes before pulling onto the highway. "I'll head to the motel. We'll be able to get access to her room. Maybe we'll find more information about her."

During the short drive to the motel, Kane drove slowly and indicated to the overgrown ditch alongside the highway. "There's not anywhere to walk safely here. She must have walked along the blacktop. It would only take someone to watch her movements for a few nights and then wait for her to leave." He sighed. "I can't see any type of disturbance but we've had rain."

"I doubt anything would stick out in that long grass. We'd need to search it." Jenna pulled out her phone. "I'll call Rio. We know which bar she was in the night before she died, so they don't need to check out the others. They can search the roadside." She made the call.

Ahead, the old motel fluorescent sign flickered VACANCY as Kane turned into the Black Rock Falls Motel. The place never changed. It was a dive stuck in the seventies. The dusty windows surrounding the office had the same yellow sunflower drapes as when he arrived in Black Rock Falls over seven years ago. He pushed open the door and stepped inside the dingy room. The ceilings carried a thick coating of yellow sludge, left from years of smoking, and although now banned in public areas, the hint of it still lingered as if it had permeated every fiber of the room.

He scanned the room, taking in the faded, yellowing posters and the old travel ads that hadn't been updated in decades. Notices pinned haphazardly in a plastic-wrapped bulletin board featured local events from years ago. He glanced at Jenna and grimaced as they approached the cluttered reception desk, its wood scarred from years of use. He moved forward and stared at the coffee-stained register book. The pages for the last few days were empty.

In the background, he could hear the sounds of daytime TV, and when he leaned over the counter, he found a TV screen with grainy images of the line of motel rooms. On the wall was an old key rack, with keys dangling from rough chunks of wood with the numbers written on with a marker. He snorted and looked at Jenna. "Does he really figure someone is going to run off with one of those keys?"

"I guess so." She hit the bell on the counter, which made a hollow clinking sound, not loud enough to alert anyone watching TV in the back room. She wiped her hand on her jeans. "Hey, anyone home?"

A large balding man stepped out from the back room. Potato chip fragments liberally coated the front of his knitted sweater. He took a gulp from a bottle of soda and his limpid eyes moved from Kane to Jenna. "Look, I've been following regulations. No one smokes out here no more. The sheets are changed regular, when the clients leave. I run this place to the book."

Kane raised one eyebrow and shook his head. "I'm sure that you're doing your best to keep everything up to date but we're not here about the regulations. We're here to remove the personal effects from room sixteen, and before you start making a fuss, Ms. Watkins is deceased." He held out a hand. "Give me the key. I'll return it when we're through."

"She's not still in the room, is she?" The man behind the counter looked to the door and then back to Kane.

"No, she isn't. Now the key, please?" Jenna glared at him.

After handing her the key, Kane followed Jenna outside to the Beast. She'd dropped the key on the hood and was frantically pulling out wipes from the dispenser. He took a handful from her and wiped his hands and then pulled on the examination gloves she thrust at him. "Are you okay?"

"Yeah, I am now." Jenna snapped on gloves and threw the wipes into an overflowing garbage bin outside the office door. "I'm not planning on taking germs from that disgusting hole back to our kids."

Kane smiled and let Duke out of the back seat to stretch his legs. The dog wouldn't go far. "I'm surprised he didn't want to come with us in case we try to sneak away with one of their towels."

"After the Triple Z Bar and now this filthy disgusting place, I'm taking a shower before I go home. You should too." Jenna headed along the row of motel rooms.

Kane followed, wondering if the council inspected dives like this, but then the motel rooms out back of the Triple Z Bar were in even worse shape. He figured if they changed the sheets and offered clean towels maybe that was enough. He stood to one side as Jenna opened room sixteen. A gust of cleaning spray escaped when she opened the door but it hadn't masked the damp mildew smell. He figured Bunny must have tried to clean the room. He glanced around at the floral wallpaper, peeling at the edges to reveal water stains. The bed was unmade and the blankets pulled back as if to air the damp sheets. He moved closer to read the rude graffiti carved into the headboard and shook his head. Some of the messages for a good time dated back to the eighties.

Discarded clothes were draped over a straight-backed chair. Kane picked up a white T-shirt with stains down the front, dumped over a pile of underwear. On a bedside table scarred with cigarette burns sat a plastic lamp with a tilted shade and a half-empty water bottle. He glanced at Jenna. "I'll take a look around. Her bag is on the table. Maybe she left some clue behind?"

"Okay, but leave the door open." Jenna wrinkled her nose. "I can't breathe in here."

The room was tiny. The closet held a few clothes. Shirts, sweaters, pairs of jeans hung over coat hangers. A pair of well-worn boots had been set neatly beside the bed on the threadbare, filthy orange and brown shag carpet. A cold breeze brushed Kane's face when he opened the bathroom door. The small window had been propped open using a coat hanger. Wet clothes hung on the shower rail. It was like stepping back in time. The avocado-colored vanity matched the shower cubicle in every way, including the dripping taps and rust stains. The toilet seat was sunflower yellow and scarred from many years of use. It was as if Bunny had just walked out. A makeup bag spilled its contents over the top of the vanity, beside a hairbrush, a can of hairspray, and a toothbrush and toothpaste.

He pulled out his phone, took photographs and retraced his steps. Jenna was doing the same as she removed items from the bag and spread them over the small table. He pulled evidence bags from his pocket, labeled them, and collected the things in the bathroom, and then moved through the room until he had everything packed. He dumped them on the bed and went to Jenna's side. "Find anything?"

"Yeah, she has a tablet and an unused burner phone still in its packaging." Jenna pointed to the table. "There's a bus ticket, along with a timetable." She stood back to show him the clothes she'd stacked in piles. "There's a paperback romance novel, a few bills hidden in a pair of socks, and this." She held up a small silver key. "She stashed something, somewhere. There are hardly enough clothes here to survive. It's as if she left in a hurry. The clothes wouldn't see her through winter. What or who was she running from?"

EIGHTEEN

After repacking the bag, Jenna placed all the other items into evidence bags. She followed Kane back to the Beast and dropped the evidence bags inside. While Kane got Duke settled in the back seat, Jenna went into the office and dropped the key on the front desk. The man dashed out from the back room and stared at her. She met his gaze. "We have collected all of Ms. Watkins' things and don't need to return." She narrowed her gaze. "How long has she been here and when was she paid up to?"

"She's been here three weeks and she's paid up to Friday. She pays when she gets paid." He took a step back. "We don't give refunds." He pointed to a greasy notice behind him. "Says here plain and clear."

Jenna rolled her eyes. "Did she sound like she planned to stay longer?"

"I'm not sure." The man swallowed. "She got a call from the Stanton Forest B and B today offering her a room." He indicated to the numbered cubbyholes behind him. "See, I left the message for her but I haven't seen her. She didn't have a vehicle and walked to the Triple Z Bar and back." He gave her a long look. "She arrives here after midnight and I leave the key for her in the breakfast hatch." He shuffled his feet. "The key wasn't in the box this morning, so I went down to her room and it was still in the breakfast hatch, so I brought it back here."

Jenna stared at him. "Didn't it occur to you that something might have happened to her on the walk back here at midnight?"

"Look, Sheriff, I run a business and what the clients do is their concern." He lifted his double chin. "I'm not her pa and what she does or where she spends her nights is none of my concern."

Wanting to get away from the motel as soon as possible, Jenna dropped a card on the counter. "If anyone calls you about her, apart from the B and B, get their details and call me right away. Understand. Right away."

"Yeah, sure." The man looked relieved.

Jenna hurried from the office, stripping off her gloves as she walked and dumping them in the garbage. She climbed into the Beast. "Let's get out of here. We'll drop the tablet to Wolfe and see if he can crack it. He'll call on Kalo to assist if he can't. Then I need to take a shower and burn these clothes."

"They'll be fine in the wash." Kane chuckled. "I'll make sure they don't contaminate the boys."

Giving him a long look, Jenna shook her head. "I'll drop them into the washing machine at the office. They'll be dry before we leave." She sighed. "Spray the Beast when we leave too. Just to be sure."

"Okay, okay." Kane pulled into the medical examiner's parking lot. "Wait here. I'll give Wolfe the laptop." He grinned at her. "I don't want to spread germs in the morgue." He grabbed the evidence bag from the back seat and slid from the vehicle.

Jenna's phone chimed. It was Rio. "Did you find anything?"

"Nope, not even a candy wrapper. No footprints." Rio

crunched through gravel. *"We're heading back to my truck now. Did you get any more info on the second victim?"*

Leaning back in her seat, Jenna stared through the glass doors into the pristine white-tiled hallway in the morgue, watching Kane disappear into Wolfe's office. "Yeah, we have a laptop and her belongings. She was traveling light. I figure she packed in a hurry and came here without any type of a plan in mind. The manager at the Triple Z Bar confirmed that she worked there but she gave her address as the Black Rock Falls Motel. We also found a key. It looks like the kind that is used in the airport lockers, or maybe at the bus station."

"So, you figure there's something more to her than meets the eye?" Rio sounded interested. A door slammed and an engine roared into life. *"A mystery within a mystery, huh? We'll meet you at the office. I can't wait to see what else you found."*

Sighing and checking her watch, Jenna nodded. "Yeah, but it's too late to hunt down the lock to this key. It could be in another county. We'll look at the list of names the bartender gave me."

"Fine by me." Rio cleared his throat. *"Our ETA is five minutes. See you there."* He disconnected.

Jenna made a few notes to put her deputies to work the following morning. She would attend the autopsy and they could hunt down and question the suspects. Four men had interacted with Bunny hours before she died. She needed a timeline and to make sure she had all the potential players lined up. Deep in thought when Kane returned, she ran the possible timeline through her mind. Kane remained silent, lost in his own thoughts as they drove the short distance to the parking lot outside her office. When the truck stopped, she turned to him. "What did Wolfe say?"

"He'll try to open the laptop, and if not, he'll call Kalo to crack it, like we figured." Kane climbed out of the vehicle and collected the evidence bags from the truck.

Jenna unclipped Duke's harness from the back seat and lifted him down. The dog gave her a lick on the cheek and she rubbed his ears. He shook all over, from his big floppy ears to the tip of his tail, stretched and yawned, and then smiled his big doggy smile at her. She laughed, recognizing the signs. "Ah, it must be time for your dinner? Yes, we are late this afternoon. Don't worry, we have plenty of food for you in my office." She used the retinal scanner and walked inside the back door and then stood to one side, holding open the door for Kane, laden with evidence bags and a backpack.

She took some of the bags from him and they headed through the office, waved to Maggie, and stopped at Rio's desk. "Give me fifteen minutes and I'll bring you up to date. We need to change. I smell like an ashtray. We'll use the conference room."

"Not a problem." Rio stood. "I'll put on a pot of coffee while we wait."

"I'll check the server in case Wolfe has updated the first victim's files." Rowley looked out from around his cubicle.

Jenna nodded. "That sounds like a plan." She followed Kane up the stairs. They dumped the evidence bags onto the conference room table and headed for the showers.

Since becoming sheriff, Jenna had encouraged her team to keep clean uniforms and casual clothes, boots, and cold-weather gear in the lockers. Visiting crime scenes could be a nasty business, as was chasing down killers over all terrains. Having a laundry room as well had made life easier. The changes she'd made and the extensive expansion of the sheriff's office had made a great difference to the comfort of her team. As she climbed into the shower, the image of Bunny Watkins slid into her mind. Who had she been running from? A killer, a stalker, or an abusive relationship? Her hands would be tied to pursue an abusive partner if he lived out of her jurisdiction. Special Agent Beth Katz and the intimidating Agent Dax Styles out of

Snakeskin Gully came to mind. Beth had the same hatred as she did for abusers. If she discovered Bunny had been a victim of domestic violence to the extent she needed to hide in Serial Killer Central, she'd ask Special Agents Katz and Styles to pay her partner a visit.

NINETEEN

He sat in his truck, his fingers cold as they circled the milkshake. He sucked on the straw, one arm leaning nonchalantly on the open window as he watched the people climbing down from the bus and collecting their luggage from the underneath compartment. He wondered if the vampires he sought understood how easy it was to pick them out of a crowd. When people arrived in town, they usually had purpose. They scanned the vehicles as they waited for a ride or had made plans to move to the next stage of their journey and, ticket clutched in their hands, moved off toward a line of waiting buses. The vampires kept their heads down, likely trying to hide the red glow in their eyes. They always started that way. They honestly believed that people are stupid, and that everyone would fall for their poor little girl act.

Most times the crowd would scatter and they'd be standing all alone with maybe a small bag or a backpack. It was as if they were testing the location by tasting the air to see if anyone would take the bait. They expected people to feel sorry for them and offer help—and oh, how they played on people's feelings, drinking down their good nature as if it were nectar. He'd witnessed it so many times. He could play the game, and although they often acted coy, very few refused his help in the end. If they were reluctant to follow him to his truck, he'd pretend to leave as if he didn't care and they'd run after him or call him back. By then it was too late for them. He always drugged their drinks and they'd either fall asleep in the truck or at the table in the diner with no memory of him. The drug he used made certain of that and by morning it had left their system without a trace.

The straw made a slurping sound at the bottom of the to-go cup and he tossed the empty container into the garbage can beside the truck. By the time he looked back at the bus, the crowd had thinned and there she was. This one was younger than the others, maybe eighteen, with long blonde hair falling to her waist. Pale skin and those big round frightened eyes. He wondered how many poor souls she'd drained the blood from and over how many centuries. She'd hide her fangs, keeping them tucked away until she had someone in her sights. The evil coming from her spilled across the blacktop and mixed with the puff of exhaust from the bus as it drove away.

He pulled out his field glasses and peered at her, noticing she had a bruise under one eye, hastily covered with makeup. He shook his head, disappointed. Most of his selections were perfect, but she had all the other attributes he needed. She looked like an angel but the innocent look didn't fool him. He would bide his time and wait for her to need him. A young blonde in the Triple Z Roadhouse alone after dark was a recipe for disaster, and he could play the knight in shining armor again. He smiled as two pickups screamed into the parking lot and hunters, still wearing their bright orange vests, spilled out. From the lack of kills in their truck beds, they hadn't had any luck and were heading to the roadhouse for a meal. They all noticed the lone girl, whistled, and offered her their company. He smiled. Some days, others did his work for him. One man, she could feed on safely, but not a bunch of yahoos.

He glanced in his rearview mirror. He'd changed his appearance. He'd chosen worn jeans, a T-shirt under a sheepskin jacket, and a dark brown Stetson, his dusty cowboy boots were worn down at the heels and turned up at the toes. He blended in with the locals as just another ranch hand. His attention moved back to the girl. She checked her purse and chewed on her bottom lip, no doubt working out if she had enough to buy a meal. As she pushed through the doors of the roadhouse, he took the wedding band out of his inside pocket and slipped it on. Believing he had a wife at home sweetened the pot. The girl would feel safe and the vampire would have two sleepy victims to hunt. He checked his watch. It was five after ten as he walked toward her. Excitement shivered through him and he breathed it in, enjoying the rush. It was almost as good as when he drove the stake into their rotting hearts.

TWENTY

Wednesday

Rio went to the whiteboard, picked up the pen and made a list of the suspects that Jenna had retrieved from the Triple Z Bar. He'd arrived at the office at six-thirty that morning and spent his time hunting down any information he could dredge up from the files. Sly Goldman, the cleaner at the Triple Z Bar, had been arrested in Blackwater a few times for petty crimes but had a rape case against him dropped, when the woman involved had refused to cooperate with the investigation. As he could possibly be one of the last people to see Bunny alive, he would be someone they would need to investigate more closely. He made the appropriate notes against Goldman's name.

The horse breeder was easy to find. Bryce Withers had his own spread, known locally as the BW Ranch. A search of his name brought up interesting articles about the charismatic man in his late thirties, who had plans to run for mayor one day. He found no priors, not so much as a parking ticket. He often hung out at the local bars too, as he was quoted in a recent article, "Get to know the working man."

A background check on Dale Cash, a ranch hand working out on the Crazy K Cattle Ranch, proved to be more interesting. His records showed juvenile misdemeanors, including drug possession, theft, and vandalism. He had a current order against him for abusing his girlfriend. The order had originated from the neighboring town of Louan six months previously. The last man on his list, Daniel McCulloch, a maintenance man at the hospital, was a surprise. A few years previously, after drugs were stolen from the local hospital, the background checks on employees had been tightened, and yet McCulloch had complaints against him, which had resulted in disciplinary actions or terminations from previous jobs. It seemed unusual to him that the hospital would employ someone with obvious behavioral issues. He rubbed his chin, thinking as he scanned the whiteboard, checking his entries.

The previous evening Jenna had given them their orders for the morning as she and Kane would be attending the autopsy. He turned as Rowley walked into the conference room. He looked tired and had a distinct smell of babies about him. No doubt, he'd been up all night with a teething child. He rubbed a hand under his nose. He didn't envy him one bit. Of late, he enjoyed being single and dating a variety of women. Seeing Raven with his ex-girlfriend Emily didn't bother him at all. He cleared his throat. "Morning. I have some background information on the suspects and where we might find them this morning. I've uploaded the information onto the server. If you download the files, we'll head out and start interviewing them as potential suspects."

"Sure." Rowley turned on his heel and headed back down the stairs.

Rio followed. He grabbed his coat and checked his weapon. As usual, on the strike of seven Maggie walked through the door and beamed at him. He handed her a list of the places they'd be heading. "I'll check in as we arrive and leave. When the sheriff arrives, tell her I've added everything I've found onto the whiteboard and the files have been updated. There's nothing from Wolfe yet."

"Okay, I'll let her know." Maggie dropped her bag on the counter and slid out of her heavy coat. "I figure snow is on the way. The sky is threatening." She smiled at him. "Stay safe out there."

He nodded and turned as Rowley came toward him, pulling on his coat. "First stop is the Crazy K Cattle Ranch." He looked at Rowley. "Do you know where that is by chance?"

"Yeah." Rowley pushed on his hat. "We'll take my truck. It's easier when I know the ranches. The Crazy K just happens to border my land."

Rio followed him to his truck. "I hope one of these leads pans out. Whoever is doing this knows about leaving trace evidence. If Wolfe had found anything, he'd have called by now. Which means it's going to be hard police work."

"I don't know how they do it but Jenna and Kane often see things I miss." Rowley backed out and headed along Main. "You do too. It's also the subtle things suspects say you all home in on and explore. I've seen Kane ask questions and the suspect seems to forget to lie or something."

Rio smiled to himself. "It's an interviewing technique. Kane makes the suspect believe he is either on his side or he feels the same way. I recall him getting down to a killer's level to make him confide in him. It worked and another killer is off the street." He looked at Rowley. "I figure he's been trained in interrogation. We know he is ex-military, not that he talks much about it, but I'm guessing that's where it came from."

After looking at the images of the suspects, Rio had an idea. "Swing by the roadhouse. I want to show these pictures to the servers and see if any of our suspects dropped into the roadhouse on Sunday night."

"I doubt it. The staff on duty at this time of day would be

different than the ones who work nights and weekends." Rowley kept driving. "Maybe try there after five, when the new shift takes over?"

Rio nodded. "Good thinking."

TWENTY-ONE

Ten minutes later, they headed through the gates of the Crazy K Cattle Ranch. As they drove along a well-maintained driveway lined with white pole fences, Rio took in the landscape. A herd of Black Angus cattle grazed on a hillside, and as they got closer to the buildings, he made out a paddock with horses, heads up looking at them. They headed to a collection of outbuildings set around a grand old ranch house with wide verandas and pulled up outside a building with the sign OFFICE. He climbed out and the smell of cows washed over him. It wasn't unpleasant, more like the smell of a ranch he recalled visiting as a child. He followed Rowley into the office and a woman in her sixties greeted them. "Morning, ma'am. I need some information on one of your ranch hands by the name of Dale Cash."

"I'm not in the habit of giving out confidential information." The woman looked at him over her half-moon glasses. "You should know that, Chief Deputy Rio. Is that a trick question?"

Rio smothered a smile. "Nope. Dale Cash has a criminal record, as I'm sure you're aware. We are not here to arrest him.

We're more interested in who he was speaking to on Monday night."

"Over half the men working here have criminal records." The woman leaned back in her chair and folded her arms across her ample belly. "Many of them just want the chance to start again. We run a tight ship here and don't allow them to get out of hand, but what they do on their downtime is their business."

"Where can we find him?" Rowley moved forward. "We need to speak to him and we're running out of time."

"Just a minute." The woman clicked on her computer keyboard. "He works with the horses, so at this time of the morning he'll be in the barn mucking out, I'd say. They turn out the horses into the corral each morning until it starts snowing."

Touching his hat, Rio turned and headed out of the door. They walked between the buildings until they found the barn. As he stepped inside the dim interior, he waited for a few seconds to allow his eyes to adjust. Three men worked together using pitchforks and chatting loudly. The banter stopped abruptly when they turned to see him. He recognized Cash from his DMV photograph: tall and broad with dark blond hair curling to his collar from under a brown cowboy hat. He dropped his pitchfork to the floor and the steel tips clunked against the concrete. Cash leaned against the handle, watching them with a measured stare. He didn't act concerned, just wary. Rio moved closer. "Dale Cash? We need a word with you."

"Why?" Cash lifted his chin, his grip tightening on the handle. "I ain't done nothin'."

"Maybe you should ask for a lawyer?" One of his coworkers tipped back his hat and his lip curled. "You can't trust law enforcement. You know that, right?"

"I know it." Cash hadn't moved and his defiant expression spoke volumes. "I ain't done nothing, Deputy. What's this all about?" He swiped at the end of his nose. "If Laura is tellin' you I been hassling her, she's a liar. I haven't left Black Rock Falls in the past two months—ask anyone. I hang around this place like a bad smell."

His workmates chuckled and Rio glanced at Rowley and then back to Cash. "I didn't say we planned to arrest you. We just need some information, is all. You can give it to us here, or we can take you downtown to speak to the sheriff." He shrugged. "It makes no difference to us. We're just doing our job. Like you, some of us need to shovel the shit from time to time."

Anger flashed in Cash's eyes but he managed to keep himself under control. Rio had hit a nerve. He reached for the cuffs on his belt and the small action had an immediate effect on Cash.

"Okay." Cash propped the pitchfork against the stall and walked across the barn toward them. He indicated to a tack room. "We can talk in private in there." Once inside, he spun around to look at them. "Okay, ask your questions but I reserve the right to refuse to answer on the grounds it may incriminate me."

Rio glanced at Rowley and rolled his eyes. "If it makes you happier, I can Mirandize you. It seems pointless when I only want to ask you about your visit to the Triple Z Bar on Monday evening. You were seen talking to a woman clearing the tables. We would like to know what you talked about."

"Many guys were speaking to her—she's a looker." Cash rubbed his chin and looked at them thoughtfully as if trying to think of what to say. "I asked her if she was new in town because I haven't seen her before. I asked if she'd like to have a drink with me later, when she finished work."

"What did she say?" Rowley rested one hand on the grip of his pistol, but his stance was casual.

"She said that she worked until after closing, finishing around midnight and she didn't make a habit of having a drink with anyone. She was too darn tired." Cash smiled. "I asked her if she'd like to have a drink with me or even a meal on one of the days she wasn't working. She told me she worked seven days a week and that she was trying to save up for some form of transport. Maybe a bicycle. I told her I will be happy to give her a ride anywhere she wanted to go but she refused." He leaned against a saddle rack and shrugged. "That was all we talked about. I left after that and came back here. We start at daybreak and I needed to get some sleep. I only went there to play pool with my buddies. We don't usually go there during the week."

Rio glanced at Rowley, who was making notes, to see if he had any questions for Cash. "Did she mention that she walked home each night?"

"I figured that was kind of obvious as she didn't have any transport." Cash snorted and looked away. "I may be shoveling shit all day but I'm not stupid." He scratched his cheek. "Why are you asking me all these questions? Has something happened to Bunny?"

"Do you sleep in the bunkhouse?" Rowley's attention had moved to Cash.

"Yeah." Cash's eyes darkened with suspicion. "Why?"

"We need to see your belongings and then we'll leave you be." Rowley straightened.

"I don't believe it." Cash shook his head slowly. "Bunny sent you here because I took her bandana? I told her I'd give it back when I next went to the bar. I was teasing her, is all."

Surprised, Rio cleared his throat. "We need it back. Why did you want it?"

"It smells good, like her." Cash waved a hand around. "In case you didn't notice, women are thin on the ground here. The two female ranch hands who work here are older than my ma." He sighed. "Follow me, I'll get it for you." He shook his head. "She didn't seem the type to cause me trouble. I figured she liked me."

Rio followed Cash to the bunkhouse and waited for him to

open a footlocker at the end of his cot. He leaned forward to peer inside. "Take everything out and place it on the bed."

"Okay. I've got nothing to hide." Cash took out a pile of jeans, shirts, a couple of winter jackets, gloves, socks, and underwear. Underneath was a Glock 22 in a shoulder holster, a box of ammo, and a red and white bandana. He handed the bandana to Rio.

Possession of the weapon was fine; Cash didn't have a felony. Rio opened an evidence bag and Cash dropped it inside. "When was that weapon last fired?"

"Last time I went to the range." Cash sighed. "Is that all? I need to get back to work before I'm missed." He stared into Rio's eyes. "Is Bunny okay? I don't believe she sent you after me."

Rio didn't blink. "She didn't." He looked away and sighed. "I'm afraid she's dead. You might have been the last person to have spoken to her."

"Dead?" Cash looked from one to the other. "What happened to her?"

"The cause of death is undetermined at this time." Rowley frowned. "Did she mention anything about her family or where she came from?"

"No." Cash shook his head slowly. "She just wanted a better life. I figured she must have hit rock bottom if she believed cleaning at the Triple Z was a better life."

Rio nodded. "You can put your things away now. One thing, did you see anyone chatting to her before you left the bar?"

"I don't know." Cash shrugged. "I left just after." He placed everything neatly back in the box. "I gotta go."

Rio nodded. "Thanks for your help." He handed him a card. "If you or any of your friends recall any information, call me."

The man took the card and dropped it into the garbage and then left without a backward stare.

TWENTY-TWO

Jenna walked into the office, glad to see that Rio and Rowley were already on the job. She went to her office to scan the files Rio had uploaded to the server. She glanced over at Kane. "I'm always impressed how much information Rio can obtain in such a short time."

"Yeah, I gather they're heading out to speak to two of the potential suspects, Cash and Withers are on the same side of town. If the autopsy doesn't take too long, we should be able to interview at least one of the others." He gave her a long look. "Do you want me to write a media release? We need information. There might be someone out there who has seen something and at the time they didn't notice something was wrong."

Glancing up from her computer screen, Jenna shook her head. "No need to. I wrote one on the drive into town and I've already sent it." She glanced at her watch. "I received a reply right away and it would have been on the eight o'clock news. I'd say if anyone has seen anything, the phones should start ringing before long."

"I hope Rio and Rowley will be back soon because there's no way Maggie will be able to cope with answering the phone all day and running the front counter." Kane leaned back in his chair. "If you want to get things organized here before we leave for the autopsy, I'll go down and lend her a hand now."

Jenna smiled at him. "Thanks, I would appreciate that. I'll give Rio a call and see how far along he is with the investigation." When Kane left the room, she made the call.

She listened with interest at Rio's rundown of the interview with Dale Cash. "So, he had a trophy?"

"The thing is we don't know if he'd gotten that from her before she left the Triple Z Bar or around the time she died." Engine sounds came from the earpiece and Rio cleared his throat. *"One thing I noticed was the man keeps his belongings tidy. His bed was made and his belongings stowed in neat piles inside a trunk at the end of his bed. Everyone who sleeps in the bunkhouse had the same setup—cot, bedside table, and trunk—but I noticed most of them were messy. He is also an impressive size, not as big as Dave but more like Carter. He wouldn't have any problems carrying a body."*

Considering everything he had said, Jenna pulled at her bottom lip. "Did you think to ask him if he was in the roadhouse on Sunday night?"

"No, I didn't. I'm sorry, Sheriff. I was kinda concentrating on the Bunny Watkins case. I have his cell phone number. I'll call him right away and get back to you." He sighed. *"We're heading out to talk to Bryce Withers, the horse breeder."*

Jenna frowned. It wasn't like Rio to forget anything. "Yeah, follow up on Cash and when you've spoken to Withers head back to the office. We'll need you both at the front counter answering phone calls. I've given a media release about the latest victim and it's already been on the news. Dave is downstairs helping Maggie answer the calls and there's no one to run the front counter." She sighed. "We're due at the autopsy at ten."

"Yes, ma'am." Rio disconnected.

She made a list of things to do and then grabbed her and Kane's coats. She looked at Duke, snug and warm and sound asleep in his basket under her desk. She bent to rub his silken head and he lifted his eyelids to peer at her. "Stay here, we'll be back soon." The dog had food and water and he'd been walked just before. He'd do for a couple of hours.

Jenna headed downstairs just as Pastor John Dimock came through the glass doors, bringing with him a strong breeze filled with the threat of snow. She glanced at her watch. She didn't have time for long discussions and forced her lips into a smile. "Pastor Dimock, what brings you here on a cold day like today?"

"I heard the callout for people for the hotline. I'm here to help." Pastor Dimock met her gaze. "Have you discovered that poor woman's name yet? How did her family take the terrible news?" He rubbed his hands together. "I'm always available to pray with the bereaved."

Zipping up her coat and pulling on gloves, Jenna shook her head. "I've put everything we know into the media release. We haven't contacted her next of kin, so we won't be releasing her name. The media release was more of a call for information. We need to discover if anyone was in the area when the body was dumped or saw anyone acting strangely."

The four phones in the office were ringing off the hook. Jenna looked at Kane who was making notes with the phone tucked under his ear. "My deputies will be along soon and be able to assist you. I'm sorry, but I really need to go now."

"That's fine." Pastor Dimock gave her a compassionate smile and turned to Kane. "I'm here to answer the hotline phones."

"Thank you. Maggie is organizing everyone, so if you need any help, talk to her or Deputy Rowley." Kane came out from behind the counter. "When you answer the phone it's very important that you take down the details of the caller first. Then write a small description of the reason for their call. Thank them and tell them we will be in contact if the information is relevant to the case. That's all you really need to know." He held the countertop flap open for the pastor and waved him inside. "The pens and the caller notebooks are on each desk. We need to go. We're late."

Jenna nodded. "Thank you. I appreciate your help."

"My pleasure." Pastor Dimock walked to a desk and made himself comfortable and then picked up a ringing phone.

Jenna hurried back through the office and out the back door to where Kane had parked the Beast. "I'm grateful for any assistance but I don't want him talking to the next of kin. That's Father Derry's job. Pastor Dimock seems to be a gossip, so we'll need to be careful what we say around him. We don't want a conviction jeopardized by sensitive information getting to the press."

"My thoughts exactly but pastors do try and help. It's what they do, so don't worry too much." Kane started the engine and they headed for the morgue. "Run it past the others as well. He might be well-meaning but we don't know him as well as the other volunteers. They know not to run their mouths." He snorted. "I guess Father Derry has run a background check on him. He usually does for anyone he has working alongside vulnerable people, so he's probably just overzealous."

Jenna stared at the doors to her office as they drove out of the parking lot. "Yeah, he would. Nothing slips past Father Derry."

When they arrived at the morgue and suited up, Jenna could hear Raven's voice clearly coming from the examination room. He was discussing various autopsy techniques with Emily and they both turned to look at Jenna when she walked through the door. They stood to one side and Wolfe was bending over the body on the gurney. "Are we late?"

"No, but as this case is identical to the previous one, we moved along with the autopsy rather than making you go through the same examination again." Wolfe peered at her over the top of his face mask. "The complete exsanguination is the same. The sharp force trauma on the neck is identical. I can't imagine why he's draining their blood unless he's drinking it, but the stake through the heart on both victims is the classic way in fiction to dispose of a vampire. I don't understand the workings of a very sick mind but I figure whoever is doing this believes he is destroying vampires." He looked at Jenna. "Have you discovered any information on her at all?"

Jenna nodded. "Yes, her name is Bunny Watkins. I have more on her than I'd hoped for, but unless you can get into her laptop, we can't get any further at this stage."

"I had absolutely no luck at all getting into her laptop. I even tried her fingerprint, but as you know, most times a dead person's finger won't work." Wolfe indicated to Raven. "Raven was good enough to fly the laptop to Kalo. It took him an hour to break the password, which makes us believe she had something to hide. It's back in my office now. The password protection has been removed, so you can scroll to your heart's content."

Glancing at Raven, Jenna smiled. "Thank you. I didn't know you were flying full-time again?"

"I've kept my license up to date and Wolfe took me out to get all the other requirements I needed. It's all good now. I've been flying alone for over a year now." He indicated to Emily. "Emily came with me this morning. We left at first light."

Jenna nodded, realizing how much she'd missed being at home with her boys. Life had gone on without them and they hadn't missed her at work at all. The team had performed like clockwork but it was different now—they had a murder to solve.

"That's why none of us has had time to look at the laptop." Wolfe had opened the chest of the victim. "See, everything is the same. The killer has this down to a fine art. Have you discovered any similar crimes elsewhere?"

"Not yet." Kane leaned closer and peered into the cavity.

"I've never seen anything like this before. We're trying to get a timeline of the victim, well both of them. It's sketchy. We discovered a bus ticket and a key. It's likely from a locker. Maybe an airport or bus station. If we can narrow it down, we might discover why this poor woman ended up in Black Rock Falls."

"Kalo is your man for that job." Wolfe removed organs and weighed them. "He has access to so many databases. Does the key have any markings, numbers, or similar?"

"Yeah, it does, a number four." Kane rubbed his chin. "Nothing else I recognized, no name. I'll take photos and send them to him."

"Women run because they're in trouble." Emily moved closer to the body. "Her prints aren't on file, so she isn't running from the law. Maybe a violent relationship?" She went to the screen array and flicked it on to display X-rays. "This woman looks fine on the outside but she suffered numerous injuries in the past. Broken wrists, fingers, her cheekbone, more than once. Look at her face. Her nose isn't straight. It was broken at one time and she has a small scar on her eyebrow. I've seen examples of domestic abuse that look the same. It's something you should consider."

Jenna had thought much the same. "I agree. It's unusual for women to just take off and run to a place like this with no set place to go. It's like they took a bus ride to anywhere just to get away."

"They might have heard of Her Broken Wings Foundation." Raven moved to lean on the counter beside her. "Maybe that's where they were heading."

Shaking her head, Jenna looked at the pale face of the victim. "I never want these women to become faceless victims. I need to know who they were and what happened in their lives to send them here."

"Find out what you can about them, Jenna, and I'll speak

for them in court." Wolfe turned to look at her. "We all do this to bring victims of crime the justice they deserve. What have you got so far?"

Determined to know exactly what happened, Jenna nodded. "Although Bunny Watkins somehow found a job and a place to stay, she became a victim. Why? I figure she must have had a little spare cash. She has worn-down nails and her dry skin and hair tells me she didn't spend anything on herself." She glanced at Kane. "Bunny is the opposite of the first victim, Darlene Travis. She lived a privileged life and left after an argument. It must have been a shock to be stranded without money." She sighed. "I figure she took a ride with the killer because she had no other option as she was being hassled by cowboys at the roadhouse."

"So, the killer must look okay." Emily looked from one to the other. "I mean he must have been a nice guy on the outside. No one is that desperate to get into a vehicle with someone who looks or acts rough."

Swallowing hard, Jenna stared at her. "Do you really believe a young woman would get into a truck with a total stranger because he's handsome or talks nice?"

"I do." Kane shrugged. "Look at Ted Bundy. He could charm the skin off a snake. He had women carrying his books and helping him. He charmed the jury until they saw what he'd done." He looked at Emily. "This is the problem with serial killers: they could be standing next to you and you'd never know until it's too late."

TWENTY-THREE

Rio organized the volunteers who arrived to answer the hotline phones and walked out from behind the counter and went to Rowley's desk. "Did you find any more information on Bryce Withers?"

"Yeah, he seems of good standing in the community." Rowley leaned back in his office chair twirling a pen in his fingers. "I can't imagine why he hangs out at the Triple Z Bar, unless he prefers the company of his ranch hands."

Rio hung his forearms over the edge of Rowley's booth. "I guess we'll find out, but we'll need to tread carefully with Withers. Without a criminal background we don't have the leverage to push hard. We'll head out to his ranch. I'll take the lead as I know how to deal with someone like this."

"Sure." Rowley stood and grabbed his coat from behind his chair. "The BW Ranch isn't far from the Triple Z Bar. Want me to drive?"

Rio nodded. "I'll grab my coat."

The weather was getting wild as they stepped through the doors of the sheriff's office and down the steps to Rowley's truck. Leaves and candy wrappers smacked into his legs as he reached the door and the cold wind bit into his cheeks. Rio glanced toward the mountains. A band of thick clouds was heading their way. He climbed into the passenger seat and Rowley headed along Main and onto Stanton in the direction of the Triple Z Bar.

When they arrived at the BW Ranch a flatbed truck was in the process of unloading palletized feed bags. Men were moving back and forth as two forklift drivers took the pallets and disappeared into a huge barn. Rio frowned at the rifles the onlookers carried. "That seems an unusual amount of security for horse pellets."

"Maybe we need a closer look." Rowley was scanning the photograph of Withers. "I figure that's him there in the sheepskin jacket. The guy beside the one with the clipboard. It looks like they're doing an inventory."

It was about that time that Withers noticed them driving toward the barn. "He's spotted us. Pull up here alongside the fence. It will give the truck room to get past us on the way out."

They stepped out as Withers came walking toward them. At about six-two with broad shoulders, he carried a Glock in a holster at his waist. His open jacket displayed a blue plaid shirt buttoned to the neck and tucked into blue jeans over a pair of dusty boots. In his forties, he fit the description Jenna had added to the case file of the man seen in the roadhouse with Darlene Travis, victim number one. Rio headed toward him. "Mr. Withers?" He indicated toward Rowley. "I'm Chief Deputy Rio and this is Deputy Rowley. We're making a few routine inquiries regarding the murders of Darlene Travis and Bunny Watkins."

"Why come to speak to me? I don't know them." Withers folded his arms across his chest and stood feet apart glaring at them. "If that's all, I have the winter feed to attend to." He glanced over one shoulder at the truck. "We've had pallets of feed go missing and we're looking at a loss of hundreds of dollars."

"If something has been stolen, you should report it." Rowley leaned against his truck. "We will be able to get to the bottom of it and you can make an insurance claim if something's missing."

"I'll take it up with the delivery driver before I do that." Withers glared at them. "Is that all?"

Rio shook his head. "Right now, we're just trying to piece together Bunny's last hours. We are aware that you spoke to her at the Triple Z Bar on Monday night. Just to refresh your memory she was cleaning your table at the time. Witnesses tell us that you spent some time talking to her. Can you walk us through that conversation?"

"Was she one of the women who died?" Withers didn't meet his gaze. "She didn't tell me her name. I noticed she was new and asked her how she managed to end up in a dive like the Triple Z Bar, is all."

"What did she say?" Rowley was making notes.

"As far as I recall, she said that the place was paradise in comparison with where she was before." Withers stared into the distance. "I didn't question her and she moved on to the next table. The last thing I need in my life is a problem. She looked like she was trouble with a capital T."

It seemed to Rio that Withers was consumed with what was going on behind him. The conversation he described would have taken a few seconds and wouldn't have come to the notice of the bartender. There had to be more he wasn't telling them. He would need to sprinkle a few lies into the conversation and see how he reacted. "We spoke to Bunny's coworkers and some of them mentioned that she seemed distracted after you'd left. Was there something bothering her?"

"How do I know?" Withers stiffened and his mouth thinned to a fine line. "I'd seen her in the bar once or twice. That was the first time she came over to talk to me. It was a casual conversation, that's all." He looked from one to the other his eyes narrowing. "You figure I had something to do with her murder, don't you? That's crazy. I didn't even ask her her name."

"You'd be surprised how many murderers don't know the names of their victims." Rowley straightened, one hand resting on the butt of his weapon. "When she left your table did you see her speaking to anyone else?"

"I didn't take any notice." Withers laughed sarcastically. "I can't believe it. I make polite casual conversation with someone cleaning my table and you turn it into a federal case. I need to get back to my men. I've spent enough time on this nonsense." He turned on his heel and headed back to the truck.

Rio turned to Rowley. "We'll head back to the office, although I'd love to take a closer look at the feed he's unloading. Horse pellets might be expensive but I'm sure he doesn't need an armed guard for them. Something doesn't smell right."

"We'll run it past Jenna." Rowley slid behind the wheel. "Seems to me he didn't want us anywhere near that flatbed." He held up his tablet. "I took a few shots of the truck; we might be able to track its origin."

Rio nodded. "It will keep for now. We need to concentrate on the murders. He's a suspect for sure. He was way too fast to deny talking to her and then he became defensive."

"He's involved in something, and we just need to find out what that is." Rowley swung the truck back in the direction of town. "I wish Kane had been here with Duke. If they had drugs hidden among those horse pellets, the dog would have gone ballistic." He glanced at Rio. "I figure we need to keep an open mind. What if Bunny discovered Wither's drug-smuggling operation and he murdered her in a copycat killing to keep her quiet?"

Running the idea through his mind, Rio shook his head. "That's grasping at straws but anything is possible."

TWENTY-FOUR

Jenna dropped into a chair in front of Wolfe's desk and took the cup of coffee Emily handed her. "Thanks, I need this."

Kane and Raven took cups from Emily and sat down just as Wolfe walked into the office.

"First up, we received a DNA sample from Darlene Travis' mother along with a recent photograph of her." Wolfe met Jenna's gaze. "I've sent a copy to your phones and uploaded it to the files. The DNA is a match." He waved a paper in his hand. "I also have the results of Darlene Travis' blood tests." He spread a document on his desk and sat down to read the results. "There are traces of ketamine in her stomach contents, none in her blood. This would suggest she'd had her food or drink spiked. Ketamine causes confusion and is used as an anesthetic for animals. It's a veterinary drug easily obtained by horse and cattle breeders, likely available to ranch hands. I know obtaining it illegally in Black Rock Falls is difficult, but it's easy to buy on street corners in Blackwater." He looked at Jenna. "This proves this was well planned and premeditated." He scanned the documents again. "Hmm, there's also small traces of fentanyl in the blood." He looked up. "I'll have more information later but it might be a few weeks. I tested specifically for these drugs as they're the most popular street drugs right now."

Before she could discuss anything, Jenna's phone chimed. It was Rio. She looked apologetically at Wolfe. "I need to take this. It's Rio." She stood and went out into the hallway. "Yes, Rio."

"A call just came in on the hotline. A couple of hikers say they believe there's a body hanging in the forest, close to the old footbridge over the river, about a hundred yards from Stanton. They entered the forest on the trail opposite the roadhouse." Rio cleared his throat. *"We've just gotten back to the office after interviewing Bryce Withers. I sent Maggie and the volunteers to grab a bite of lunch. We're kinda stuck here at the moment."*

Jenna checked her watch. "We'll go. We're just about done here. We have Raven with us as well. His dog will find a body if it's there."

"Rowley is taking their details. They're on Stanton waiting in a blue Silverado. They'll give you directions." Rio cleared his throat. *"I'll tell them you're on the way."*

As Rio disconnected, she sighed. It was Halloween week and there'd been two murders. People often saw things that didn't exist. Jenna hoped this wasn't a waste of precious time as she had suspects to interview. She headed back to Wolfe's office to bring them up to date. "As we've left Duke in the office, I'll need you to come with us, Raven. I assume Ben will be able to track down a body?"

"Yeah, he's good." Raven rubbed the dog's ears. "I've trained him well over the years. The only thing he has difficulty in is being a dog." He grinned at Jenna.

"I'm coming too." Emily jumped to her feet. "Give me a minute to change and to pull on my hiking boots. I have my backpack ready to go."

"She's right. Y'all might need a medical examiner to process the scene if it's a body." Wolfe stood. "Make sure you take your satellite phones and call me. I'll bring the van around to collect the body." He looked at Raven. "I have spare survival packs. I'll grab one for you." He looked at Jenna. "I assume you have yours in the truck?"

"I have mine in my truck too and my phone." Raven smiled at Wolfe. "I'll follow Dave."

"Here, take these." Wolfe took down a box of energy bars from a shelf and handed them to Kane. "I can hear your stomach growling and Raven's is trying to outdo it. You'll miss lunch. You can eat some of these along the way."

Jenna opened the box and handed a pile to Raven with a roll of her eyes. "Now I have two hungry deputies to worry about. Are you ever full?"

"After Thanksgiving dinner." Kane chuckled. "You?" He looked at Raven.

"Same." He handed Jenna her coat and then Kane his before slipping on his own. "Come on, Ben. We have work to do."

Cold wind buffeted Jenna as she ran to the Beast and jumped inside. She pulled on her gloves and shivered. "The temperature is dropping so fast I wouldn't be surprised if we had snow before long."

"I just hope it holds off while we're in the forest." Kane started the engine and they headed along Main and onto Stanton.

Thick clouds had stolen the sunlight, making the midday drive more like late afternoon as the forest closed in around them. The vehicle was just where Rio said it would be opposite the roadhouse. They all climbed out and approached the two women seated inside. One held a rifle across her knees. Whatever she'd seen in the forest had disturbed her. The door opened and one of the women climbed out. Jenna approached her. "You called the hotline about seeing a body?"

"Yeah, we believe we did, although it's quite dark in there today." The woman pointed to the entrance to a well-known hiking track. "We took this track and as we passed that old bridge that goes over the river, we went past a huge boulder and noticed something in the trees. It looked like the pink back of someone hanging by their legs, head down. We turned around and ran back to our truck and then called 911. Someone from the hotline picked up the call."

"How long ago was this?" Kane had moved beside her. "Did you see anyone on the trail?"

"Maybe twenty minutes, maybe less, and no, we didn't see anyone." The woman's hand trembled as she brushed hair from her face as the wind twirled it around her head.

Jenna nodded. "Okay, thank you. Did you give your details to Deputy Rio?"

"Yes, we did." The woman backed away. "Can we go now? That vampire slayer might be close by."

Trying not to roll her eyes, Jenna glanced at Kane and then back to the women. "Yes, we'll take a look but vampires don't exist. That's just a rumor set off by people to spook everyone over Halloween." She looked from one woman to the other and handed them her card. "If we need any more information, one of my deputies will be in touch."

Jenna waited for the women to drive away and turned to the others. "Okay, let's go."

TWENTY-FIVE

Emily glanced up and grimaced. Dark clouds bounded across the sky, threatening rain or early snow. By the sudden drop in temperature, she reckoned it would be snowing by the end of the week. She settled her backpack on her shoulders and reached for her forensic kit. Her hand brushed over Raven's as he lifted it and hooked it over one shoulder. "I'll carry it."

"I'm sure you can." Raven looked at her and raised one eyebrow. "Do we need to have this argument every time I want to do something for you?"

She stared at him for probably a few seconds too long, taking in the overall strength of the man, his good looks, and charm. He could be a serial killer if she didn't know better. "I figure being the oldest kid in the family, and taking responsibility for carrying stuff is just something I do without thinking." She smiled at him. "Thank you, I appreciate the help."

"My pleasure." Raven waved her ahead of him into the dark forest.

Emily paused. It was as if everything inside of her was screaming at her not to go in there—but she must. An eerie stillness cloaked the forest as they walked. The birds suddenly fell silent and the only sound was the slight rustling of leaves as Kane and Jenna walked ahead of her. The trail became steeper as they climbed and steam puffed around her with each breath. In the silence her breathing appeared loud and her steps heavy. Ahead mist swirled across the pathway distorting her vision and changing the shapes of trees along the trail. She stopped walking and fear gripped her as something appeared to be crawling out of the leaves, but it was only the mist moving around an old rotten log. She took a few deep breaths as Raven caught up to her.

"Everything okay?" Raven scanned the forest. "Don't worry, Ben will alert us if anyone is near."

Glad to have Raven and the dog close by, Emily nodded. "Yeah, the mist is making me see things, is all." She peered along the trail. "I can barely make out Jenna."

"See the large boulder just ahead the women mentioned? Jenna probably went around it and into the forest." Raven ushered her forward. "Look left just ahead and you'll see them."

Stepping carefully over exposed roots and a tangle of dead bushes, Emily turned into the forest, just making out the fluorescent yellow writing on the back of Jenna's jacket reflecting in the dim light. "I see her."

Shadows closed around her and she increased her pace along the narrow path, but all around her branches reached out to tangle in her clothes and pull at her hair. A light breeze brushed cool against her heated cheeks and twirled the mist, making it dance across the pathway in spirals. With it came the unmistakable stench of death. Ahead in the gloom a slowly swinging shape emerged from the mist. It appeared to be human, naked and hanging by its feet.

"Hold up." Raven's hand closed around her arm. "Kane will make sure it's safe."

Brushing his hand away, she turned to look at him. "If it's a body, I need to go and examine it."

"Wait for the all-clear to go in." He moved closer to her. "It could be a trap."

Unease crept over Emily as she stared into the dark forest watching Kane step closer. The beam of his flashlight revealed a pale curve of flesh. She followed the light down to the gaping slash across the neck and the round snout and large nostrils of a pig. She turned to Raven. "It's a pig. A pink pig. How did that get into the forest?"

"They escaped captivity many years ago and seem to be able to outwit the predators." Raven shrugged. "I've killed a few myself to eat." He shook his head. "Whoever killed this one left it to rot. I wonder how long it's been here." He walked toward Kane and looked back at Emily over one shoulder. "It wasn't field-dressed here. The ground below is clean."

"No footprints we can use either." Kane ran his flashlight over the surrounding ground. "It's been disturbed by animals trying to get to the carcass." He unwound the rope and lowered the pig so Emily could examine it. "Do you need to look at it, Em?"

Emily pinched her nose. "A pig? It doesn't need an autopsy. Someone cut its throat. Case closed."

"What's that?" Jenna pointed to the pig as it swung back and forth as if someone had pushed it. "There hanging down from its neck."

"It's a gold locket." Kane pulled out his phone and took photographs of the pig and the locket. He bent and unclasped the chain and held it up in gloved fingers for Jenna to see. "I recognize it."

Trying to ignore the acrid smell of rotting pig, Emily moved closer and a shiver slid down her spine. The killer had been here. This was his idea of a sick joke. "Me too. It's in the photograph we have of Darlene Travis." She stared at Jenna and then scanned the shadows. "He's here, isn't he? This is a trap."

"If he'd wanted to kill us, he would have tried by now."

Kane's voice was just above a whisper. "We've been out in the open, and anyone who can aim a rifle could have hit at least one of us by now. I figure this is a ploy to keep us out of town, for whatever reason."

"How would they know we'd take the call?" Raven looked skeptical. "Or the women would spot the pig and call it in?"

"Because he has a trail cam close by." Jenna waved a hand at the densely packed pine trees. "He could place it anywhere along the trail and we'd never see it. He doesn't need to be here; he'd pick up the feed on his phone."

Three gunshots rang out and echoed through the forest. Both men went for their weapons and pushed Emily and Jenna to the ground. The forest floor vibrated and the sound of distant hoofbeats thundered toward them. The loud cracking of branches breaking was getting louder by the second.

"Stampede. Get up, run. We can't turn the herd. There's no room. We'll need to make it to the bridge." Kane grabbed Jenna's hand and they sprinted toward the river.

"Come on." Raven took Emily's hand. "Run."

Leaping over fallen logs and dead bushes, Emily ran. Ahead, Jenna and Kane made a sharp left and bounded through a clearing. They ran along the edge of the ravine. She stared down in horror. Thirty or so yards below them, the river pounded toward the falls. Cold air cut painfully into Emily's lungs as she ran, the agony increased with each breath. Muscles in her legs screamed with overexertion as she gasped for air. She couldn't stop to take a breath. The noise of the stampede thundered behind them and Raven's hand held her tight. He ran so fast she could hardly keep up with him. Roots tangled around her feet and the next moment she fell. Without a word, he stopped, picked her up, tossed her over one shoulder, and kept running. She gasped, trying to pull air into her lungs. "Put me down."

"Look behind you." Raven picked up speed.

Her chest bounced painfully against his shoulder. Tree branches tore at her clothes and hair and whipped her cheeks. Her ribs ached but she lifted her head to look behind her and fear gripped her by the throat. A wall of elk, some of them with bleeding stumps where they'd torn off their antlers against the dense trees in their desperate rush to get away, headed straight for them. In seconds they would be crushed to death. There could be no escape. Where was Kane heading?

"Go, follow Jenna across the bridge." Raven skidded to a halt and dropped her to her feet at the edge of the ravine.

An old footbridge, the cables rusty and the wooden slats wet and covered with moss, swung across the boiling river. A huge rusty sign with red writing warned DO NOT CROSS.

Emily gaped at the rotting dilapidated footbridge, and then at Kane and Jenna. Her friends moved swiftly, picking their way slowly from rung to rung. She couldn't make her feet move toward the open holes where the slats were missing. How could she hold on? One of the guide ropes hung down toward the river. Panic gripped her as she looked down. Beneath her, the river bubbled and churned and ahead the old bridge swung dangerously back and forth. To her horror, green slimy slats fell away behind Jenna and tumbled end over end into the bubbling firmament below. Terrified, she cried out paralyzed with fear. Even with Raven's encouragement, she couldn't make her feet move. "I can't."

"You must. It's our only chance." Raven stepped past her, grabbed her hand, and pulled. "Walk in my steps. If the elk try and follow, they'll destroy the bridge. Hold on tight to me. Move it. Now!"

TWENTY-SIX

Glad of her leather gloves, Jenna gripped tight to the rusty metal cable that formed the side of the bridge. Below her the rapids roared like thunder and water soaked her hair and face. Everything was slippery and with each step, her boots slid on the green slime coating the rotting wooden slats. Ahead of her, Kane yelled encouragement and gave her instructions: where to move each foot and how to slide her hands along the railing. Underfoot, the bridge shook as the elk smashed through the forest. The trees appeared to bend as they ran in blind fear. She glanced behind her. Raven was in the lead, dragging Emily behind him. Her face was contorted with fear.

In a rumble like thunder, elk burst through the forest in a snorting mass of brown, with wild eyes rolling. The thick musty scent of them washed over Jenna and she gaped in fear as they came closer, ripping apart the forest. With the ravine in front of them, they had nowhere to go. Hooves slid over the rocky edge as more rushed from behind. The ones in front lost their footing and dropped out of sight into the swirling, bubbling water below. Jenna cried out in terror, her scream echoed by Emily as a massive bull elk jumped onto the bridge. The slats disintegrated below it and the proud creature tumbled into the river with its legs still running. Behind it, masses of animals formed a thick wall and forced the ones in front into the ravine. The bridge shook from the impact of elk jumping at the bridge in a frantic effort to get to safety but there was nowhere for them to go but down.

"Keep moving before the bridge collapses." Kane's voice drifted to her above the chaos. As she looked back toward him, a board disintegrated under Kane's foot and he dropped, vanishing into the mist. Horrified, she screamed unable to believe her eyes. "Dave. Oh, dear God, no."

Where was he? Afraid to look, she gritted her teeth and peered over the edge expecting to see him floating away with the elk but only mist and turbulent water tumbled through the ravine. Panic gripped her. She couldn't breathe and then movement under her feet caught her attention. She dropped to her knees and stared through the slats. "Dave?"

She sobbed in relief when a hand appeared through the broken boards groping for purchase. To her horror, Kane's gloved hand slipped but before she could reach for him, his fingers dug into the cable beside the missing slats. The bridge swung and bucked. He wouldn't be able to hold on with his fingers for long. She looped one arm around the metal cable running from handrail to the slats and grabbed Kane's arm with both hands. "I've got you. Hang on."

Above the noise, Raven was yelling at her. When his hand closed around her arm, she shook him off and gripped tighter vowing to die before she let Kane go.

"You're not strong enough." Raven lay flat along the broken slats, one leg hooked around the horizontal cable. "I'll pull him up. Go help Emily."

Trembling, Jenna moved slowly back to give Raven room to move. The bridge jolted and swung erratically. Her feet slipped on the soaking boards and for a moment her feet hung in midair.

With effort she dragged herself back onto the shuddering bridge and waved Emily forward. Her friend's face was ashen and when her wide eyes turned in her direction, Jenna's heart went out to her. Emily wasn't going to move. Behind Emily, streams of terrified elk jumped at the bridge in a suicidal attempt to get to safety. Each effort shuddered through the dilapidated bridge. It tipped sharply sideways and Jenna clung to the railing. In front of her Raven had lifted Kane enough to get his hand onto the rusty metal cable running from railing to slats.

Don't drop him, please don't drop him. Jenna held her breath as Raven leaned down the hole and, muscles bulging, dragged Kane's other arm back through the gap. With both Kane's hands on the cable, Raven grabbed one of the straps on Kane's backpack and hauled him through the shattered slats.

Tears streamed down her face as Kane pulled himself up and straddled the broken slats, gasping for air. He'd lost his hat and a cut on his cheek bled in a curtain of red. Jenna could see an angry bleeding gash peeking through a rip in his jeans below the knee. Raven lay on the bridge, his chest heaving, and then he rolled over and reached under the bridge emerging with Kane's black Stetson.

"It somehow got caught on the end of a hanging slat." Raven sat up slowly as the bridge lurched again.

"Thanks. That's the best hat I've ever owned." Kane indicated to Emily frozen on the bridge. "Can you help Em? She's not moving." He slapped the hat on his soaked head and held out his hand to Raven and pulled him to his feet.

"Don't worry." Raven edged past Jenna. "I'll get her."

TWENTY-SEVEN

Shaking with shock and emotion, Jenna stared at Kane, unable to speak or move. It was as if she'd stepped into a nightmare. Nothing seemed real. Underfoot the bridge shifted and she couldn't make her hands release the cable. Water ran down her face and into her collar, freezing her to the spot. The sounds of the panicked elk had lessened. Some had turned away from the edge of the ravine and were moving back into the forest in a rolling wall of brown. Clouds of water vapor closed in around them, and as the bridge moved underfoot, it was as if they were riding a surfboard on clouds. Through the mist she could just make out Raven, working his way back to Emily.

"Jenna." Kane's sharp voice shook her back to reality. "Look at me." He stood for a few seconds, breathing heavily, and then held out his hand. "I know you're afraid but we need to get over this bridge. I'll lift you over the gap." He met her gaze. "I won't let you fall."

She looked back the way they'd come and then past Kane but she couldn't see the other end of the bridge. "Can't we go back? The elk have calmed now."

"There is no bridge to walk on and this end might not last

much longer." Kane held out his hand. "We need to move before it falls into the ravine. Think of the boys, Jenna. They need us. We must get home to them. Come on. Trust me. This is the best way to go."

Heart pounding, Jenna edged closer, looking only at him and not the rolling water and certain death below. She took a deep breath and let go with one hand and grasped his fingers. Between Kane's legs the jagged hole spanned about three slats wide and she'd easily slide through it. "I'm scared."

"I know you are but it's an easy jump. You can do it." Kane's other arm was hooked around the cable. "Count to three and jump."

She turned her hand to take hold of his wrist and his fingers closed around her forearm. She bent her knees. "One, two, three." She let go of the cable and jumped.

Her toes barely made the slippery moss-covered slat, and teetering back, she grabbed tight to Kane's arm and then grasped the cable beside him. "I'm okay."

"I've got you." Kane stepped across the void behind her, gathered her in against him and held her close. "Take a few breaths and then move forward slowly. Test each slat before you stand on it. Keep one arm looped around the cable."

Concerned, Jenna looked at him. "Where are you going?"

"Nowhere, but I'll need to help Raven get Emily across the gap." He indicated along the swaying bridge. "Raven is behind her. She's terrified."

Jenna didn't move. Kane's face was pale and his expression granite as if he had slipped into combat mode. She frowned. "Are you okay?"

"I'm the luckiest man alive. I figure someone was watching over me. My hand fell onto the broken cable or I'd be in the water." His mouth lifted in one corner. "I'm banged up some but I'd feel better if you were moving to safety."

He never admitted anything hurt, not ever. Something was

wrong. She shook her head. "They're almost here. I'll grab Emily when she jumps over. She'll come to me."

"Then anchor yourself like I'm doing." Kane frowned at her. "I'll take her weight. You just steady her when she lands."

Trying to look calm and in complete control, Jenna smiled at Emily. "Come on, Em. Let's get off this darn bridge." She held out a hand. "Dave will help you and I'll make sure you don't fall."

"Don't look down." Kane straddled the hole again and held out his hand. "Hold on to me and jump. You won't fall."

"You don't look so good." Emily looked over one shoulder. "Raven, will you help me, please?"

"Sure." He took Kane's place and swung her across the gap.

When Kane grabbed Emily and set her down on the bridge, Jenna caught him wincing. As he came up behind her, she turned to look at him. "Tell me what's wrong. Where does it hurt?"

"My shoulder is dislocated. I felt it go when I grabbed for the cable." Kane urged her forward. "Raven will be able to pop it back in when we get to solid ground." He sighed. "I figure I have a splinter in my leg. It hurts more than it should. Apart from that I'm just dandy." He gave her a lopsided smile. "There's no hiding anything from you anymore, is there?"

Testing each slat as she moved across the swaying bridge, Jenna shook her head. "The combat face was the tell. I figured you were hiding something from me and you're sheet-white. I've seen you injured before and that's rare."

"I don't scare easy but I admit falling through the bridge I came close." Kane kept one hand locked on her arm. "The next bit will be dangerous, it's uphill and the boards are all slime. You have both sides of the guide rail to hang on to, so use them and slide one hand and then the other. Never let go."

It seemed to take forever to make their way along the slippery, whining, shuddering bridge, but eventually they made it to the other side and collapsed onto boulders alongside the ravine. Jenna turned to Raven. "How long since you've fixed a dislocated shoulder?" She indicated toward Kane with her chin. "He's too stubborn to ask you."

"I'm not." Kane shook his head. "Just resting, is all."

"You need those cuts tended to as well." Emily slid off her backpack and pulled out her medical kit. "I carry everything we need here. Do you need morphine for the shoulder?"

"Nope." Kane leveled his gaze on her. "Once it's back in, it won't hurt as much. You'll need to cut open my jeans. I figure I picked up a splinter in my leg." He pointed to a hole in his jeans just above the bleeding cut below. He looked at Raven. "Shoulder first."

Jenna wanted to hold Kane's hand as Raven manipulated his shoulder but she just moved closer. She heard a pop as it slid back into place, but Kane didn't make a sound. He stared into space as if zoning out. Raven made him move his arm and then wanted to place his arm into a sling.

"No, I'll be fine." Kane rubbed his shoulder. "It's happened before. The cold wet clothes will help with the swelling and I'll ice it when I get back to the office."

"Sit still." Emily cleaned the cut on his cheek. "It's just a scratch. You don't need a bandage." She cut open the leg of Kane's soaked jeans and her mouth fell open. She indicated to Raven. "This one needs a clean and a couple of sutures but that needs surgery. It's not going to pull out and it will leave splinters behind."

Jenna's heart raced at the sight of a thick splinter of wood embedded in Kane's calf.

"I'm sure Raven has fixed worse than that in combat zones." Kane frowned. "I need it out so I can walk out of here." He looked at Jenna. "Call someone to meet us on the fire road." He indicated a trail through the forest. "It's that way. Give them GPS coordinates. They'll find us."

"Okay." Raven scanned the area. "Over there. The boulder is flat and big enough for you to lie down." He lifted Kane under one arm and helped him to the rock and then turned to Emily. "My kit has everything we need. Numb him up and get to work on the sutures. I'll do the splinter."

After making the call to Wolfe, Jenna called Rio and brought him up to date. "Get the drones up and look for anyone carrying a rifle. We figure someone spooked the elk herd on purpose. Contact the game warden and ask him to check out anyone hunting in that area. I don't believe it's a designated hunting area. It's a hiking trail."

"Do you figure they'd still be hanging around?" Rio sounded skeptical. *"How long have you been stranded on the bridge? They could be long gone by now."*

Jenna frowned. "Maybe but do a search anyway. If hunters were passing through, they'd have checked in with the game warden. They might have seen someone. Talk to him first." She paused a beat. "Tell the warden that elk have fallen into the ravine. They'll need to send someone to remove the carcasses when they reach the lake."

"Okay. I'm on it." Rio disconnected.

Deciding to keep Kane distracted as the doctors went to work, she went to his side. Kane lay staring at the sky, his hat lying on his chest as if he didn't have a care in the world. She wondered how many times in his secret past he'd been worked on in the field. Teeth chattering, she edged closer beside him, trying to share heat. It was freezing and everyone was soaked through. She took his hand. "Tauri will want to know everything that happened. Do you figure it's too disturbing to tell him about the bridge?"

"We can tell him about the stampede and escaping on the bridge." Kane's eyes moved to her face. "Not about me falling through." He suddenly smiled. "Jackson will say I have an 'ouchie' and to kiss it better like you do." He squeezed her hand.

"Do all moms kiss things better? I recall my mom doing that to me, but not my dad. He'd say, 'Suck it up and be a man.'"

"You never say that to our kids." Jenna rested a hand on his chest as Raven cut into his leg. "You're very loving to our boys."

"It's a different world now." Kane sighed. "But I don't rush over and make a fuss if they fall over. You don't either. We both wait those few seconds to see if they get up and keep going first."

Jenna nodded. "Yeah, well I've seen kids that cry every time they fall over when they're not hurt. I noticed early on that Jackson waits to see our reaction first, if it's okay with us, then he just carries on unless he bangs his head or whatever."

"Bringing Up Kids 101, huh?" Raven looked up at them. "Are your shots up to date. Tetanus, for instance?"

"Yeah." Kane lifted his head. "Why?"

"The hunk of wood you had embedded in your leg has a rusty nail in it." Raven was stitching the wound. "I've got it all and it's going to be fine. The muscle wasn't damaged as first I thought but it will be sore for a week or so. Ten days for the sutures and a course of antibiotics. You're not allergic to anything are you?" He tied off the last suture.

"Nope." Kane frowned. "Why?"

"When we've bandaged you, you'll need to drop your pants. I have a shot that needs to go into your backside." Raven grinned. "Sure you don't want morphine?"

"I'll be fine." Kane frowned and sat up slowly. "I have pain meds for my headaches. If I need anything, I'll take them." He looked down at the damage. "Can you use waterproof bandages? I'll need a shower when I get back to the office and get into some dry clothes."

"Not a problem. You must keep this leg elevated for a day or so or it will bleed. Okay?" Raven shivered and packed up his bag. "I'm sure glad I have a change of clothes at the office too. I'm wet through."

Jenna's phone chimed. It was fortunate she'd decided long ago to never leave home without the satellite sleeve. "Yes, Rio."

"I called the game warden and he heard the shots and went to investigate. He found a couple of kids shooting rodents. They had no idea their shots had spooked the elk herd until it was too late. They swear they didn't see them. He let them off with a warning. Oh, yeah, and he'll organize the elk cleanup."

Jenna sighed. "Okay, it was a shot in the dark. Good about the cleanup, and before I forget, the body was a pig. It's been here a day or so and it was wearing Darlene Travis' locket. A stampede went through the area, so it's pointless doing a retrieval. We figure it was a distraction to get us away from town. Is it all quiet there?"

"Yeah, the hotline calls have slowed. Do you want us to follow up on the other suspects?"

There was no way she could drag Kane around interviewing suspects right now. "Okay, thanks." She disconnected.

"I'm good to go." Kane stood and pushed on his wet hat. He went to pick up his backpack and Raven grabbed it. "There's no need. I'm good."

"I'm your doctor right now, which makes me in charge." Raven raised both eyebrows as if waiting for an argument. "That shoulder could slip right back out under the weight of this. I'll carry it and no arguments." He slung it over one shoulder. "Lead the way."

Jenna grinned at Kane's stubborn expression. "I'm sure Wolfe will want to check you over too."

"You called Wolfe?" Kane snorted. "I'm not dead yet."

TWENTY-EIGHT

As Rio drove to the hospital, Rowley checked his notes on the next suspect. Daniel McCulloch, a maintenance worker at the hospital, had a sketchy past. Complaints had been leveled against him and he'd been fired from his last job. The mention of drugs stolen from the hospital concerned him, mainly because of the drugs discovered in the stomach contents of the first victim. Drugs could be stored and used on another victim and as McCulloch had only arrived in Black Rock Falls in July, it put him into the timeframe. As Jenna and Kane had mentioned, killers of this type usually moved around to avoid detection. They only lived in an area long enough to look as if they belonged and then moved on once they'd committed the crimes. He turned to Rio. "When you called the hospital, did they say anything about this guy?"

"Nope." Rio turned into the parking lot and turned off the engine. "I asked if he was there today and where could we find him. I didn't want to cause him any trouble. He might be innocent and trying to make a clean start here." He gave Rowley a long look. "You need to take all this into consideration when speaking to a suspect. Us being here and talking to him can cause problems."

Rowley had to admit Rio had the experience. He'd made detective and had the street smarts. He'd learned to listen to his pearls of wisdom on the job. "So how do you make sure it doesn't cause a problem?"

"I usually say we found something valuable we figure belongs to him or something generic or tongues start wagging." Rio picked up his phone and slid from the truck.

They entered the hospital by the front doors, and the smell reminded Rowley of the morgue. People lined up at the counter waiting for a number and others moved past in wheelchairs or were being pushed on gurneys to the ER. He couldn't feel an ounce of happiness, even though the staff had covered the front counter with cobwebs and jack-o'-lanterns, and a skeleton sat beside the desk in a chair reading a newspaper as if waiting so long to be seen they'd died. The brightly colored orange and purple bunting just seemed to make it weird, as if laughing at sadness.

Rowley bypassed the line to speak to the woman behind the counter and she directed them to the boiler room. The moment they pushed through the glass doors the overpowering odor of bleach surrounded them. They followed the signs on the walls along brightly lit hospital corridors and down a flight of stairs.

As they moved down the dim staircase the fluorescent lights buzzed overhead and flickered, distorting the view of the steps below. The intermittent bright flashes against the stark white walls disoriented Rowley and he gripped the handrail. "Maybe we should remind him to change these fluorescent tubes before someone breaks their neck falling down the stairs."

"I'll be looking for the elevator on the way back." Rio headed down to another level. "This looks like the right floor. The stairs don't go down any farther."

Stale air filled the bottom floor as if the ventilation system wasn't working properly. A dingy hallway stretched out before them but a sign showed them the way. They walked past medical equipment carts lined up against the wall. Most of them needed repair and had a slight covering of dust. Rowley pushed through a heavy door mounted with a sign in bold red letters that warned MAINTENANCE AREA—NO UNAUTHORIZED ENTRY. The door opened easily and led to more stairs and into a room humming with the sound of machinery. As he moved deeper into the area, the overpowering smell of oil burned his nostrils. He spotted McCulloch tinkering with a pipe. The man wore grimy coveralls streaked with oil. As they approached, Rowley cleared his throat. "Daniel McCulloch?"

The wrench tumbled from the man's hand as he jerked to his feet, surprise and fear etched in his expression. Tall with broad shoulders, he fit the suspect's description. Dark hair peeked out from beneath a dirty ball cap and wide brown eyes shifted nervously. He lifted a grease-covered hand and he reached for a rag hanging from a back pocket. "You startled me. What do you want?" McCulloch looked from one to the other.

"We'd like to ask you a few questions about your visit to the Triple Z Bar on Monday night." Rio glanced around. "You can speak freely. I figure we're alone."

"What's this all about?" McCulloch frowned. "Is it breaking the law having a drink after work?"

Rowley took out his notebook and pen. "No, Mr. McCulloch, we are investigating the death of Bunny Watkins. How well did you know Ms. Watkins?"

"She died?" McCulloch's Adam's apple moved up and down and he tightened the grip on the rag in his hands. "The waitress, right?"

"She cleaned tables and mopped up spills. She didn't work behind the bar." Rio rested his hands on his belt. "But you'd know that, right?"

"I seen her around." McCulloch's eyes darted from Rowley to Rio. "I didn't know her."

Rowley glanced at his list of questions. "You were seen speaking to her at the Triple Z Bar the night she died. What did you talk about?"

"I don't recall talking to her at all." McCulloch shrugged in a feeble attempt to appear casual but the rag trembled in his hands.

"I'm sure if you cast your mind back to Monday evening, you would be able to remember." Rio rested one hand on the handle of his pistol. "Do you recall if she appeared to be distressed or worried about anything during your conversation?"

"Nope." McCulloch wiped a grimy hand down his face. "If I don't recall speaking to her, how would I remember if she had a problem or not?"

Rowley exchanged a glance with Rio. "The customers at the bar that evening mentioned that you were there until closing. Did you leave around the same time as Bunny, and if so, did you notice who she left with?"

"No, I didn't leave at closing. I left a short time before, and no, I didn't see Bunny leaving the premises." McCulloch was getting irritated and shoved the rag into his back pocket. "I'm sorry if she died, but I didn't have anything to do with it."

Running through his notes, Rowley sighed. "So, you left the bar. Did you see anyone hanging around the parking lot?"

"Only the cleaner, Sly." McCulloch ran a hand through his hair. "He was leaning against the wall near the trash cans smoking."

"We pulled your files." Rio narrowed his eyes. "Can you explain why the hospital hired you despite the disciplinary actions against you at previous jobs?"

"I guess they needed a maintenance worker." McCulloch shrugged. "That was a long time ago. Why are you concerned about that now?"

"Have you had any recent issues or warnings since you've been working here?" Rio pushed on. "You see we're also following up on stolen drug incidents from a few years ago. Were you connected to those thefts in any way?"

"No and no." McCulloch's eyes flashed. "That was in the past when I was young and stupid. I'm good at my job and I don't get into trouble."

Rowley made fast notes and then looked up. "Where did you go after you left the bar? Can anyone verify your movements?"

"I went home, and no, I don't have anyone at home to verify my movements." McCulloch made a show of looking at his watch and sighing. "If that's all. I have a heavy workload."

Recalling Jenna's question, Rowley held up a hand. "One other thing. We have CCTV footage of a man fitting your description entering the roadhouse on Sunday night around midnight. Was that you?"

"Nope." McCulloch shook his head. "If I want a meal, I go to Aunt Betty's Café. Look I really need to get this fixed."

"Okay, Mr. McCulloch." Rio handed him his card. "If you remember anything else we need to know about that night, call me." He turned and headed for the door.

Folding his notebook, Rowley followed. Outside in the hallway he turned to Rio. "What do you think?"

"He's way too nervous." Rio headed toward a band of elevators and pressed the button. "I figure we keep him on the list. He's the right size, if we're going on the description of the man seen with Darlene Travis."

The elevator doors slid open and they climbed inside. Rowley pressed the button for the ground floor. "From what I've seen so far, they all are."

TWENTY-NINE

With every muscle screaming, Kane made it to the fire road. He rested his left arm inside his jacket for support and held Jenna's hand along the way, trying to reassure her that he was fine, but this time his body had taken a beating. He'd struck his back, upper thighs, and knees during the fall; his shoulder had taken his full weight as he fell; and the transfer to his right hand had taken every ounce of strength he possessed. Luckily, he generated strength at a fast rate, but being human meant that the bruising, pulled muscles, and damaged tendons might take longer to heal if left untreated. He needed to surrender himself to Wolfe for a course of treatment. He grimaced. Admitting he needed help wasn't in his vocabulary, but Jenna needed him beside her to catch this killer.

Wolfe's truck was parked at the tree line and he jumped out to greet them with blankets. As he handed one to Kane, he pulled him to one side. "I'm injured. Dislocated shoulder, knees are damaged, thighs took a hit on a metal bar, and I could have broken ribs. My back is cramping." He looked into Wolfe's gray eyes. "I need a quick fix. This case is too dangerous for Jenna to handle alone."

"You got it." Wolfe nodded. "Head okay?"

Kane rubbed his chin. "Yeah, that's the only place I didn't hit."

"Get in the truck." Wolfe climbed in and looked at the others. "I'll get y'all back to where you left your vehicles and then take Emily home." He looked at Kane. "Take a shower and then I want you in my office. I'll do scans of your shoulder and make sure there's no ligament damage." He frowned. "It's me or waiting at the hospital. Make up your mind. My patients don't mind you jumping the line."

Smiling, Kane looked at him. "Yeah, that's fine. Just don't forget I'm breathing."

"I'll do my best." Wolfe chuckled. "I must admit, sometimes when I'm working on a live patient and they talk to me it gives me a start." He took the next bridge over the ravine and headed back to Stanton. "Emily mentioned it was a collaborative surgical team working on you. You'll need antibiotics for two weeks. Splinters with nails are bad news."

Kane nodded. "Yeah, I've been through similar before. That's what's good about a bullet: it burns its way through."

"I irrigated the wound with saline solution and gave him a shot of penicillin." Raven leaned forward from the back seat. "I see just fine, and Em held a flashlight on the incision to make sure I removed all the debris. I excised a good part all around the splinter. I'm sure it will be okay."

"I've no doubt y'all did a great job." Wolfe glanced at him in the rearview mirror. "I'm confident both of you are skilled, but Dave here believes he's unstoppable and sometimes goes against doctors' orders. I'm just enforcing the need to take his meds and get some rest."

"I'll handcuff him to the bed." Jenna giggled.

Turning painfully in his seat, Kane looked at her. "That's not a good idea. Unless you plan on using it for firewood anytime soon."

Kane's muscles cramped during the ten-minute drive to the Beast. He waited for Raven to head off and then Wolfe before he turned to Jenna. "I'm sorry but you'll need to drive."

"That's okay." Jenna opened the passenger door for him and he slid inside. "You're coming into my locker room and I'll help you undress. I won't take no for an answer. It's bad, isn't it?"

Shaking his head, Kane smiled at her. "Dying or losing a limb is bad, this is an inconvenience. It slows me down, is all. Wolfe has many things to help me recover fast. Once we're through, take me home and let me sleep. I'll be good as new when I wake." He wriggled his right hand. "My right side is fine. I can hold my boys, eat, and draw my weapon. It's all good."

"Why don't you update Rio so he knows what's happening?" Jenna handed him his phone and started the truck. They took a slow drive back down the mountain to the office. "Tell him we're only dropping by to change and then we'll be heading home once we've seen Wolfe. Put him in charge. He'll have Raven, so he won't miss us for the rest of the day."

Reluctantly, Kane made the call. He didn't want to go home but he did need treatment and the drugs would make him inefficient and there'd be no way he could get out of taking them with Wolfe standing over him. "We'll be dropping by for a shower and then heading to Wolfe's. Before we go, Jenna needs an update on the suspects' interviews. Did you discover anything interesting?"

"Yeah, the three we interviewed so far all fit the description. Two have priors, as you know. They all could be involved. None of them sticks out. All are smartasses. None of them admit to knowing Bunny outside her workplace or admit to being near the roadhouse on Monday night."

Kane exchanged a knowing look with Jenna. "Okay. If you have time to interview Sly Goldman this afternoon, leave Rowley to run the office and take Raven with you. He'll be able to answer any questions on what happened today. I need to have a few scans and then rest up. We'll be back in the morning."

"Okay. I'll call the sheriff with an update later today." Rio disconnected.

Sighing Kane looked at Jenna. "He likes being in charge."

"Maybe, but he knows I'm the sheriff and that's all that matters." She flicked him a glance as they turned into the office parking lot. "If he challenges me for sheriff at the next elections, it's all good. If I win, I stay; if I lose, we're heading for that island in the sun."

THIRTY

Duke greeted them as they headed through the office. The dog did his happy dance, his thick tail wagging in circles and his tongue lolling out in a happy grin. Jenna bent to give him a rub on the head. "It's good to see you too, Duke. Better still will be going home to see the kids soon. You'll like that won't you?"

Whistling came from the utility room as they headed to the sheriff's locker room. Jenna glanced inside to see Raven pushing his clothes into one of the washer-dryers. She nodded at him as Kane followed her into the locker room. "It looks as if Raven has already showered and changed. Did I take that long driving down the mountain?"

"Well, you drove slowly." Kane eased himself down onto a bench seat. "I wouldn't expect you to drive like a maniac. You haven't driven the Beast for some time."

Jenna ignored him and busied herself pulling off his boots. By the time he stepped into the shower she could see the extent of his injuries. He had bruises all over. She said nothing and turned on the shower. "I'll be in the next cubicle if you need me."

Shivering, Jenna peeled off her soaking boots and clothes.

She dropped all their wet sopping clothes into a large plastic bag. She'd take them home to wash and dry. The boots she placed beside the radiator to dry. She showered like lightning and wrapped a towel around her as Kane stepped out of the shower. She smiled at him. "I sure hope Wolfe can wave his magic wand and take away some of the pain. I wouldn't like to be in your body right now."

"I'm alive." He cupped her cheek and smiled at her. "That's all that matters. I'm starving so that's a real good sign."

She dressed quickly and collected up the towels. "I'll dump these into the washer-dryer. Why don't you grab an energy bar and a cup of coffee? It's going to be some time before we get home and we haven't had lunch."

"Okay, and I'll call Susie. She'll have a takeout order ready for us by the time we head home. I'm not planning on cooking tonight and you'll be tuckered out by the time you've fed the horses."

Jenna headed for the door. "Okay."

Ten minutes later they'd arrived at the morgue and Wolfe went to work using his medical equipment to check every inch of Kane's battered body. Sipping her to-go cup of coffee and nibbling an energy bar, Jenna stood beside Wolfe as he scanned Kane. Images came up on a screen and he pointed out injuries. He turned to smile at her. "There's nothing to worry about but he'll be sore for a few days. He'll want to move the shoulder but it needs time to heal. I'll give him a corticosteroid injection along with a long-acting local anesthetic. It will relieve the pain for a time but it will get sore again. The joint is very inflamed and will take time to settle. Although I can't see any permanent damage there. The key to his full recovery is keeping the joint immobilized. You know how stubborn he is, but if he doesn't follow my instructions, it could lead to permanent damage and weakness in that arm. He would have considerably less strength." He narrowed his gaze at her. "He listens to you and you've nursed him through worse than this. I'll follow up the steroid injection with anti-inflammatory pain medication that won't affect his concentration." He sighed. "We'll ice it as well."

Concerned, Jenna folded her arms across her chest. "If he does all this, how long to full recovery?"

"Normal people would feel much better in one to two weeks but can't do vigorous exercise or lift heavy weights. The next couple of weeks they usually can start gentle exercise but won't regain full use of the arm for at least ten to twelve weeks. But knowing Kane as I do, he'll be back to full strength in less than six weeks—if he follows my instructions."

Nodding, Jenna waited for Wolfe to tell Kane to get off the scanner bed. "He knows his body. I don't believe he'll risk permanent injury but he's stubborn. Why does he have a faster recovery rate than most people? Is there something I need to know?"

"No." Wolfe grinned at her. "He's one hundred percent human but he's trained his body not to respond to pain and other things like cold and wet. He can hold his breath underwater for a long time. He would survive torture and never give in. He moves faster, reacts faster than a normal man, because he's been highly trained and he keeps up his training. All these things are taught and he is the best at what he does. The fact he is in such great physical shape is the reason he survived. How many people do you figure could survive that fall? He hung on to the cable with a dislocated shoulder. It's mind-blowing when you think about it. Most people would say it's impossible but there he is alive and with minimal damage considering the injuries he sustained." He switched off the machine. "I'll need to inject him under ultrasound, so head along to the door marked IMAGING and I'll get the injections ready."

Emily came along the hallway as Jenna stepped out of the room. She smiled at her. "He will be fine. No permanent damage."

"That's good to know. I have his meds here. I picked them up from the pharmacy on my way." Emily handed a paper sack to Jenna. "Make sure he takes the anti-inflammatories on a full stomach or they'll give him a bellyache. The penicillin, he needs to take the entire course." She walked beside her. "The others are sedatives. You should give him one once he's eaten so he gets a restful night's sleep—today and tomorrow night as he'll be in pain and he won't complain. Sleep is better than suffering. Watch his leg as well. Any redness, bring him here fast."

Peering into the sack, Jenna lifted each bottle of medication and examined it. "Okay." She walked beside her and wondered about Wolfe's middle daughter. "I haven't seen Julie for a time. How is she doing at college?"

"She's away on a course at the moment." Emily smiled at her. "She is trying to decide her career path. She's at a conference right now. I figure she wants to work with children. She'll be coming home in a day or so. She is flying in from Helena."

"There you are." Kane stepped into the hallway wrapped in a robe. "Next I get stuck with needles." He smiled at Emily. "Thanks for stitching me up. You did a great job. I doubt I'll have a scar."

"Anytime. Just take the meds and rest." Emily gave him a hard glare. "Even a tough guy like you can't fight septicemia." She squeezed his arm. "And I need my Uncle Dave, so do as you're told."

"I will." Kane grinned. "Just for you."

Half an hour later, Jenna had collected the takeout from Aunt Betty's Café and they'd headed home. Along the way Kane demolished two hamburgers and fed Jenna fries. The injection that numbed his shoulder had put him in a really good mood. He'd even listened to Wolfe's stern instructions about what he could and couldn't do. Jenna looked at him. "Now you've eaten, take the meds in the yellow bottle. Those are anti-inflammatories and will help with the pain and bruising. You don't need to take the antibiotics until the morning."

"Hmm, and these others are to make me sleep." He buzzed down the window.

Jenna slammed on the brakes. "If you throw those out of the window, I'll call Wolfe to come by each day and give you a needle to put you to sleep."

"I'd like to see him try." Kane snorted and then buzzed up the window. "I don't need drugs to sleep, Jenna. I sleep just fine. Who will protect you and the kids overnight if I'm in a drug-induced sleep?"

Jenna glared at him. "I'm fine at protecting my kids, and in case it slipped your mind, Raya is a highly trained FBI agent. We have a home like Fort Knox. No one is getting inside our home. To make a full and fast recovery you need to sleep and heal. You're taking the meds even if I need to crush them and add them to your food, the same as we do for Duke."

"Were you ever trained as a military interrogator?" Kane raised one eyebrow.

Jenna shook her head. "Of course not."

"You could have fooled me." Kane leaned back in his seat and closed his eyes.

THIRTY-ONE

Surprised when Rio asked him to accompany him, Raven climbed into Rio's truck and they headed for the Triple Z Bar. Along the way he read the notes Rio had compiled for Sly Goldman. "None of the victims had been raped. Why would you consider this man to be a suspect?"

"The only evidence we have to hand at the moment is finding people who were speaking to Bunny the night she died. The bartender noticed four men, so we've been interviewing them and they all fit the description of the man seen at the roadhouse with Darlene Travis." Rio headed the truck along Stanton Road. It was late afternoon and long shadows crossed the highway. "Goldman started his shift at four. The manager and the bartender are aware that we're on our way to speak to him. There won't be any problems."

The truck bounced across the parking lot and stopped outside the Triple Z Bar. Raven grabbed his notebook and climbed out. The smell of stale sweat, beer, and chili oozed out from the swinging doors. He turned to Rio. "I'll need another shower when I leave this place."

He followed Rio to the bar and the barman pointed out a

tall broad guy who was carrying a garbage bin filled with beer bottles toward the backdoor. "Goldman has seen us and I didn't notice a reaction. Unless he's outside running for his life."

"I'll head out of the front door and you follow him. There's an alleyway behind the bar where they keep the dumpsters. If I can't see him, I'll meet you there." Rio headed off at a fast pace.

Weaving through the tables of people doing their best to ignore him, Raven made his way to the back door. In the alleyway Goldman was placing bottles into a crate. He glanced up as Raven walked toward him. The alleyway stunk of garbage and urine, as if it was used as the local toilet. He sidestepped a puddle of vomit and went to stand a short distance from Goldman. "Mr. Goldman?"

"That would be me." Goldman turned slowly and studied Raven's face for a few seconds. "What can I do for you, Deputy?"

At that moment Rio's boots clattered on the cobblestones as he walked along the alleyway. Raven indicated to him. "That's Chief Deputy Rio and I'm Deputy Raven. We have a few questions to ask you about Bunny Watkins."

"What about her?" Goldman wiped his hands on his jeans and straightened. His gaze shifted from one to the other. "She works here as a cleaner and started a few weeks ago, as far as I know."

"We've discovered her body." Rio paused as if waiting for a reaction but it didn't come. "Sheriff Alton was in the bar speaking to people about the murder of Bunny and Darlene Travis. You were seen talking to Bunny the night she died. Do you recall what you spoke about?"

"She asked me if I could empty the garbage bins." Goldman raised an eyebrow. "I told her if the boss employed her to clean, it meant taking out the garbage as well, and that I had enough to do without doing her job as well."

Jackass. Raven frowned. The request seemed normal to

him. Bunny was only a small woman and the bins filled with bottles appeared to be heavy. He made a few notes and looked at him. "I gather you've been working with her for a time? Did you notice if she appeared to be upset or worried when you spoke to her?"

"Yeah, she always had something to moan about. Most times it was about walking back to the motel each night in the dark." Goldman snorted. "Like she was trying to get me to give her a ride. I don't need being seen with trouble like her."

"What exactly do you mean by that?" Rio rested his hands on his hips and stared at him. "Was she turning tricks?"

"Not that I'm aware but why would she ask me?" Goldman shrugged nonchalantly. "I figure it's kinda obvious that I don't have any spare cash."

Raven rested his thumbs inside his belt. "I noticed you had some run-ins with the law in Blackwater but you seem to be keeping your nose clean in Black Rock Falls. Although being likely the last person to see Bunny alive, I figure the rape case against you in Blackwater is likely going to cause you some attention from law enforcement." He noticed Goldman flinch but he covered it well.

"That was a misunderstanding, is all." Goldman pushed a dirty hand through his hair. "We both had a little too much to drink and things got out of hand. She came to her senses and dropped the charges against me."

"People who were here that night made mention that you didn't seem to be yourself. Had you noticed anything unusual going on?" Rio lifted his chin and when Goldman shook his head, he glanced at Raven. "I guess that's a no. So, what time did you leave the bar? Did you see Bunny leave?"

"I left before her. When the place is empty, she locks up." Goldman shook his head slowly. "The boss doesn't trust me to do that job." He shifted uneasily. "I did see someone in the parking lot, but many of the drivers sleep in their cabs when they're having a rest stop."

"Can you describe him?" Rio took a step closer. "Tall, short, wide, skinny?"

"It was dark, I only got a glimpse of him, is all." Goldman's eyes darted from one to the other and he shuffled his feet. "Someone was out there. I'm not sure. I only saw a shadow moving, tall and broad and wearing a long coat. I didn't stick around. I jumped into my ride and took off."

Raven exchanged a glance with Rio. "Did you see Bunny with him?"

"Nah, Bunny was still inside when I left." Goldman shook his head. "Like I said before, she stayed behind to lock up. I was long gone by then."

"Okay, what about Sunday night?" Rio searched his face. "Did you work that night?"

"Nope." Goldman shrugged. "Why? Someone else go missing?"

"Did you drop by the roadhouse for a meal, late on Sunday night, maybe speak to a young woman?" Rio leaned closer. "Maybe shared your burger with her?"

"I was there between eleven and midnight, maybe." Goldman closed his eyes as if steadying himself or maybe searching for a reply. "I purchased a burger, fries, and a chocolate milkshake. I was working until then at a function at the Cattleman's Hotel. Ask anyone, they saw me."

Raven folded his notebook and pushed it inside his pocket. "Don't leave town. We might be back to ask you a few more questions." He handed him his card. "If you see the man hanging around the parking lot again, call me." He followed Rio out of the door.

As they walked to the truck, Raven glanced at Rio. "He acts like he's guilty of something or he's hiding something."

"Yeah." Rio swung behind the wheel. "Any one of them could be guilty or innocent. We need more than circumstantial evidence to get an arrest warrant."

THIRTY-TWO

He'd waited until full dark and then, hidden in his truck in the forest, he buzzed down his window and stared across the road at the corn maze. At the entrance two bales of hay stood to each side with grinning jack-o'-lanterns barely visible under the sliver of moonlight. Come Halloween they would light the lanterns and offer the public a chance to walk through the maze to discover the center, where candy would be laid out for the children. This time they would find something much more exciting. He opened the door slowly, making sure the interior light didn't illuminate the body lying beside him.

He gathered her into his arms, surprised how much lighter she'd become. Without the blood, her face appeared hollow, like a recently shed snakeskin. Stanton was deserted, with most people asleep in their beds and no one around to hear his boots clatter across the blacktop. The wind rustled through the cornstalks like waves on the sea and as he entered the maze they shivered as if watching him. Underfoot, dead stalks and yellow leaves littered the ground, their denseness covering his footprints. It was all part of his plan. His illusion. To most people, a vampire slayer was nothing more than a myth—until they met him.

When the weight of the body shifted in his arms, he glanced down at her face. Empty eyes stared back at him and her slightly parted blue lips almost smiled. She no longer resisted him. He'd tamed her, bent her to his will, and she was no longer a threat. "Soon you will be at peace. I will make sure you will not rise in the morning."

Darkness spread out before him but he'd memorized the way to go. He'd watched the men cut the maze earlier and place the two hay bales in the very center. They'd spread a Halloween tablecloth over them, ready to be covered with candy. Halloween props, severed hands, skeletal heads with flashing eyes, and grinning jack-o'-lanterns decorated the pathways, but none would be as good or more memorable than his.

With each step the cornstalks seemed to reach out to pull her from his arms as if she had the power to make them live again. Like her, they were just the shell of a once-living thing. He laid her down and stood back, staring down at her. The nightgown flowed down over her legs, making her appear to be innocent—perfect. With care, he arranged her hair, using his comb to smooth it down over her shoulders. He watched as the breeze moved it, making her seem almost alive but he'd never allow that to happen. He pulled the stake from his back pocket and, taking it in his gloved hand, raised it high before plunging it deep into her heart.

No blood, only a sigh came from her body. He lifted her arms and folded her hands below the stake and then raised her chin and arranged her hair again, to display the vampire marks. He knelt beside her, inhaling his creation, imprinting the image of her in his mind and wondered how the sheriff would react when she found her. A wolf howled in the distance and he smiled. Like him there was never just one wolf. Men like him roamed the country, ridding the world of vampires. It soon would be time for him to go. One more and he'd be gone—until next year.

THIRTY-THREE

Thursday

"Da-dee. Da-dee. Da-dee." Jackson pounded his tiny fists on the side of the bed and then pulled at the blankets.

"Mommy said to let him sleep." Tauri's voice crept into Kane's muddled dreams.

As Jackson let out a scream of protest, Kane opened one eye and looked at him. "Where's Mommy?"

When Jackson giggled and pointed over one shoulder, Kane leaned over the edge of the bed and scooped up his son in his good arm. The giggling, squealing toddler gave Kane a sloppy kiss on the cheek and snuggled down beside him. Tauri sat carefully on the edge of the bed. He smiled at him and noted how careful Tauri was to avoid hurting him. "Morning. What are my two handsome sons doing up this early?"

"It's not early. Nanny Raya came by to cook breakfast for us." Tauri frowned at him. "Mommy is tending the horses and told me to stay here and look after my brother. She said Jackson was not to wake you."

Kane sat up, slowly assessing the damage from yesterday's

fall. He didn't like wearing the sling but had to admit that it did help with the pain, and Wolfe's warning of possible permanent damage if he didn't allow it to heal made him acquiesce to his demands. He needed to be ready for any circumstance and strong enough to protect his family and do his job. His high tolerance to pain and discomfort was a blessing when he had multiple injuries and he'd had them many times before. "It's okay." He kissed the mop of black hair on Jackson's head. Oh, how he loved his boys, and moments like this were so special. "I'm glad you woke me and I'm happy to see you." He ruffled Tauri's gold-streaked hair, making him giggle. "I don't get much time to see you before you go to school. What did you have for breakfast?"

"Pancakes, strips of bacon, and maple syrup, and Jackson had scrambled eggs. He likes eggs."

At the thought of food, Kane's stomach growled. "Did Raya make any extras for me?"

"Yes, and she told me to tell her when you woke up so she could bring you in breakfast." Tauri nodded slowly. "She said I must ask you first."

Raya, their nanny and a trained FBI agent, took her job very seriously. She had her own apartment, where she cared for the boys in their absence. She took Tauri to school and spent the day with Jackson. She had become like a grandma to the children, but she kept the boundaries and gave Kane and Jenna their privacy and space. She preferred to eat her meals in her apartment. Kane figured she liked time to turn off and rest after caring for the boys. Having her own apartment also meant she had her own privacy as well. She rarely made breakfast but was always there in an emergency. "Yes, I'd like breakfast, but I'll need to wash up first. I'll go to the kitchen when I'm done."

He deposited the giggling Jackson onto the floor, and Duke crawled out from under the bed and yawned. Kane smiled at him. The dog never left his side anytime something was wrong. "Duke, look after the boys. I'll be right back."

When he emerged from the bathroom, dressed ready for work, Jenna stared at him. He plucked a strand of hay from her hair and kissed her. "Morning. What's that look for? Did I forget to comb my hair?"

"You're not thinking of working today, are you?" Jenna eased past him into the bathroom. "You need to be at home resting."

Kane smiled at her. "Much as I'd love to stay home and care for Jackson, I'll get more rest at work. He's been jumping all over me since I opened my eyes." He sighed. "He's used to me lifting him up and swinging him around. He doesn't understand that I'm hurting." He gave her a long look. "I can still be useful at work and I can still draw my weapon. My right hand is just fine. The stitches in my leg are a little tight but I can drive and walk." He rubbed his stomach. "I'll grab some breakfast. Have you eaten?"

"Yeah, I ate with the kids." She sat down and pulled off her boots. "Raya makes great pancakes but yours are better."

Kane chuckled and headed out of their room and along the hallway, hearing the boys chatting to Raya. He went to the coffee pot and poured himself a cup. "Morning, Raya. Thanks for making breakfast."

"I'm happy to do it until you're better." Raya poured pancake batter onto the griddle.

The air filled with the buttery aroma of pancakes and the bacon crisping in a pan. Kane sat at the table. "That would be very helpful. The boys need a good breakfast and Wolfe insists I rest my shoulder."

"Indeed, you should." Raya took two strips of bacon cooling on a plate and handed one each to the boys. "Sit and talk to your daddy." She lifted Jackson to his booster seat at the table. "Don't feed Duke. He's had his breakfast and then some."

"Mommy makes cookies and black toast." Tauri wrinkled his nose. "The toaster caught fire the last time, so I helped her and the next time it turned out just fine." He looked at Kane. "She turns down the toaster dial so it doesn't burn but then the bread is still white and she puts it down again and forgets about it." He shook his head. "I told her not to mess with the dial."

Grinning Kane leaned toward him. "Do you want to know a secret?"

"I do." Tauri leaned closer.

Kane lowered his voice. "That's why I cook. Mommy has too many things on her mind to worry about toast."

After waving goodbye to Raya and the boys, Kane locked the house and headed for the Beast. It was parked right outside where Jenna had left it the previous afternoon. He shook his head. Wolfe had slipped him a sedative and by the time he'd gotten home, he could hardly make it up the steps and into bed. He'd slept like a log. The bitterly cold wind brushed away any cobwebs as he climbed into the truck. The drive through town took longer than usual with many people slowing along Main to peer at the ever-growing Halloween decorations. The sign for the Halloween Ball now had a red sticker across it saying SOLD OUT. He glanced at Jenna. "I'm glad you purchased the tickets early."

"I needed to get a stack. Everyone is going. I hope Julie makes it; she's due home any day now. She left her SUV at the airport, so unless she has a problem getting a flight, she should be home soon." Jenna gathered her things as they pulled up outside the office. "I'll head upstairs. Can you ask the guys about any updates? Rio was going to interview a suspect. I'll see if Wolfe has uploaded any more info and meet you in the conference room."

Feeling a little useless with his arm in a sling, Kane smiled at her. "Not a problem."

People buzzed around behind the counter answering the

hotline calls. Rio had updated the media release the previous night and the following few days were usually busy. The pastor was again manning the phones along with a couple of the usual women. Kane stopped at the counter and spoke to Rowley. "Any updates?"

"Rio has. He's in the conference room with Raven updating the whiteboard." Rowley leaned closer and dropped his voice. "The pastor is becoming a fixture. I figure he means well, but he asks so many questions it drives me insane."

Kane frowned. "About the cases?"

"Yeah, he has been here working the phones but wants to chat whenever someone calls in. Then there's the other new guy." Rowley indicated to a tall young man with broad shoulders answering calls at one of the desks. "That's Doug Lowe. He wants to help too. He never stops asking questions."

Kane eyed the man in his peripheral. "Well, we do need help with the hotlines."

"That would be fine but he wants to be more involved and said if Jenna deputizes him, he'll go around to the bars and truck stops asking about the suspect you're looking for as an undercover agent." Rowley rolled his eyes. "I said I'd pass on his suggestion and I don't discuss the cases with him either."

Glancing at Doug Lowe currently making notes after a call, Kane slipped behind the desk and went to speak to him. "We really appreciate your help but going undercover for us isn't possible. We couldn't risk your life with a potential serial killer in town. Thank you for the offer." He didn't wait for a reply and had turned to go when Lowe raised his voice.

"Deputy Kane." Lowe came up behind him. "I've been considering becoming a deputy. I don't mind working nights if necessary. I'm a good shot and know hand-to-hand combat. How do I sign up?"

Not wanting to reject the offer of help, Kane turned slowly back to face him. "We're not looking for anyone just now but there's an application online. Fill it in and we'll be in touch when a position becomes available."

"Perhaps if Doug is free at night, he could come with me on my rounds?" Pastor Dimock smiled benevolently. "There's always God's work to be done?"

Although Kane wondered how a young woman would feel about two strangers approaching them at night in Serial Killer Central, he smiled. "I'm sure helping the less fortunate is what you do best." He looked at Doug Lowe. "If doing charity work is something you'd like to do, I'm sure Father Derry will be able to discuss this aspect with you. Thanks again and now I must get back to work. I'm needed upstairs." He turned and walked from behind the counter and headed up the steps.

He explained the conversation to Rowley and Jenna. "They seem to want to get involved." He dropped into his office chair. "I understand wanting to help man the hotline, but they seem overkeen." He frowned. "The problem is they both fit the general description of our suspect." He ran a hand down his face. "Am I seeing too much into this?"

"We can't be too careful. We know that some psychopaths like to insert themselves into investigations. I'll make a note to ask Kalo to do background checks on them." Jenna smiled. "Does that make you feel better?"

Kane blew out a sigh. "Yeah, thanks."

THIRTY-FOUR

Jenna glanced up as Kane walked into the room, and she beckoned him forward. "Kane's just walked in. I'll put you on speaker and bring him up to date." She looked at Kane. "The victims have been positively identified and are who we believed. The local PDs from their counties have been very helpful and are currently interviewing family and friends for background information we can use to discover why the women headed here. Over to you, Shane."

"Okay, first, Kalo found the origin of the silver key you found in the motel room. It belongs to the Black Rock Falls bus station. The lockers are used by travelers, so can be taken up to a month at a time. I suggest you go and take a look. Secondly, I looked over Bunny's tablet and found an email to a friend that mentioned she'd taken everything she could carry and left her apartment. Apparently, her ex-boyfriend had been beating on her for years, hence the old injuries. She took out a domestic violence order against him but he's hunting her down. She mentions having proof of his violence toward her in a safe place. So, I figure she's left it in the locker at the bus station."

"I doubt that has anything to do with the current murders." Kane rubbed his chin. "Poor woman, she never got justice."

Jenna shook her head. "If we get the evidence to the DA in her hometown, maybe they can prosecute him." She picked up her landline. "Rowley, grab the silver key from Bunny Watkins' possessions and head down to the bus station. See if it opens one of the lockers. Number four is on the key. There might be information in there on a domestic violence case." She disconnected. "He's on his way. What else do you have for me, Shane?"

"I've added all the drug information to the files but basically the tests I ran on the stomach contents of both victims confirmed the presence of a date-rape drug." Wolfe moved around in his office chair, making it squeak. *"We've seen the use of these types of drugs in previous cases. They work very fast and can first incapacitate the victim and then render them unconscious."*

Jenna's jaw tightened and she flicked a glance at Kane. "So, you were right all along. He drugged the victims before killing them."

"I checked the mouths for bruising or evidence of force-feeding and found nothing. Since the victims ingested it voluntarily, he likely added it to their food or drink. This would tie in to him being seen at the roadhouse. It would be a perfect place to slip a drug into their drinks."

"So, they never had a chance to fight back." Kane leaned on the desk. "I noticed the absence of defensive wounds. Did you find anything else to prove that there was a struggle?"

"I found no scratches, bruises, or any signs whatsoever of a struggle on either victim." Wolfe blew out a sigh. *"I don't believe they were just subdued. I figure they were completely incapable of resisting."*

"If he's using a sedative this strong, it means he's calculated. He doesn't want panic—he wants control." Kane's mouth turned down. "What about the bite marks?"

"I examined the bite marks under a scanning electron microscope. It gives me extremely high-resolution microscopic images of bite patterns and potential sharp force trauma weapons." Wolfe cleared his throat. *"In my opinion the puncture wounds are too precise—too perfect to be animal bites. I found no tearing or irregularity you'd expect from a dog, for instance, with long canines. Whatever inflicted this damage I believe was artificial."*

Leaning back in her chair, Jenna considered the implications. "Are you sure?"

"Yeah, I'm very sure." Wolfe tapped on his keyboard. *"Just to be certain I used a forensic light source, which identifies bruising, saliva traces, and hidden injuries that might not be visible under normal lighting. I also discovered traces of metal residue embedded in the flesh around the wounds. I believe the killer used a modified hollow tool designed to mimic the bite of a vampire and has the ability to extract blood."*

Trying to get her mind around this well-organized psychopathic killer, Jenna raised both eyebrows at Kane. "So, we're looking at someone who isn't just obsessed with vampires—he's engineered the means to make their killings appear real. Do you figure he's doing this to scare everyone?"

"I have no idea what his motives are, but I can tell you the depth of the wounds suggests the device was very sharp and forcibly inserted but controlled. This would tell me he's done this several times before and he knows exactly how much pressure to apply." Wolfe could be heard filling a cup with coffee and adding the fixings. *"Another thing of interest is, I don't believe the blood was spilled—it was siphoned through a mechanism connected to the fangs. There's no indication of a sucking motion that would bruise, so both victims were alive when they were drained."* He drew in a breath. *"Both cases are identical. It's ritualistic and he's perfected his method. I figure he's been killing for some time. Have you discovered any similar cases?"*

Jenna shook her head as if he were in the room with her. "Not yet, but we've uploaded all the information we have to date and circulated it statewide. I'll ask Rio to send it out to law enforcement throughout the country. If he's been doing this for a time, bodies must be showing up each Halloween. My worry is what he's been doing for the rest of the year."

"I'm not sure I want to know." Wolfe sighed. *"If no one has caught him yet, he may be the smartest serial killer you've faced so far."*

"Did you discover any evidence on the locket?" Kane drummed his fingers on the table.

"It's clean, as in washed-in-alcohol clean. Not even a trace of the owner. All I discovered was trace evidence from the pig. Nothing human." Wolfe's chair squeaked as he ran it across the floor. *"I can find no reason why he placed the locket on the pig. This guy is an unknown quantity. Y'all stay safe out there."*

Jenna smiled. "We'll do our best." She disconnected and looked at Kane. "This guy is some scary freak."

Kane stood. "You can say that again. I guess we give the bad news to the team."

Jenna collected her tablet and followed him to the conference room. The aroma of freshly brewed coffee filled the room and she noticed a plate of fresh donuts on the counter. The deputies had arrived before breakfast via Aunt Betty's Café. She brought Raven and Rio up to date with Wolfe's findings. "I hope the interviews gave us a prime suspect. We need a break in the case."

"Yeah, we've spoken to everyone on the list now." Rio stood and went to the whiteboard. "I figure we have three out of the four we need to look at more closely. Maybe investigate their backgrounds and see if any of them have the skills to make metal fangs."

"Unless they got something from an undertaker?" Raven

leaned back in his chair. "They use very wide catheters to pump the blood from corpses and then fill them with formaldehyde. He could have picked up something like that from a medical salvage sale."

She led Kane to the whiteboard and they stood beside Rio as he added notes. "This looks interesting."

"I figure the interview we had with Sly Goldman was the most interesting. He spoke to Bunny the night that she died as he was working alongside her, but he left a few minutes before she did and noticed someone in the parking lot. He described him as tall, wide, and wearing a long black coat and a cowboy hat. It's the same description as the one we received from the server in the roadhouse. If it is, and he is the killer, we have him implicated in both murders."

"Another interesting thing came from his interview." Raven stood from the conference table and walked over to them. "Goldman visited the roadhouse on Sunday night around the same time as the man was seen in the roadhouse restaurant with Darlene Travis. He mentioned he went there for a meal after work, but he didn't notice the man or Darlene."

Jenna scanned the whiteboard. "How would you describe Goldman?"

"He fits the description of all the others in the killer's profile. They're all tall and broad in various degrees." Rio leaned his hip against the desk. "When we spoke to McCulloch, the maintenance worker at the hospital, I found him to be very defensive. He moved around and appeared to be nervous, and when we started questioning him about Bunny, he got annoyed. The one thing of interest that came out of his interview was when he left he noticed Goldman outside the Triple Z Bar leaning against the wall and smoking."

"Do you figure Goldman tried to throw the suspicion away from him and onto someone else?" Kane looked from one to the other. "Maybe he knew that he'd been spotted outside and decided to conjure up the suspicious man in the long coat?"

Running a scenario through her mind, Jenna nodded. "What if he'd been outside watching to see if a potential victim got off the last bus? He admits she went there after work on Sunday and there's a clear view from the parking lot at the Triple Z Bar to the roadhouse. The bus station where the buses stop is well lit and so is the ticketing office. When you think about it, the wall outside the bar would be a perfect place to keep a watch on that area."

"Which would mean that Goldman could be our prime suspect." Kane folded his arms across his chest. "Although Cash and Withers are interesting guys. From reading the interview comments about Withers being charismatic and overfriendly, he fits into the mold as well. Although he doesn't seem the type to be hanging out at the Triple Z Bar. Is it that he likes hanging out with his staff or he doesn't have any friends of his own?"

"I figure he's a rich guy who started off poor and prefers the company of cowboys." Rio tossed the marker pen from hand to hand. "He's charming. I guess women would see him as trustful. The charm is overpowering. I wouldn't discount him at all."

Jenna slid one hip onto the tabletop and frowned. "This guy Cash, who took Bunny's bandana, he has priors in assaulting women and yet you haven't red-flagged him. Why?"

"He appeared to be genuinely shocked when he knew that Bunny was dead." Rio shrugged. "I searched his footlocker, and he carries a weapon, which is perfectly legal. I didn't see anything there that would indicate he has any drugs. He answered all our questions and appeared a little angry we'd disturbed him. He believes we were there because of complaints against him from women. My thoughts were, we would need to keep our eye on him for any type of domestic abuse or attempted rape, but this isn't the man that we are looking for, is it? Although he fits the description, his attitude doesn't fit the crime."

"Then we won't dismiss him completely. We'll just keep him on the list but consider the others as our prime suspects." Kane moved over to the counter and poured two cups of coffee. "Has anything interesting come from the hotline calls?"

"Rowley has looked over them and hasn't found anything of great interest, but he sent all the paperwork here so we can go over it." Rio replaced the whiteboard pen in the holder and turned back to the conference table.

Jenna took a cup from Kane and sat down. "I figure we need to look more closely at these suspects. As Wolfe believes they've been committing murder for some time in the same way, we need to track their whereabouts over the last couple of years, if possible, especially around Halloween. If murders are reported in other counties or states and we can link them, we'll know they're involved. We can trace employment records. They all need to work, apart from Withers, so for him, maybe try to discover from his sales if he delivered any of his horses personally and where. There must be records of sales for tax purposes or whatever."

"I'd like to search their homes and vehicles." Kane sank into a chair making it groan. "But a hunch won't get us a search warrant." He glanced at Jenna. "This is going to be a long day."

The door opened and Rowley came in carrying an evidence bag containing a large bulging envelope. Jenna stood and held out her hand. "You found something."

She pulled gloves from her pocket and snapped them on and then opened the evidence bag, unsealed the envelope and emptied the contents on the table. Images of Bunny with bruises, cut lips, and broken arms spilled over the table. Each had a doctor's report and signed statements from witnesses. Two thumb drives with evidence against Peter Jorden, labels attached to them. Sifting through the statements, Jenna lifted her gaze to Kane. "We have an address of this animal. Bunny has collected evidence over four years or so. Would you contact the DA in Missoula and tell him what we've found?" She pushed the documents back into the evidence bag and handed it to him.

"It would be my pleasure." Kane stood and took the evidence bag. "I hope Peter Jorden ends up in our town. I figure I might have a few words to say to him."

THIRTY-FIVE

Getting home after six wasn't Jenna's plan, but Raya had fed the boys and by the time she'd tended the horses with as much assistance as Kane could offer, they were both bathed and ready for bed. They both liked to spend time with the boys after work. Jackson liked to cuddle and Tauri wanted to tell them about his day. They held back on the dinner they'd collected from Aunt Betty's. Wendy knew what they needed and had packed a few days' microwavable meals. Once Jackson had fallen asleep in her arms, she carried him to bed. Tauri, now the bigger brother and very responsible for his age, decided to follow and they both went to tuck him in.

They discussed the case over dinner. Although they'd made headway, tracing the suspects over the last year, they had no cases to line them up against. The horse breeder, Withers, moved around all over, collecting horses from different sales and selling his own. He was a definite possibility for the killer and fit the description. Jenna would follow up on him in the morning. After dinner, they'd just finished clearing the table when Jenna's phone chimed. It was Rio. "Is there a problem?"

"Might be." Rio yawned explosively. "Sorry, ah, Atohi

Blackhawk called. He noticed a pack of wolves moving toward Stanton. It's unusual for them to be this close, especially with deer and elk high in the mountains at the moment. He had concerns about them coming into town, so he followed. The wolves' interest confused him. Alongside Stanton in that section, there's nothing but cornfields, and gray wolves don't waste their time with mice when there's plenty of deer to eat. When the pack headed back up the mountain, Blackhawk and a few of his friends continued along the trail looking for carrion and they found something unusual. He figures there's a bad smell coming from the corn maze and he couldn't find anywhere alongside the field to indicate an injured deer or elk stumbled in and died. So, because of the current murders, he called it in. I drove past the maze this afternoon and the entrance is blocked with hay bales, with a KEEP OUT notice. I didn't see anything unusual apart from a few Halloween decorations. Do you want me to do a walk-through?"

Jenna exchanged a look with Kane, who was already on his feet and heading for Raya's apartment door. "No, don't go in without backup. We're on our way." She thought for a beat. "Wait near the roadhouse for us. I don't figure you should be out there alone. Where is Blackhawk?"

"He's heading back to the res. They've been hunting and wanted to get home." Rio cleared his throat. "Do you want me to call him and ask him to come back?"

Jenna pushed her feet into her cold boots. "No. I'll call him if necessary, but we need to check this out. We'll see you in fifteen minutes." She disconnected.

As she pulled on her duty belt and collected her coat, Raya came into the family room. Jenna smiled at her. "So sorry to disturb you. We need to check out a possible murder scene."

"That's what I'm here for." Raya settled on the sofa with her knitting. "I'll watch TV until you get back."

"I've just put on a fresh pot of coffee." Kane checked his

weapon. "The spare room is made up if you need to crash." He picked up a Thermos and handed it to Jenna. "I'll leave the sling at home tonight. I don't want to look like an easy target. I'll drive. I don't do shotgun so well and it's nothing to do with your driving. It's just I'd like to get there before daybreak." He flashed her a smile and then bent to rub Duke's ears. "Guard the house, Duke. We'll be back soon."

It would be pointless arguing with him about driving. Jenna nodded and headed for the door. She disarmed the security and went outside. A gust of freezing wind smacked her in the face. Tiny ice shards bit into her cheeks and she tucked in her chin and ran to the garage. "Snow isn't too far away."

"Yeah, that's all we need right now." Kane slid behind the wheel and they headed along the driveway, through the gate, and onto the highway.

Black glossy ice patches reflected in the lights as they drove along the blacktop. Darkness surrounded them until they turned onto Main. In town, mist curled across the road, creeping from the river. It always gave her the shivers over Halloween. The bright although macabre Halloween decorations gave the town a festive feel, and although Jenna understood the chance of facing another murder scene, she couldn't help smiling at the craziness of some of the displays. Orange lights gave the entire street a strange glow, and the skeletons danced with flashing eyes and chattering jaws as they approached. They drove past a coven of witches, posed around a green bubbling cauldron, all cackling, their long white hair flowing in the breeze. Each store they passed by had something different and imaginative. Every year the displays grew larger and more complicated and now they had a haunted house, already being touted as having a resident ghost due to the poor murdered soul found there.

Rio was waiting for them alongside the road opposite the roadhouse when they arrived and they drove in a convoy to the corn maze just outside of town. They climbed out of their vehicles and Jenna turned in all directions, scanning the local area with her flashlight. The forest stretched out in an endless pitch-black mass and anyone could be watching them, but she didn't see any wolf eyes reflecting in the dark. She turned to Kane and they walked to the entrance of the maze. "It's a maze. How are we going to find what's making that smell?"

"I guess we split up." Kane dragged a bale of hay from the entrance. "I'm sure we've all been in one of these before. They usually have a few dead ends, and you keep coming back to the beginning and starting again. I'd say as this has been set up for the kids, it won't be too difficult." He turned to look at Jenna. "Or we can all go together. It's your call."

Although the idea of walking into a maze in the pitch black wasn't her idea of fun, Jenna aimed her flashlight along a pathway. "It would be quicker if we split up. Call out if you find anything."

Mist swirled around Jenna as she stared into the darkness for a few moments, listening. The air carried the scent of damp earth and mold but the overpowering smell of death came on the breeze. Fear gripped her as Kane and Rio disappeared into the darkness, leaving her alone. Taking a deep foul breath, she aimed her flashlight across the tangled pathway and took a few steps. On each side the cornstalks stood tall and yellow. With each step their dried leaves whispered in the wind, sounding so like hushed voices. The hair on the back of her neck prickled. Glancing over one shoulder, she moved with care through the towering stalks. She gasped when her flashlight beam sliced through the darkness and landed on a severed hand, crawling from a pile of damp earth. Heart pounding, she shook her head. "It's just more stupid Halloween fun for the kids."

As she moved deeper into the maze, the way became littered with scary props. Huge spiders, cobwebs, and bats came at her from every angle. She sidestepped a cackling witch in a rocking chair and kept moving. With each step forward, darkness closed in around her in a solid suffocating wall. Strange, unsettling noises came from all directions and suddenly a wave of fear gripped her and she couldn't shake off the feeling someone else was close by, watching her. Rustling sounds came from the corn but she couldn't tell if it was Kane or Rio moving through the maze or someone coming straight for her. Disoriented, she fought the desire to turn and run back to the entrance.

The bad smell intensified, becoming more unbearable with each hesitant step. Something dead was close by. Trembling, she stopped, pushed the flashlight between her knees and pulled on a face mask and gloves. The flashlight slid from her grip and rolled away into the corn. The darkness was immediate and closed around her, amplifying every small sound. She gasped and dived after the flashlight, crawling on her hands and knees. The light had rolled just out of reach among the cornstalks. In pitch black, she scrabbled forward, fingers outstretched. She sobbed with relief when her fingers closed around the handle. Nerves at breaking point, she backed out of the corn and straightened slowly, moving the beam all around to make sure no one had followed her. The wind had picked up and the field of corn rustled and moaned. A wolf pack howled in the distance and she swallowed her rising fear and turned at the next corner.

Ahead, a small clearing intentionally carved into the maze opened up and she stopped midstride as her light moved over a young woman laid out on two hay bales. Transfixed, Jenna's hand trembled as she held the flashlight steady. Was this real or just another prop to scare the kids? The unmistakable smell of decomposition seeped through her face mask. She took a hesitant step forward, taking in the ritualistic position of the hands cradling the stake plunged through the heart, the marks on the neck. It was the same as before. The killer had struck down another innocent young woman.

She wanted to cry out for the injustice, the tragic waste of life. How could she stop this maniac? Her training kicked in and she stepped back, not wanting to contaminate the scene. Unease slid over her. This woman hadn't died here. The ground and all around was clean. Could the killer be close by, watching her reaction, and enjoying the horror on her face? She wouldn't give him the satisfaction. She moved back, scanning all around her, and then raised her voice and turned her flashlight up into the air. "Dave, Rio. Over here."

Footsteps came running and corn broke and crackled all around her as Kane pushed his way through the wall of the maze. She gripped his arm, glad to see him. "It's a body. The same as before."

"I'll call Wolfe." Kane pulled out his phone.

Behind her, she made out the sound of Rio as he ran along the pathway toward her. He rounded the corner and stopped. His flashlight illuminated the grotesque scene. She turned to look at him. "It's just as well you decided to call this in, or this poor woman would have been eaten by the wolves."

"It looks exactly the same as the last two." Rio moved his flashlight over the body and around the ground beside the hay bales. "I can't even see a footprint. This guy sure knows how to pick places to dump his bodies."

Jenna nodded. "I'd figured he made a mistake when he left the locket with the pig." She waved a hand toward the forest. "I hoped Wolfe would find something incriminating but it's another dead end."

"Maybe there was evidence on the pig we missed. Once the elk went through there was no evidence left and by morning the wildlife had taken the rest." Kane rubbed his shoulder. "At first, I believed the pig was to distract us, but all the women so far have been taken after dark. So, he had some other motive."

"Really?" Rio looked from one to the other, his face dark under his Stetson. "It's kind of obvious to me. The killer knows about the old bridge and it's all over town that the elk have been moving down this way. I figure he used the pig to lure you into the forest and then he paid kids to stampede the elk. He would know the only possible way to escape would be to cross the bridge." He gave them a long look. "He wanted you all dead and I figure he almost got his wish."

THIRTY-SIX

Rio's words percolated through Jenna's mind as she waited for Wolfe and his team to process the scene. The killer had suddenly become more dangerous. It was obvious that he was living some deluded fantasy about vampires but how did Jenna's team come into the equation? She'd spent some time over the last couple of days reading as much information about this type of unusual behavior as possible. She wanted to get inside his mind to discover his next move but that was proving more difficult by the moment. This killer wasn't following any particular behavior. She didn't know if he drank the victim's blood because he believed it gave him power or if he was influenced by myths and legends or books that he'd read.

It seemed, like most of the serial killers they'd hunted down, this guy had his own individual fantasy when it came to murder and he was using the vampire slaying as an excuse. During her time dealing with serial killers, she'd discovered that all of them had blamed somebody else for what they'd done. None of them could admit the fact that they were mentally ill. Many of them believed that what they were doing was happening everywhere else in the world and nobody cared. In fact, many of them believed people should be grateful.

As Rio and Webber carried the body to Wolfe's van, she hurried to his side. "It looks the same as the others, doesn't it?"

"I'm afraid so." Wolfe scanned the corn maze. "He sure knows how to select a place where it's difficult to leave any evidence." He indicated to the ground. "This walkway is so littered with debris that I'd never be able to prove anything we found here belonged to the killer. I wonder how many people have been walking up and down placing the props and Halloween decorations in the last week." He looked at Jenna. "Do you have any suspects?"

Nodding, Jenna followed him back to the road with Kane close behind. "Yeah, we have a couple that look promising but everything we have on them is circumstantial evidence. It doesn't make the investigation any easier. Unless I have someone stake out the roadhouse over the next few days and hope he strikes again. However, we don't know for sure if that's his hunting area. He seems to be changing it up each time."

"I'm hoping that we'll get more information from the victims' local law enforcement agencies over the next few days." Kane moved beside Wolfe. "If we get some idea of why the women were in Black Rock Falls, maybe we'll be able to trace exactly where he ran into them."

"It could be totally random." Wolfe removed his gloves, balled them up and shoved them into his pocket. "I've read about killers like him, whose fantasies are triggered by certain people. They have a type. In this case, maybe, he sees a thin pale-skinned woman and something in his twisted mind tells him she is a vampire and needs to be staked. He believes he is saving people by removing her from society."

"Maybe he's been reading too many vampire slayer books and it's an identity problem." Kane rubbed his chin. "We've dealt with another Halloween killer who believed by murdering young women at Halloween, he gained years on his life. He must have gotten that idea from a novel. Now we have this one, who by his ritual must believe he's preventing the vampires rising the next morning. The thing is, he's got his story mixed up. In all the stories I've read about vampires, it takes a vampire to create one."

Jenna nodded. "True, so do you believe this killer created his own vampire bloodletting machine, or whatever, and believes he's a vampire?"

"Then he'd be creating them, not murdering them." Kane rubbed his chin. "If that's his motive, it doesn't make sense."

"Ha, y'all can't make these people logical." Wolfe leaned against his van. "Their minds work in a way necessary for them to validate murder. He sees vampires as a particular type of woman. I figure he is consumed with the old movie type of female vampire, with long hair and flowing white gowns, so he creates one in that image and believes by draining her blood and staking her, he's saving her from damnation."

Running a hand through her hair, Jenna stared at him. "By murdering her?"

"Unfortunately, yeah, I believe so, but what makes sense to us means nothing. He might see his reason for killing completely differently. There's no logic in what they do—that's what I've deduced over the years working with you, Jenna. Their minds work on a completely different plane to ours." Wolfe pushed away from the van. "It's late. I'll call you in the morning and we'll schedule an autopsy." He wiped a hand down his weary face. "Another family lost a daughter tonight. The killer must have left a clue behind, something we can use to stop him. If it's there, I'll find it."

THIRTY-SEVEN
HELENA

Friday

Zipping up her jacket against the cold wind, Julie Wolfe stepped down from the bus and followed the others toward the conference hall. She'd spent the last two weeks at a child-focused conference in Helena to explore ideas for her career. She had her degree in psychology and needed to know which were the best options for her going forward. Some of the interesting jobs she could work toward were in the Child Protective Services or as a family support specialist. It had been difficult to make any type of decision. She didn't have her sister Emily's drive to become a medical examiner and had been making up her mind for ages.

Since moving to Black Rock Falls after her mother died of cancer, she had seen how many children were abused in the foster system throughout the country. Due to Jenna's diligence this type of abuse didn't happen in Black Rock Falls, but children still needed a voice in their future. She had been seriously considering becoming a youth advocacy coordinator. The idea of supporting young people and ensuring they have access to resources, education, and protection would make her happy. She could obtain certifications in youth advocacy and child welfare to strengthen her qualifications before applying for a suitable position. After attending keynote speeches, she decided to join a networking roundtable, where she'd have the opportunity to speak to professionals one-on-one.

As she headed toward the door of the conference center, a motorcycle roared into the parking lot. A man dressed in all leather slid from the back of his Harley like a black snake. He removed his helmet and smoothed his collar-length glossy hair as he turned to look at her. Julie's stomach gave a twist at the thought of what her father would say if he knew she'd been talking to a bad-boy biker. She'd met Rhett Lawson when he'd sat beside her in most of the same seminars. He'd mentioned studying at MU and, like her, he couldn't make up his mind which career path to follow. They'd got to chatting and she'd discovered that he'd been raised in many foster homes and had vowed to make sure no child had to endure what he'd suffered after his parents died in a plane crash when he was just two years old. There were many students from MU at the conference but they seemed to avoid him like the plague. Two girls she'd known for years warned her not to speak to him, saying he had a bad reputation. Julie made up her own mind about people and had found Rhett to be quiet, softly spoken, and incredibly smart. He was two years her senior but she wasn't planning on marrying him.

Julie lifted a hand to wave at him and caught a flash of white when he smiled. "Fancy seeing you here again. Are you interested in pursuing a career in youth advocacy or counseling?"

"In fact, I am." Rhett shrugged. "I'm overqualified. I already have a couple of degrees up my sleeve and the counselors keep trying to push me in different directions but it's not what I want to do." He chuckled. "They figure I don't fit the mold of a counselor because of how I look and the snake tattoo looped around my arm." He walked backward, watching her as if gauging her reaction. "What they don't understand is kids who were raised like me don't trust suits or the school principal types. They relate to guys like me, and I can help them. I just need someone to give me a chance to prove it."

Concerned by the lack of understanding he'd received his entire life, Julie frowned. "You're highly qualified and that counts more than what you look like." She waved a hand in the air. "You should see the deputies riding around Black Rock Falls on the weekends, all in leather and riding old Harleys. They have their own biker club—my dad is a medical examiner and he's right there in the thick of it. Maybe that's where you should apply for a job. I am and I know they are crying out for suitable staff for the Her Broken Wings Foundation. They work with women from abusive relationships and traumatized kids all the time."

"That sounds like a plan." Rhett grabbed his things from the saddlebags. "Black Rock Falls, huh? Now that's a coincidence. My folks came from there. I don't know anything about the place but they ran cattle and a trustee is in control right now. Maybe when I turn twenty-five, I'll go and see what my inheritance looks like."

Julie smiled. "It's a beautiful place to live but has a problem with serial killers." She sighed. "It's the kids I want to help. I always have and now I figure I've finally found my path in life."

"I'll buy you lunch if we can discuss Black Rock Falls and the foundation." Rhett gave his head a slight shake. "It's strange how my roots are in the town where you live. Maybe we were meant to cross paths?"

Laughing, Julie walked beside him. "They say spooky

things happen over Halloween but this is my last day in Helena. I'm flying out late tonight."

"Then if you don't mind exchanging numbers, I'd love to keep in touch." Rhett pushed black hair from his face. "It's been really great chatting to you this week, Julie."

Wondering if her dad would approve of Rhett, Julie pushed the concern to one side and smiled. "Yeah, I'd like that."

THIRTY-EIGHT
BLACK ROCK FALLS

Jenna stared out of the office window at the turbulent sky wondering what was happening with the weather this year. Last night when they'd been out in the corn maze, she'd been sure it would be snowing by the morning, but the heavy black clouds rumbling across the tops of the mountain told a different story. The weather pattern had changed in the last couple of years. Violent storms, earth tremors, and flooding had become a regular occurrence rather than a once-in-a-century weather event. She turned to look at Kane, who was working at his desk. "It looks like there's a nasty storm coming. The dark clouds have been building up all day."

"I guess then I better keep Duke close by or he'll be a shivering pile of Jell-O." Kane leaned back in his chair and stretched his long legs. "I figured we would have heard something from Wolfe by now. Do you want me to call him?"

Jenna shook her head and walked over to the hooks behind the door to grab her coat. "No, he'll call when he wants us. As the murders are identical, there's not really anything different for us to observe. Right now, I want to take a walk through town and then stop by Aunt Betty's for lunch. The townsfolk are on edge and maybe seeing us on patrol might calm them down a little. Although, if there's a bad storm coming, it's going to wreak havoc with the Halloween decorations—and so close to Halloween too. I hope it blows through and doesn't do any damage."

"Yeah, so many kids are waiting patiently for Sunday night. It seems a long time coming this year with the murders spoiling everything." Kane stood and took his coat from Jenna. "When you called Jo this morning, did she give you any insight into the killer that we haven't already discussed?"

Shaking her head, Jenna pulled on gloves. "Not yet. She's looking at the recent case and working with Wolfe today and then she'll give us her recommendations." She sighed. "It's good to have a special agent who is a top behavioral analyst on speed dial when we need her. I'm at the overthinking stage with this case. Nothing is coming together."

"Rio, Raven, and Rowley are trying to piece together the victims' last hours and reasons for being in town and more on the suspects' whereabouts before arriving in Black Rock Falls. With that information, we might be able to sync it with one or more of the suspects or murders in other states or counties. Then I figure we lean on them, follow them, or whatever to make sure they know we're watching them. Maybe after Halloween, the killings will stop. The one responsible will most likely leave town and we'll have him."

Jenna shook her head. "You're optimistic today, Dave." She swung open the door and Duke dashed to her side, his thick tail wagging. "I figure he's saving his best until last. The Halloween night murder would be the ultimate in his twisted mind. He could scare the entire town and he'd do it just to prove his point—that vampires exist. We need to catch him before he has a chance to kill again." She gave him a long look. "Somehow."

The threatening sky had turned Black Rock Falls into dusk, making the bright decorations cheerful in the gloom. On the way to Aunt Betty's, they stopped to chat with the townsfolk and examined the displays outside every store along the sidewalk. With terrible murder scenes replaying in her mind, the craziness of Halloween and the laughable displays lifted Jenna's spirits. Whenever she found it difficult to catch a killer, she blamed herself. As sheriff, it was her responsibility to bring murderers to justice. Young women should be safe in her town, even if climbing from buses or walking home. She worked very hard to catch the killers but they always seemed to slip through and kill one more time. These monsters destroyed families and added another memory she'd rather forget. She glanced around the town, searching for anything unusual or out of place, but no one lurked in the alleyways or watched from trucks parked alongside the road.

"Don't let it get you down, Jenna." Kane brushed against her. "We have the best minds working on this case. We'll get a break soon. I'm sure of it. I've told you many times before, one day the killer will make a mistake. The last kill was almost identical but the marks on the neck appeared rushed to me. Maybe he's getting sloppy?"

Jenna pushed open the door to Aunt Betty's Café and ducked beneath the legs of a giant spider, which had become a Halloween favorite along with its many babies scattered in cobwebs all over the diner. She glanced at the sheriff's table at the back and smiled to see Raven in deep conversation with Emily. She turned to Kane. "That's a good sign. I hope they get together. It's a match made in heaven."

"Don't meddle." Kane narrowed his gaze at her and guided her to the counter to order. "It's a slow burn and they last the longest, just like us."

They ordered the specials and headed to the table. Jenna smiled. "It's good to see you, Em. Have you any news on the autopsy?"

"We drop by here to get a break from the murders most

days." Emily smiled up at her. "It's nice to clear your mind and start afresh in the afternoon. We've been discussing our costumes for the Halloween Ball on Sunday night. Have you decided what to wear?"

"We might be chasing down a serial killer." Kane removed his jacket and dropped into a chair. "But I'm going as the Grim Reaper this year, if we go. I know it's in bad taste after all the murders but that's all they had left in the store in my size—and I got a skull mask thrown in."

Jenna smiled at her. "I have a witch costume and Tauri is going as a ghost. He's been moaning and dragging chains around the house all week." She chuckled. "Jackson is mystified but he has an amazing sense of humor for his age, so we hope he won't find anything disturbing, but we'll keep them both well away from anything graphic."

"I've told them none of it is true." Kane's hand closed around his empty coffee cup and he waved to Wendy as she went by carrying a pot. "They understand dress-up, so it should be fine."

"I'm so looking forward to going this year." Emily lowered her lashes and her cheeks pinked. "We selected our costumes together."

"I'm Thor, and Emily is an ice princess." Raven leaned back in his chair. "I hope the ball goes ahead. It brings everyone together in the town."

Loving seeing Emily and Raven finally dating, Jenna nodded as Wendy came by to pour coffee. "Oh, it will go ahead, with or without us. It takes more than a serial killer to stop the ball. Same as the trick-or-treating. If we're held up, we have Raya and your family to watch over our boys."

"Ah, there's nothing better than a full rack of ribs with all the trimmings on a cold day." Kane smiled at Wendy as she came back to the table and emptied her tray. "I could eat these every day."

"They're a favorite and we have them twice a week as specials now." Wendy stood to one side as another server placed plates in front of Emily and Raven. She looked at Jenna. "I'll be right back with your meal, Jenna."

Nodding, Jenna stared at the array of side dishes Kane had ordered with his huge meal. "So, the fall didn't affect your appetite?"

"Never." Kane grinned at her and tucked a napkin under his chin. "I figure my appetite increases when I've been injured. I need the energy to regenerate after the damage."

Blinking, Jenna looked at him. Whoever said they need to regenerate? He always sounded like some type of lab experiment. She'd seen him shot in the head, electrocuted, and buried alive and yet he came back. He might be sore now, but in a week or so he'd be stronger and fitter than before, mainly because after any injury he worked hard on getting back in shape. After Jackson was born, he'd encouraged her to get back into their workout routine, and because of it, she figured she coped with the stress of being a new mother. Her meal arrived, and everyone fell silent, all enjoying the ribs. She'd just wiped her hands and mouth when her phone chimed. It was Wolfe. "Hey, Shane, we're at Aunt Betty's. Do you have anything for me?"

"Yeah, small things but significant." Wolfe yawned. *"Sorry, it's been a long couple of days. If you schedule a conference call this afternoon, along with Jo, I'll bring you up to date. What's the special at Aunt Betty's today?"*

Jenna pushed her plate away and sipped a glass of water. "Ribs, and do you want all the team involved?"

"It would save time." Wolfe tapped away on his keyboard. *"If Emily is there, ask her to bring me some takeout. Three specials, Norrell and Webber as well."*

Leaning back in her chair, Jenna sighed in contentment. "Not a problem. I'll set that meeting up for two-thirty. It will give you time to eat." She disconnected, gave Emily the message, and waited for Kane to finish the last bite. "I believe Wolfe has found something. We're having a conference call at two-thirty." She turned to Raven. "The entire team."

"Sure." Raven stood. "I'll drop Em back to the morgue and be right there." He patted his leg and Ben, his K-9, crawled out from under the table alert and ready to work.

"I wonder what he's found." Kane wiped his mouth and stood. "Or maybe Jo has found something interesting about the killer?" He shrugged slowly into his coat. "I guess we're going to find out."

THIRTY-NINE

By the time they'd walked back to the office, the street lights had come on. The temperature had plummeted, and Jenna's cheeks became stiff with cold. The sky looked angry and way in the distance lightning streaked across the sky. People were covering the displays with tarps and staring at the dark clouds. One woman stopped Jenna. "Is there a problem?"

"No, I just wondered if you'd heard a weather report." The woman frowned. "They said likelihood of rain at noon and look at the sky. That's a bad storm and we're getting no warnings."

Shaking her head, Jenna glanced into the sky. "It doesn't look good but it's some ways away. Maybe it will blow over."

"I hope so." The woman picked up her grocery bags and hurried along the sidewalk bent against the wind.

The moment Raven returned, Jenna collected the team in her office and set up the computer for a conference call. It was good to see Agent Jo Wells and her partner, Ty Carter, as they always came to Black Rock Falls for Halloween, and Tauri had become close friends with Jo's daughter, Jaime. "I know we're in the middle of a case but it would be great to see you here again.

The cottage is ready and waiting for you, if you're planning on coming."

"We wouldn't miss it and I don't figure Jaime would be very pleased to stay in Snakeskin Gully over Halloween. It's very boring there." Jo turned to Carter sitting beside her. *"When can we leave, do you think?"*

"Saturday night or Sunday morning, depending on the weather." Carter moved a toothpick around his mouth. *"The weather doesn't look so good out here at the moment."*

Jenna nodded. "Same here. I figure we're in for one heck of a storm."

When Wolfe joined the meeting, they got down to business. Jenna leaned on her desk and stared at the computer screen. "I know you've been discussing the cases. Have you discovered anything of interest that we can use to catch this killer?"

"I've analyzed each case, taking into account the killer's escalation." Jo stared into the camera. *"The corn maze crime scene portrays the same ritualistic intent, but according to the time of death, he spent more time with this one than the others. He didn't risk leaving the body out where the wolves could consume it. I believe you discovered it not long after it was left in the corn maze. He risked being seen, which means he's becoming bolder and more confident."*

"I have the victim's name." Wolfe stared into the camera. *"Her fingerprints came up on the database. Her name is Gabby Turner. I've discovered something significant about her that's different from the other two victims."* He leaned forward on his desk. *"The wounds on the neck were contaminated with what I believe is the blood from the last victim. Previously to this, the tools he used to make the marks on the neck and draw the blood were sterilized. Apart from that, I found absolutely no trace evidence whatsoever."* He sighed. *"It tells me that he was in a rush to get this one drained of blood. Also, it's of interest that this is the only one that has a slight bruise on her face. This one had a* bruise just under the left eye, but it was covered with makeup. As the killer hasn't used makeup on the victims' faces previously, I can only assume she wore makeup when he abducted her."

"Why is this significant?" Raven's eyes narrowed. "She meets all the criteria of his last victims."

"She doesn't." Jo shook her head. "The others were perfect, no injuries to their faces. This makes me believe he was anxious to find another woman to kill. He decided to overlook the bruise, which would go against his vampire ideal. He'd believe they never age and recover from injuries immediately, and yet Wolfe mentioned the bruise was over a week old. This tells me he's moving into another phase."

Jenna raised one eyebrow. "Can you explain in more detail?"

"Before this murder, his previous two victims had reinforced his delusion. They had pristine skin with no visible signs of human frailty and then we come to the last one. Why did he choose her when the bruise disrupted his illusion, as in his mind, vampires regenerate and should be flawless?" Jo's lips pursed. "The move is out of character. It's a sign he's losing control. In my opinion, he'll risk everything to get his next kill. It's his ultimate as it gets closer to Halloween. He needs to be gone from Black Rock Falls."

Jenna leaned back in her chair, twisting a pen in her fingers. This was all very good information but it didn't get her any closer to the killer. "Have you profiled this man? We assume he is over six feet tall with broad shoulders."

"I have some information on this killer." Carter cleared his throat. "Although we have no reason to believe that the cases are linked, a year ago three women were found in Austin, Texas, with bite marks on their necks and drained of blood. At the time there was a cult known for blood drinking, and although the local law enforcement interviewed everyone suspicious, they couldn't get enough evidence for a case against anyone. It reminds me of *this case as from reading the documentation there's nothing to link any of the victims to the killer."*

"I took this case into consideration when I was profiling the killer." Jo scrolled through her tablet. *"The fact that he is tall and broad it makes perfect sense for him to move around in states where his size wouldn't stick out."* She looked directly at Kane. *"You've traveled all around the US. Where do you find the biggest guys?"*

"Montana, South Dakota, Alabama, Tennessee, Utah, and Nebraska maybe." Kane shrugged. "It's not something I worry about."

"From what I've seen, this man is methodical and cautious. It also suggests a deep awareness of how he's perceived." Jo checked her notes. *"Wolfe figures he's been doing this for a long time and yet has remained undetected. I would say we're looking at a man between thirty-five and forty years old. Someone who adjusts his occupation, clothing, posture, and speech pattern to blend in seamlessly. He hides in plain sight and no doubt carefully studies the places he intends to go for his next murder spree. This would make him even more difficult to track. His ability to disappear into the background is a calculated and deliberate act."*

Intrigued, Jenna nodded. "So, we should concentrate our search for similar crimes anywhere where the men are over five-ten to six feet. Starting with the states Kane suggested?" She pushed both hands through her hair. "The problem is this won't help us catch the killer in Black Rock Falls."

"It will." Carter smiled around his toothpick. *"From what I understand, you've been chasing down the employment records of the men you suspect did this. This information means that you can eliminate people who do the same job. For instance, the horse breeder. Although he travels around, he's still a horse breeder and high profile. He's recognizable and not hiding in plain sight."*

Scanning the files on her tablet, Jenna nodded slowly. "Ah,

yes and the other three, the maintenance man, Daniel McCulloch; the ranch hand, Dale Cash; and the cleaner at the Triple Z Bar, Sly Goldman; all have a variety of casual occupations. I just figured they took what jobs they could to survive, but if I look at them with your profile in mind, any one of them could be the killer."

"*That would be my assessment.*" Jo smiled. "*Another thing, if we look at the opposite to this perp, we're talking about a disorganized killer. It would be unlikely they would map out their next kill. They're more opportunistic. I don't believe for a minute this person restricts themselves to Halloween. This is a sideline for him, a fantasy, or something that's triggered each year by a childhood memory. He needs to follow the same path each year because of something he has either seen or believes to have seen during his childhood. This guy is well organized.*"

"He figures he's doing his bit for society." Carter shook his head. "*The fact that he doesn't rape or touch them in any other way leaves his other crimes open to interpretation. This guy is way too clever to commit the same type of crime everywhere he goes. The problem is it might not be until we track him down that we discover the extent of his killings.*"

"*I believe he will stage his last killing soon and be gone by Halloween.*" Jo reached for a glass of water on her desk and sipped. "*In his mind, he's given the vampires enough warning to stay away from the town. If you intend on catching him, it's going to be over the next two nights. Come Sunday, he'll be gone.*"

Milling over what they had said, Jenna glanced around the table at her team. "So, we take Withers out of the equation and that leaves three suspects. We know where they live and if he's going to strike, it's usually late at night. Suggestions?"

"Trail cams would work the best. We could set them up on the roads leaving where they live and take shifts watching them overnight." Kane raised both eyebrows at Jenna. "We have a stack of them on hand. It wouldn't take more than an hour to set them all up." He indicated toward the window. "But we'll need to do it before this storm hits. I don't figure anyone will want to be out when that comes to town."

Jenna nodded. "Yeah, make it happen. I'll call Raya and ask her to collect Tauri before the storm and take Duke home with her." She looked at Raven. "Is Ben good with storms?"

"Good as gold." Raven smiled. "I'll help set up the trail cams and then shoot home to feed my dogs. Then I'll take the first shift."

"There's no need to be in the office." Kane smiled. "The webcams feed to our phones. If there's any movement, they send a notification. We can all go home and monitor them from there."

Glad to see him volunteering, she ended the call. "See you all soon. She turned to the team. "It's kind of you to offer, Raven, but Rowley, you take the shift until eight because it's difficult to have alarms going off with kids. If Raven can do eight to one and Rio one to five, we'll take over from then until we're all back in the office. There's a storm brewing. Don't go anywhere without your satellite phones." She looked at Kane. "You organize the trail cams, and Raven, go with Rio to get them up at the hospital and the ranch. We'll handle the Triple Z and roadhouse. Don't forget, direct them to the road only, not a private residence. We're only watching traffic. Which reminds me, the vehicles currently registered to the suspects are in the files." She looked at Rowley. "You chase down their vehicles and then see if you can get any details on the last victim, Gabby Turner."

"Yes, ma'am." Rowley stood.

Jenna looked at Kane. "Let's go."

FORTY

As Jenna headed out to the Beast, the wind howled around, buffeting her and making it difficult to walk. The temperature had dropped and so had the visibility as the dark clouds rolled in and day turned to night. Raya had arrived a short time earlier and they'd taken Duke down to her vehicle. The bloodhound hated storms and he would feel safer hiding under their bed at home. She needed to explain to Tauri why he'd been taken out of school early. Her little boy had straightened in the seat and told her he would be the man of the house and take care of everyone if the storm came by. Jackson had been sound asleep in his car seat, his cheeks still flushed from teething. She'd kissed his fat cheeks and ran her hand through his silky black hair, but he'd slept on in blissful ignorance of the brewing storm overhead. A pang of worry gripped her as Raya drove away. She wrestled with the truck door as the wind tried to rip it away from her grasp and climbed inside. "I hope they make it home before the storm hits."

"They will." Kane stared at the sky. "I figure it's some time before it gets here. Have you ever counted the thunder after lightning flashes? When you see a flash of lightning, count the seconds before you hear a rumble of thunder. Then divide the seconds by five. That's a good indication on the distance you are from the storm. It's heading toward us and they're driving away from town."

Nodding, Jenna watched Raya's truck until it vanished in the traffic. Along the sidewalk the Halloween decorations were waving and churning as if the skeletons were dancing around the light posts, their teeth chattering like castanets. She turned in her seat as Kane headed in the opposite direction. "I figure we need to cover the road outside the Triple Z Bar and another one facing in the opposite direction so we pick up anyone who's going into the roadhouse." She frowned. "We can't be seen doing this. If the killer is anywhere around, he'll go underground until he can disable the trail cams."

"We'll have plenty of cover in the forest to place the cameras anywhere you need them. The trees will cover them and no one will even know they're there." Kane accelerated along Stanton and out of the town limits.

An eerie light fell across Black Rock Falls. Above, the sky resembled a turbulent sea, black and churning. Clouds heavy with rain rushed toward them as if goaded along by the lightning zigzagging across the mountaintops. Light rain fell across the blacktop and it seemed that everyone was rushing to get under cover. The highway leading to Black Rock Falls had traffic backed up, and impatient drivers were risking their lives overtaking the eighteen-wheelers trying to outrun the storm. The blinking fluorescent lights outside the roadhouse and the Triple Z Bar blazed out in the distance. As the Beast passed the bar, a line of eighteen-wheelers drove into the roadhouse, and in another hundred yards, more of them rumbled into the Triple Z Bar parking lot. With a motel out back, it had become a popular place for truckers to stop during bad weather.

"I'll turn into the fire road just ahead and we'll go in on

foot." Kane left the highway and they bumped along a fire road deep into the dark forest.

The fire road ran parallel to Stanton and would give them access to a view of the Triple Z Bar and the roadhouse. Jenna stared at the GPS screen. "If you stop about twenty yards ahead, we should be able to walk through the forest and attach the trail cams."

"Okay." Kane slowed to a stop, jumped out, and grabbed the cameras from the back seat. "You can wait here if you like."

Jenna stared at him. "You're not planning on climbing trees? I'll do it. You're injured."

"I can pull myself up with my right arm." Kane shook his head. "You'll get blown out of the tree, Jenna. Don't worry, I heal fast. Wait here. I'll be fine."

Shaking her head, Jenna grabbed a flashlight and followed him from the truck. "No way. It's pitch black in there. I figure you'll need someone to hold the flashlight while you secure the cameras."

They moved swiftly through the forest, and Kane selected a suitable tree and climbed with ease. Sudden violent bursts of wind circled around them, and the forest gave a mournful moan as branches creaked and dead leaves rose up in spirals as if the dead were escaping from their graves. A chill shivered down Jenna's back. She'd been through many storms but this one put her nerves on edge. She wondered if this strange weather event would forever after be called the Halloween Storm. Lightning flashed, illuminating the forest for split seconds as Kane climbed down from the tree. "That's not the safest place to be in the middle of a storm."

"One more to go." Kane took her arm. "Jump back into the truck and we'll drive. It's more dangerous walking along the fire road right now." He glanced up. "That's a weird storm. Black clouds with green. Maybe it's hail." Another gust of wind buffeted them. "I guess we'll find out soon enough."

As they stepped out of the truck a wall of rain crashed down on them and underfoot the dirt paths turned to mud. Gusts of wind pushed Jenna's hood from her head and within seconds soaking wet hair stuck to her face. She pulled the hood up again and, turning away from the wind, secured it but water had leaked down her collar and trickled down her back. She followed Kane deeper into the forest. The wind howled around them snapping the smaller branches of the trees and turning them into missiles. Ahead she made out the sign outside the Triple Z Roadhouse blinking in the darkness. She raised her voice to be heard over the wind. "Can you see anywhere where there's a clear view both ways?"

"Yeah, this one will be fine." Kane walked around a tall pine with many lower branches. "Easy to climb too. Keep your flashlight facing the ground." He turned on a penlight and held it between his teeth as he climbed.

Jenna held her breath with each lightning crash. The violent storm raced toward them. She counted the seconds between flashes and the thunder shaking the ground beneath her feet. Loud cracks and the smell of pine rushed toward her as the wind broke trees like twigs. She raised her voice to be heard. "Hurry. We need to get out of here."

Seconds later, Kane dropped down beside her, took her hand, and they ran through the forest. The fire road resembled a muddy river as they splashed their way toward the Beast. They dived inside and Jenna reached for the towels she kept on the back seat and handed one to Kane. His face was wet but his Stetson hadn't moved but dripped water from the rim. "I figure my hoodie would keep me drier than my hat but it didn't. I'm soaked through. You look dry apart from your face. Shoulder okay?"

"I'm fine and it's a great hat but the rain has leaked through my jacket in a few places. I figure I'll need to change the dressings on my wounds when we get back to the office." He smiled at her. "Don't worry about the storm. We're safe and dry in here." Kane dried his face and hands and then checked the camera feed. "Everything is set and the other cameras are in place as well." He peered out at the lashing storm. "I'm glad you sent the boys home. They'll be safer at the ranch and Duke will hide under our bed until I get home." He started the engine. "See if you can get a weather update. If we lived along the coast, I'd be concerned. That sky looks worse than a hurricane but it doesn't resemble a twister." He flicked her a glance. "This close to Halloween some of the people are going to believe it's some evil curse rolling across the sky." His mouth turned up at the corners. "People sure seem to get spooked around Halloween."

FORTY-ONE
HELENA

Light rain was falling when Julie stepped out of the conference hall with Rhett at her side. She glanced across the parking lot for the bus. "The bus is late again. I need to get back to the hotel and pack."

"I'll give you a ride if you're not scared of motorcycles." Rhett smiled at her. "You might get a little wet but I have a spare slicker in my saddlebags if you want to wear it."

Julie smiled. "I would appreciate a ride, and the slicker, thanks. I've ridden with my dad before. I like motorcycles. My dad has a Harley."

"He is a man of great taste." Rhett chuckled.

She turned on her phone and messages came in. "Oh no, they've delayed my flight to Black Rock Falls until ten tonight."

"The storm is heading that way." Rhett frowned. "Why don't you get packed and we'll go and have a meal? I can drop you at the airport. The rain will be gone by then."

Surprised by his generosity, she smiled. "That would be great." She stared at her phone. "Give me a second. I need to send a message to my dad. He's expecting me this afternoon."

She handed him her backpack. "You sure you'll be able to carry my bag as well?"

"Yeah, it will fit on the back." Rhett pulled out a spare helmet from the saddlebags and went about fitting their backpacks into the space.

Although she had no reason not to trust Rhett, Julie turned away and thumbed a message to Wolfe. She mentioned the storm delay and that she was getting a ride with Rhett and included his full name and license plate. He appeared to be a nice guy, but living in Black Rock Falls, she'd become suspicious of everyone. Not long after she'd sent the message a reply came back, telling her the storm looked bad and that he'd run Rhett's name and get back to her. She wanted to roll her eyes but her dad was just looking after her. She pulled on the helmet and smiled at Rhett. "If it doesn't bore you, you're welcome to wait with me while I pack. It won't take long."

"I figure you'll need to shower and change as well." He raised both eyebrows. "I sure do. I've been damp all day. I'll drop by my dorm and come by in an hour." He pulled on his helmet. "It will give us plenty of time to find a place for dinner. There's a nice diner not far from the airport. We could go there." He climbed onto the motorcycle. "Jump on." He started the engine.

Nodding, Julie slid on behind him. "That sounds like a plan." She held on tight and they roared out of the parking lot.

FORTY-TWO
BLACK ROCK FALLS

Trees bent and the rain lashed at the Beast as they headed back to Stanton. Jenna winced as tree branches flew through the air inches from their truck. As they approached Stanton, all they could make out was a wall of traffic. Everyone was trying to get back to town. "Oh, a traffic jam. Now what?"

"We go back and take the fire roads." Kane turned the truck around. "The Beast can handle the mud, don't worry."

Staring ahead at the streams of muddy water, Jenna shook her head. "I'm not worried but the storm is getting crazy."

Wild wind swirled debris around them as they headed along the fire road and then in a rush hail bounced off the Beast like buckshot, ricocheting into the windshield. The wipers moved back and forth in fast motion, but ice piled up on them, slowing them down. Visibility dropped to almost zero as a wall of rain battered them. Fear gripped Jenna and she clung to the seat as lightning flashes and rolls of thunder came simultaneously. The trees bent over, struggling against the massive gusts of wind, and stuck in the middle with no place to hide, Jenna glanced at Kane, hoping he could get them out of trouble.

The storm surrounded them like a giant entity hell-bent on destruction. A blinding flash of lightning zigzagged so close it startled Jenna. It cracked like a whip and in a puff of smoke struck a tall pine, splitting it in half and sending the smoking fiery top hurtling toward them. It crashed down across the road and sizzled in the fast-flowing water. As Kane slammed on the brakes, Jenna gripped the seat. "Oh, no."

"Hang on." Kane spun the wheel, taking the Beast off road, and they bounced through thick vegetation alongside the fire road to bypass the smoking tree. "We can get back onto Stanton at the end of the next fire road. We should be close to town and hopefully be able to overtake the traffic."

Starting to worry about her kids, Jenna looked at him. "This is real bad. I hope the boys and Raya are okay."

"She knows to go into the panic room if there's a problem. The house could blow apart and that would still be standing." Kane squeezed her hand. "They'll be fine. I figure this is just wind and hail. It's not a tornado. You gotta trust me, Jenna."

Holding tight as Kane negotiated around more fallen trees, she looked ahead and breathed a sigh of relief as the lights of town came into sight, but the full force of the wind and hail hit them when they arrived at Stanton. The forest had shielded them to some extent, but all around, the damage was evident: trees down, road signs ripped out and tossed to one side, debris spilling across the highway. Vehicles lined the side of the road, some with their windshields broken, others with drivers too afraid to continue in the deluge. Others, their lights blazing, continued a slow procession into town. Jenna wanted to stop but she needed to get help. "There's too many for us to assist. I'll call out emergency teams." She made the calls.

"We need to get back to the office and start organizing help." Kane hit the lights and sirens and they hurtled along the wrong side of the highway. No one headed toward them. Everyone was trying to get back to town.

As they reached Main the street lights flickered on and off but the sidewalk was deserted. Thank goodness, everyone had taken shelter. The traffic moved faster in town with more people heading along side streets. Soaked bunting littered the blacktop and small jack-o'-lanterns bounced along the sidewalk like grinning orange balls. The wind howled and intermittent flashes of lightning made the Halloween decorations come to life in grotesque displays. The next moment, in sprays of white like a firework, a transformer exploded, followed by three more. Alarms sounded and then darkness came in an instant. The town fell eerily quiet. In another flash, Jenna gaped in horror as the wireless tower exploded. She stared at Kane. "This means we have no communication."

"The satellite phones will work." Kane drove into the sheriff's department parking lot and stopped beside the back door. "I can see everyone's vehicles out front. We're the last back."

To Jenna's relief, her dark office suddenly lit up like a beacon, the emergency generators had come online. "I'm so glad you upgraded the generators. Will we have enough power?"

"We stored power in our solar batteries all summer." Kane pushed down the rim of his hat and climbed out. As they ran to the door he smiled at her. "We'll be fine."

Coat swirling in the wind, Jenna stood at the door, hoping the retinal scanner would work. She leaned in and the door clicked open. In the hallway they met Rio, flashlight in hand. She stamped her wet boots on the mat and looked at him. "Everything okay?"

"Yeah, but we were wondering how we were going to get out of here, before the generator kicked in." Rio frowned. "An alarm sounded and then all the doors locked at once."

"We'll be okay for a time but go through the office and turn off any lights we don't need." Kane removed his hat and slapped it on his wet jeans. "Just keep the light on in the main foyer for Maggie and we'll all work in the conference room."

Jenna headed for the front desk to speak to Maggie and Rowley. "I've contacted all the emergency services on the way in and everyone is aware of what's happening. We'll only have satellite communication. Call your families to make sure everyone is okay. They all have satellite phones, don't they?"

"Yeah, I called Sandy before the blackout." Rowley smiled. "The moment she noticed the storm she took the kids into the storm shelter. It was the old root cellar but we made it comfortable after last year's crazy weather events." He held up his satellite phone. "Everyone has their phones switched on. Apart from a few broken windshields, I don't figure anyone has suffered any major damage. It seems calm now."

"Don't hold your breath." Kane dropped his wet Stetson onto his desk and shrugged out of his soaking jacket. "I figure we're going through the eye of the storm." He turned to Jenna. "You need to get out of those wet clothes. I'm going to take a shower." He headed for the stairs.

Nodding, Jenna looked at Rio. "Did you find out any information about Gabby Turner?"

"I did." Rio leaned against the counter. "Her mother reported her missing this morning from Butte. I called her for more details and she's sending a DNA sample by courier. Gabby has been constantly abused by her boyfriend. Her mom believes she ran for her life."

Sadness gripped Jenna. How many times had women believed in a happy-ever-after only to discover the man they loved was a monster? She pushed wet hair from her face. "Okay, I'll get changed. We'll wait out the storm and then see what happens. If by seven no one is calling for assistance, we'll need to go home and check our families. If any calls come before seven, figure out if we can help, if not pass them on to the right department. The mayor assured me he has all hands standing by."

"That's good to know." Rio headed through the office switching off lights. He glanced over one shoulder. "Seems to me, the weather is the least of our problems. With everyone blacked out, the killer is going to get free rein for his next victim."

FORTY-THREE

Julie traveled light. She discovered a long time ago to compact all her clothes into a small carry-on suitcase and her backpack. After being the only survivor of a crash in the mountains almost two years ago, she'd vowed never to get onto a flight again in bad weather. She waited on the sidewalk outside the hotel and stared into the distance toward Black Rock Falls. The sky still appeared to be angry, with black billowing clouds along the mountain range. If the weather forecast was bad by ten tonight, she would go back to the hotel and book another night's stay. There was no way she would climb onto an aircraft and head into another storm. Halloween was still two days away and she had plenty of time to get home, and with her father's credit card tucked inside her pocket, she wouldn't starve. He had insisted she stay at a good hotel during her visit to Helena rather than stay at the hostel with the other students. She wouldn't have cared, but as her father was overly security conscious, it saved arguments by just going along with him, and she had to admit that she enjoyed room service.

She heard Rhett's motorcycle before it roared around the corner and slowed outside the hotel entrance. He climbed off and took her bag and secured it inside a hard-shell, lockable storage compartment mounted behind the seat. She would ride wearing the backpack and took the helmet he offered her. He looked nice. He wore black jeans and a tee under his leather jacket and he'd shaved. She could smell his cologne. "Thanks. If the weather's bad, I'll stay another night and go in the morning."

"Then I guess I'd better wait with you at the airport to make sure you catch the flight." Rhett smiled at her and climbed on his motorcycle. He turned to look at her over one shoulder. "Jump on, I'm starving."

In a mix of nerves and excitement, Julie climbed on the back. They took off and the rumble of the engine vibrated through her. As the wind tugged at her jacket, she eased her grip around Rhett's waist. She hardly knew this man but already counted him as a friend. She trusted him to keep her safe and that was a rare commodity and not something she'd known from outside her family circle or, more specifically, Jenna's team. Every one of them she would trust with her life and had done. Their brief encounters at the lectures and over lunch occasionally had given her an insight into him. He'd had a very hard life, and worked many different jobs to put himself through college. She hadn't realized how much they had in common until recently. As she'd listened to him asking questions at the seminars, it was everything she needed to know. It was as if they were both traveling in the same direction. They had the same goals and that was to help children.

They arrived at what Rhett had described as a diner—it was a snug little Italian restaurant and he'd made a reservation. When they were escorted to a table with a red and white tablecloth and handed the wine list along with a menu, Julie removed her coat and gloves and smiled at him across the table. "How did you know I loved Italian food?"

"You seem to like the same things as I do, so I took a chance." Rhett grinned. "I usually eat on campus as the food is exceptionally good, but sometimes I come here. I know the owners and they've been good to me over the years, giving me work and treating me like part of the family."

Julie nodded. "I must have been very lucky to have my father pay for my tuition. It must have been very difficult for you to keep going all these years to follow your dream."

"To be honest, being at school was the best place for me as most of my time in foster care was terrible." Rhett sighed. "Studying became an escape that I needed. I did well and applied for the MUS Honor Scholarship. It's a four-year renewable scholarship that pays for all my tuition. I need to keep hitting the right goals, but I don't mind the hard work because eventually I'll be doing what I love."

Handsome, hardworking, smart, and he owned a Harley, what more could a girl want? Julie squeezed his hand. "I wish I'd met you back then when we first started at college. I've been very much of a loner. I don't follow fashion trends or crazy fads. My sister Emily is the bright star in the family. I always thought that I wanted to be just like her, but I don't. I want to be just like me." She chuckled.

"Me too." Rhett opened his menu. "We make our own trends."

The ate a scrumptious meal, talked about their futures, and made plans to keep in touch. It was Julie's first real date. She'd had coffee dates and met a few guys at college but none of them attracted her like Rhett. When it was finally time to board her flight, she wished she'd had more time to get to know him. "The storm passed through Black Rock Falls and did some damage, but the airport is fine and my truck is waiting there for me. It's a short drive home, about half an hour. I had a super time, Rhett. I'll miss you."

"I'll miss you too." He hugged her and kissed her on the cheek. "I'll FaceTime you and tell you what's happening and I'll be in Black Rock Falls after graduation. That's if you want to show me around?"

Julie hugged him back. "I'd love to. Hey, we may end up working alongside each other."

"You never know, and while I'm there, I'll need to track down a lawyer." He shrugged. "It's probably nothing but I need to know what my parents left me. Although why they made sure I wouldn't inherit until I turned twenty-five is still a mystery."

The last call for the flight came through announcements and Julie picked up her bag. "Then we'll solve it together. See you in May."

"See you, Jules."

FORTY-FOUR

Always a little jittery about flying since the plane crash, Julie walked up to the check-in counter and handed them her ticket. The woman tapped away on the computer and then looked up at her and frowned. "Is there a problem? I only have carry-on luggage."

"Not with the flight, no, but I have a note that says Black Rock Falls has suffered significant storm damage and there is no power or phone reception at this time." The woman met Julie's gaze. "Do you have someone meeting you at the airport because you won't be able to call anyone for transportation."

Not worried about a power outage, Julie nodded. "I left my truck at the airport. I'll be fine. I only live a short distance away."

"That's good to know." The woman handed her a boarding pass.

Butterflies were having a festival in her stomach by the time she took her allocated seat. There were only two other people on the small aircraft, and she sat alone at the back. Her preference to sit in the rear of the plane had saved her life not long ago and she always continued to take the seat nearest the tail. She glanced out of the window as they took off and saw one lone motorbike weaving its way through Helena toward the college and wondered if it was Rhett going home. She stared as the motorbike got smaller and smaller. The plane climbed above the clouds and she leaned back and closed her eyes. It had been an incredible couple of weeks. She met many new friends and had considered all her options for her future. It had been easier when Rhett had joined her. He seemed to know all the right questions to ask. She wondered if she would ever see him again. It's not as if they had started a romance or anything but he'd been the only boy she'd ever been able to sit and talk to for hours. They had so many things in common. They liked the same music, which was a variety of country and rock. They enjoyed the same food and she had to admit that after watching her dad and Kane spend hours rebuilding old Harleys, motorcycles had become her passion. She would own and ride one in a second.

The flight became unnervingly bumpy just before they landed in Black Rock Falls. As she pulled her suitcase toward the parking lot, darkness crept in all around her. Only two small light posts illuminated the entrance to the parking lot but she found her truck without much trouble. She glanced up at the sky. Black clouds still obscured the moon and the smell of rain and dampness hung heavy in the air. It would be good to get home. She dumped her bags on the back seat and then climbed behind the wheel. As she drove out onto the highway, a wall of black surrounded her. It was only a little after eleven and yet the highway was completely deserted. This was very strange as Black Rock Falls was a busy town and traffic passed through on the way to Blackwater.

Her headlights picked up the damage from the storm. Broken tree branches, leaves, and pine cones littered the highway and long lines of Halloween bunting littered the edge of the road as if they'd been picked up and carried for miles.

Deep water swirled along the gullies by the side of the road and in some places water had spilled across the highway, causing her to slow down and test the way. Relieved when she picked out a small glowing light at the Triple Z Roadhouse, she accelerated a little. In about fifteen minutes she would be home and then the engine gave a cough and splutter. She stared down at the gas gauge and moaned. The needle was just above empty but she should have enough to get her to the roadhouse where she could get some gas. They had lights, so maybe they had a generator to work the pumps. Only five minutes away the engine stopped and she rolled to a halt. Something in the back of her mind reminded her of a conversation she had with Kane about her truck. He had insisted that she never let it run out of gas because it might be difficult to start. He had shown her how to spray something somewhere and then start the engine so it could suck the gas through or something, but she really didn't take too much notice because she always had her dad or Kane to come and help her if necessary.

She climbed out and went to the back seat to pull out a pair of hiking boots from her luggage. She'd worn a pair of fancy cowboy boots to go to dinner with Rhett. She dragged on her thick raincoat and pulled the hoodie over her head. After grabbing the flashlight from the glovebox, she headed to the roadhouse. It didn't take too long before she climbed up the driveway. Bedraggled Halloween decorations hung limply around the roadhouse. Garbage bins overflowed with trash and rainwater. One side of the roadhouse held a line of pumps and a convenience store with a variety of items from milk to gas cans. It was a kind of one-stop shop, although the prices were much higher than normal. She walked up and down the aisles until she found a gas can and took it to the counter. The weird aroma of coffee, roadside food, and gas seemed to move around her. Tiredness dragged at her. She needed a cup of coffee to keep her awake. The coffee likely tasted like mud, but if it had caffeine in it, it would do. "Are your pumps working?" She looked at the skinny, oily haired man standing behind the glass partition and held up the can. "I need this and a gallon. I ran out of gas. I'll take a coffee from the machine as well."

"Yeah, you can pay here and fill the can as you leave. Pump number two." The man gave her a disinterested stare and pointed at the card scanner. "Scanners out. You got cash?"

Julie nodded and pulled bills from her pocket. Carrying cash was another of her dad's rules. She took the change and pushed it back into her jeans pocket. The door behind her slid open and footsteps echoed on the tile. She turned as a tall broad man wearing a cowboy hat that appeared a little too large for him walked up behind her. She ignored him and headed to the coffee dispenser. As she filled her coffee, the flickering neon sign outside cast erratic shadows across the driveway but beyond that everything was pitch black. She waited for what seemed like ages for the coffee to fill the cup and then fitted a top to the to-go cup.

She sensed someone beside her and turned suddenly, cup in hand, to see the man in the cowboy hat collecting a cup and fixings from the display by the machine. She bent to pick up her empty gas can and somehow, they collided. The cup tumbled from her grasp and hot liquid splashed across the floor and all over the man's polished boots. Horrified, Julie looked at him. "I'm so sorry." She grabbed napkins and thrust them at him. "Here maybe you can clean the coffee from your boots?"

"It was my fault. I wasn't looking where I was going." The man ignored the napkins. "I insist you let me replace it."

Too tired to argue, Julie nodded. As the coffee machine dripped slowly into the man's cup, Julie climbed onto a stool in front of a narrow counter overlooking the pumps. To her surprise, he placed the fixings on the counter beside her and then turned back to the machine. She stared out of the window at the truck alongside the pumps. She guessed it belonged to him as he seemed to be the only person around. She cleared her throat. "It looks like a massive storm went through here. Were you here at the time?"

"Yeah, it was nasty." He handed her a cup. "The town took a beating. There are a few trees down here and there and water all over the roads. Halloween decorations and displays are strewn all over Main. The power has been out for hours and we have no phone service, so I don't know if anyone was injured. People seem to be staying close to home." He gave her an inquiring look. "I don't see a vehicle. Did you walk here or did you come in on the last bus?"

Figuring he was just being neighborly, she sat and sipped her coffee. With luck, she should have the energy to walk back to her car in a few moments. "I ran out of gas. I'll drink this and then fill up this can and walk back to my truck. I figure it's only about a quarter of a mile away."

"My wife does that all the time." He chuckled and stirred sugar and cream into his coffee. "I'm forever driving out to rescue her." He raised one eyebrow. "Don't you have anyone in your life to come and rescue you?"

The coffee was sending a warm glow right through her and she wanted to sit and drink the entire cup. Roadhouse coffee wasn't as bad as she imagined but she needed to get home. "I do but I don't have any way of communicating with them right now but I'm a big girl. I can handle carrying a can of gas for a quarter of a mile." She slid from the stool, tossed the half-filled cup into the trash, and picked up the can. "Thanks for the coffee."

FORTY-FIVE

Outside, the hum of the generator masked all the noise around Julie. She walked quickly, eyeing the strange shadows created by the flickering signs. They seemed to move as if someone was hiding there waiting for her. Exhausted, she glanced around, searching the shadows as she pumped the gas. Alone, she'd become vulnerable and, carrying a can full of gas, she'd be slow and ripe pickings for a serial killer or a hungry bear. She screwed on the lid to the can and lifted it with a moan. It was heavier than she figured or she'd suddenly lost all her strength. She started when a scraping of boots came from the darkness and spun around but it was just the man returning to his truck.

"That looks heavy and it's starting to rain again." The man stood beside the door to his truck. "Can I give you a ride back to your vehicle?" He gave her a reassuring smile.

Hesitating, Julie stared at him. Overwhelmed with tiredness, the idea of walking along the highway alongside the dark forest frightened her, but she'd made it to the roadhouse okay. The highway was deserted and she could think of no reason why she wouldn't get back safely. She stared into the distance and saw only black. Her attention moved back to the man. He appeared to be rooted to the spot waiting for her to answer as if he'd got all the time in the world. "I don't think so. I don't know you."

"Sure, but if that's your truck I passed on the way here, it's not five minutes by car, three maybe, and you look tuckered out." He shook his head. "I feel bad about leaving you alone. I couldn't live with myself if something bad happened to you."

She swayed, feeling so desperately tired that she couldn't keep her eyes open. Suddenly his offer made sense. She handed him the gas can. "Thanks."

"It will be my pleasure." He stowed the gas can in the back of his truck and opened the passenger door for her. "It's strange how people meet, isn't it? You needed help and I came along just at the right time."

Mouth suddenly dry, Julie's vision blurred and her dad's voice screamed in her head. He'd lectured them about date rape drugs and how they felt. She blinked. Had this man slipped something into her coffee? She needed her dad, Jenna, Dave, anyone to help her. A memory slid into her foggy brain.

Your tracker ring is now like a satellite phone; you can get a signal out anywhere.

She pressed her ring, waited ten seconds, and pressed again. One press went to her dad, two went to everyone on the team. She lifted her hand as if to push back her hood. "I'm parked about a quarter of a mile from the roadhouse. It was so kind of you to give me a ride. I can't believe how sleepy I feel. I figured the coffee would have revived me after the walk."

"Then sleep." The man smiled at her. "I'll wake you when we get there." He started the engine.

Julie's hand went to the handle and she pushed the truck door open and fell onto the wet driveway. "I'm trying to get away, Dad. I'm running down the ramp from the roadhouse to the highway. I figure this guy is going to kill me."

With legs like lead, Julie ran but it was like running in slow motion. The truck was on her before she got to the end of the ramp.

"You're not getting away from me. You'll never rise again." The man jumped out, grabbed her, and tossed her back inside.

She screamed and kicked out at him, landing one in his groin. When he buckled, she dropped to the ground and crawled away. "Hurry. He's going to kill me."

Staggering to her feet, she ran into the shadows, trying to find a place to hide, but he was up and had seen which way she had headed. She dodged and lurched from one place to the other as if in a drunken stupor but then she heard him chuckle from behind her. Pain shot through her head from a single hard punch. Dizzy, she fought with rubber limbs as he lifted her and tossed her over one shoulder. In a few strides he was back at his truck. This time he tossed her into the bed. She hit the metal hard and all the air rushed from her lungs.

"You can't win." He reached for a toolbox and grabbed a roll of duct tape. "You're mine."

The drug was paralyzing her and she had one last chance before she passed out. Her words sounded slurred and she tried hard to make sense. "Silver pickup, Montana plates, heading north. Tall broad man wearing a cowboy hat and shiny boots. I'm in the back of his truck. *Daddy, help me.*"

FORTY-SIX

Wolfe threw himself behind the wheel of his pickup and spun his wheels backing out of the garage. Beside him, Emily was staring at the GPS screen. He'd been sitting at the kitchen table drinking coffee with Norrell, Raven, and Emily when the satellite phones chimed a ringtone that chilled him to the bone. The sound they all dreaded. It meant one of them was in mortal danger. His heart missed a beat when Julie's name flashed on the screen and he'd grabbed his coat and weapons and ran to the garage with Emily close behind. Raven was up and out the door in seconds and in his truck parked at the curb. They all understood the threat and would take deadly force if needed to resolve it. Anger and fear rushed up his throat as he turned onto Main. He could make out Raven's taillights ahead. He was moving fast, lights and sirens blaring.

"I have her, heading north on the highway." Emily held the satellite phone. "Hang on, Julie, we're coming."

Banging his hands on the steering wheel in frustration as he barely missed a fallen tree, Wolfe swallowed the lump in his throat. "It's my fault. I should have dropped everything and picked her up from the airport."

"It was her choice, Dad." Emily turned in her seat to look at him. "She's not a kid; she's a grown woman."

Wolfe snorted. "Grown women don't get into serial killers' vehicles." Wolfe shook his head. "How many times have I told y'all not to trust strangers? Do I need to tattoo it into your brains?" He sucked in a breath. "If he's hurt her, I'll kill him. Y'all know that?"

"Calm down before you wreck the truck." Emily cleared her throat. "Just concentrate on driving. Leave the rescue to the team."

Mind set on getting to his daughter, Wolfe pushed his foot to the metal, skidding around corners. Julie was in trouble and her slurred messages coming through the speakers meant he had minutes to save her. He counted time in his head as he dodged fallen branches and animals running across the highway. He glanced at Emily. "You stay in the truck. I don't want to risk your life. Anything might happen. My shotgun is behind my seat. You know how to use it. Don't talk, just fire the darn thing if he comes at you."

"Rowley should be heading toward her and Rio behind us and then Jenna and Kane close behind." Emily gripped the grab handle. "It's not far now."

Wolfe stared into the darkness. "I hope Raven kills the lights and sirens. It's better if he doesn't know we're after him."

He kept his foot flat on the accelerator, vowing to allow Kane to improve his engine. He needed the extra speed right now. He rarely needed to get to a corpse in a hurry, but it was as if he could get out and run faster. Ahead, Raven's lights vanished and he breathed a sigh of relief. They hit the highway and aquaplaned over water across the road. The back of the truck slid out and he fought to keep it from rolling into the gully.

"We can't help her if you wreck the truck, Dad." Emily's jaw was set. "Everyone is heading toward her. Look how close

Dave is. He's only minutes behind us and moving at light speed." She stared at the map with the blinking positions of the team. Each of the flashing lights in their names on the screen indicated they were gaining on them.

Wolfe overtook a lone eighteen-wheeler and bumped over a wash of rocks and debris on the blacktop. He stared out of the window searching ahead for lights. "How much farther?"

"Julie has gone off road. Maybe into the forest. Raven is close, maybe one minute behind." She pointed ahead. "There, see, he's following. There must be a road on the left into the forest."

Standing on the brakes, Wolfe slowed to follow Raven along a secluded forest track. They bumped along surrounded by dense forest. Ahead, the dirt road widened and Raven's truck roared past the silver pickup. He slid to a stop, his truck blocking the trail. The door flew open and Raven rolled out shotgun in hand and started firing, taking out the tires of the silver truck heading straight for him. The red blaze of the shotgun and smell of gunpowder greeted Wolfe as he thrust open the door and, leaving his headlights blazing, jumped out and ran toward the pickup.

Hurling himself into the back of the pickup, he stared at Julie, suddenly afraid. She wasn't moving. Her long blonde hair covered her face and spread out like a fan all around her. His hands trembled as he fell to his knees and smoothed the hair from her face. He checked her pulse and sat back breathing heavily. She was alive and would likely never remember what happened. He took in the bruise on her face and the tears still wet on her cheeks and his blood boiled. Anger raged through him. Through the buzzing in his ears, he heard Raven yelling at the driver to get out of the vehicle. He climbed from the pickup as Kane's black truck slid to a halt behind his SUV. Both Jenna and Kane ran toward him weapons drawn.

"Is she okay?" Jenna ran toward the pickup and climbed inside.

When it came to his girls, reason flew out of the window. Ignoring Jenna and disregarding Raven's screams of "he's got a gun," he wrenched open the driver's door, and as the interior light came on, he saw uncertainty in the man's eyes, not fear but surprise. Without a second thought he closed one hand around the muzzle of the weapon, wrenched it from the coward's hand, and tossed it on the ground.

"I'll come quietly." The man appeared calm. "There's no need for violence. I was just trying to help is all."

Wolfe glared at him. "By drugging her?"

He grabbed the man's coat collar in both hands and dragged him out of the vehicle. Before his feet hit the ground, Wolfe pulled back his fist and slammed it into the man's face. "If you've hurt her, I'll tear you apart and bury you so deep even the worms won't be able to find your body." He looked over one shoulder as Kane came to his side. "Y'all will help me, right?"

"Where do you want me to dig the hole?" Kane grabbed the man, turned him around, slammed him into the side of the truck, and cuffed him.

"What about right here?" Raven picked up the man's weapon with a stick. "The ground is nice and soft. We'll have him six feet under in no time." He stepped forward and frisked the man. He held up a hunting knife and a container of medication. "Well, here's the proof we need. Kidnapping carries a twenty-year sentence and I'm sure when we go visit your home, we'll find enough evidence to charge you with murder one."

"How about you read him his rights, Dave?" Jenna jumped down from the pickup and went to Wolfe's side. "Your daughter needs you now. Leave him to us."

As Kane turned the man around to read him his rights, Jenna shone her flashlight into his eyes and gasped. Wolfe stared at her surprised expression. "Do you know him?"

"I don't believe it." Jenna shook her head, shock on her face. "Yeah, I know him. He was right under our noses the entire time." Her mouth turned down. "Pastor John Dimock. He's been answering hotline calls at the office." She kept the light on his face. "So, this is how you help people, by drugging them and then draining their blood?" She turned to Raven. "Put him in your vehicle. Rio's just arrived. He can ride with you back to the office. I'll drive his truck."

"Sick freak." Raven grabbed Pastor Dimock and, after removing Ben, thrust the prisoner inside the back of his truck. "Can you take Ben with you, Jenna? Pastors aren't on his menu—although it's not a bad idea."

"Come on, Ben." Jenna took the leash, shaking her head.

Breathing heavily, Wolfe turned to see Emily on her knees beside her sister, her pale face streaked with tears as she removed the duct tape from her sister's wrists and ankles. He turned back to Jenna. "I guess the pastor gets to live another day but don't call on me if he's hurt. I've seen what that animal is capable of and I'll refuse."

"You won't need to. As soon as I've interviewed him, I'll ship him off to County." Jenna squeezed his arm. "Julie is alive and that's all that matters. Take the girls home. We'll talk in the morning."

Wolfe dropped down the tailgate of the pickup, climbed in, and lifted Julie into his arms. "It's okay, sweetheart. Daddy's here now. I'm taking you home."

FORTY-SEVEN

After watching Wolfe leave, Jenna put Ben into the back seat of the Beast, glad that the K-9 took her orders. She walked up to Rowley, who'd just arrived and gave him the details. "You might as well head on home. We'll need you in the office first up. It's going to be a long night and we can handle it from here. Thanks for responding so fast."

"Anytime. Is Julie okay?" He glanced behind him as Wolfe's headlights disappeared into the darkness.

Jenna sighed. "I hope so. She's been drugged. A date rape drug most likely. She has a bruise on her face but her clothes are intact. Likely she won't remember anything."

"Maybe that's for the best." Rowley frowned. "I'll be in the office at seven as usual." He headed back to his vehicle.

Jenna turned to Rio. "I want you to ride with the prisoner. I'll drive your ride back to the office. It's pointless us all working half the night. I'll need you in the office early to get the transcripts of the interview over to the DA and to get the search warrants for his home and vehicle, plus any outbuildings on his property. I'll send the prisoner to County. I'm not risking leaving him here overnight."

"That makes sense." Rio nodded. He handed her his keys and headed toward Raven.

Jenna walked toward Kane, who was leaning on the pastor's pickup. "Hold up. We'll need a search warrant before we touch anything."

"I know, I was just looking." Kane nodded. "I'll call a tow truck to collect it, seeing that Raven shot out the front tires. If the phones are still out, I'll drop by Millers' Garage and ask them." He indicated inside. "He has duct tape and rope in plain sight. He's been a busy boy." He took the keys and locked the pickup.

Jenna nodded. "Yeah, Jo always said you could have a serial killer standing right beside you and you'd never know. This guy has been volunteering in the office since the first murder."

"Yeah, some of them are so confident they try and insert themselves into the investigation." Kane led the way back to the Beast, rubbing his shoulder. "I'd never have suspected him. He barely spoke to anyone but you and Rowley."

Tossing Rio's keys in her hand, she nodded. "Yeah, he was charming and seemed genuinely interested in helping but he asked way too many questions. He drove Rowley nuts. Of course, Rowley kept his mouth firmly shut. He didn't like him at all." A disturbing thought crossed her mind. "You don't figure he was lining me up for his next victim, do you?"

"I guess we'll never know." Kane waved as Raven drove past. "I'll walk you to your ride."

Jenna leaned into him and smiled. "Ever the gentleman. I'm so lucky to have you, Dave."

She pulled her satellite phone from her pocket and called Kane. He gave her a quizzical smile as he answered. Jenna laughed. "I need to chat with you on the way back to the office. Put your phone on speaker as the Bluetooth isn't working."

"Sure." Kane opened the door to Rio's truck. "Don't go

speeding on the way back to the office now, will you? Remember you have a cop on your tail."

Jenna started the engine and backed some way along the road before turning around and heading back along the highway. Through the phone, she could hear Kane singing and she smiled. He usually sung in the shower and had a good voice, but she figured he was singing to keep her company, rather than discuss the case. During the drive back to the office, Jenna realized just how much damage the storm had inflicted on her county. Bedraggled Halloween decorations piled up alongside the highway and plastic jack-o'-lanterns bobbed along in the water flowing alongside in the gully. She wondered if the townsfolk would be able to get everything back together before the big day on Sunday. She hadn't walked through town since the storm and would as soon as she came back into the office tomorrow. As they got closer and turned onto Main, she noticed trucks along the side of the road with crews repairing the fallen electricity lines. Perhaps by the morning they would have power and, hopefully, phone service. Without phones they had no idea if anyone was in trouble or injured by the storm. She hoped that neighbors would check on each other.

At the office Raven and Rio had taken the pastor to the interview room. Using her satellite phone, she called the county jail to arrange for them to collect the prisoner. She explained the urgency and the threat that he posed to the town if he escaped. They would be sending a team to collect him within the next two hours. She sent Rio home and they all went down to the interview room to speak to the prisoner. She set up the recording devices and introduced everyone in the room. She sat opposite, hopeful that Pastor Dimock would act like a normal serial killer and want to boast about why he murdered the women.

Raven had handcuffed the prisoner to the ring on the table but Jenna wasn't taking any chances and had Kane sit on one side of her and Raven on the other. The pastor appeared a little roughed up. His clothes had mud stains from the takedown and his left eye was swollen and turning blue all around. She considered her line of questioning. "Pastor Dimock, we've read you your rights. You've refused medical attention and now I need to ask you again for the record, do you want to speak to us voluntarily or do you want me to call a lawyer for you?"

"I'm innocent, why would I need a lawyer?" The pastor clasped his hands on the table in front of him as if in prayer.

Jenna nodded. "I'll get to that, but first, where were you heading when we apprehended you? You told me you lived at the shelter."

"I needed you to feel sorry for me." The pastor smiled. "It worked, didn't it? No, I have a cabin and a barn. I take the vampires to my barn where no one can hear them scream."

"No one felt sorry for you, Dimock." Kane eyeballed him. "We tolerated you, is all. The thing is, we caught you, didn't we? We stopped your killing spree."

"Did you?" The pastor turned his attention to Jenna. "One thing I need to ask you, Sheriff. You are accusing me of murdering someone. Is that correct?"

Wondering what game he was playing, Jenna nodded. "Yes, I'm interviewing you in regard to the murders of three women. Darlene Travis, Bunny Watkins, and Gabby Turner."

"Well, Sheriff, is it a crime to murder someone who is already dead?" The pastor smiled at her. "I don't think so." He met her gaze, the smile still playing on his lips. "Those women were already dead. The living dead, vampires. I stopped them feeding on the living. You shouldn't be arresting me, you should be giving me a medal. I saved your town."

Ignoring the absurdity of his question, Jenna lifted her chin slightly and narrowed her gaze at him. "If you truly believe you're saving the town from the threat of vampires, why not come out and tell me about it? You were in the office helping out. Why the secrecy?"

"Not many of us can see them." The pastor leaned back in his chair relaxed as if without a care in the world. Then he leaned forward suddenly and the chains on the handcuffs rattled against the metal ring attached to the table. "Do you believe in monsters, Sheriff?"

I'm looking at one. Jenna remained motionless. She'd never allow him to read her disgust of him in her body language. "I keep an open mind. If you truly believe vampires are in our town, how come you're the only one who can see them? Don't you believe that if other people had seen them, they would have reported them to us? I mean, you say that you see them but even you didn't bother to come and get assistance from law enforcement."

"The moment you recognize one of them, they'll turn you. Why can't you understand?" The pastor rolled his eyes as if losing patience. "They're already feeding on people. Most times it's the elderly. They sneak into nursing homes and drink their blood—not enough to turn them—just enough for a meal."

Jenna couldn't believe what she was hearing but tried to make sense of it all. "So, what is it about their behavior that makes them stand out to you?"

"They're always alone." The pastor attempted to open his arms wide but, restrained by the cuffs, he just closed his hands and met her gaze. "They appear vulnerable, lost or in trouble. Most of them have long hair and very pale complexions and are usually slim."

"Don't you believe men can be vampires too?" Kane's intent gaze moved over him. "If so, why haven't you murdered them?"

"I wish I didn't have to speak to foolish people who don't understand." The pastor tossed his head in annoyance. "There is only one male in this town and he sends his females to get him suitable candidates for feeding. He uses his glamor so no one can see him. His powers are endless. A mere mortal like me wouldn't have a chance against him."

"Surely, they would need to be fed on a regular basis?" Kane watched the killer with an unwavering stare. "What makes you believe they only feed over Halloween?"

"They can remain dormant for centuries, but they rise at Halloween because it's a time they can slip into society and nobody recognizes them." The pastor moved around on his chair. "I do, and I take them out before they turn anyone."

Clearing her throat, Jenna flicked a glance toward Kane. "Why don't you walk me through your first kill, and tell me, what made you certain your victims were vampires? You see, your last victim, Julie Wolfe, I've known since she was a small child. It seems you made a big mistake with her."

The pastor looked at her, shaking his head as if in sympathy. Then he blew out a long breath as if he might just as well give them the facts to finish the interview.

"They always arrive in town after dark." The pastor leaned forward staring at Jenna. His eyes danced as if reliving the moment gave him a thrill. "Most times they're in trouble or acting as if they haven't got enough to buy themselves a meal, or the friend they were expecting to arrive didn't show. They always have an excuse of one thing or another to find someone who will feel sorry for them. I'm just a Good Samaritan and buy them a coffee. I slip a drug into it so they don't cause me any problems. I offer them a ride to anywhere they want to go and by the time they're inside my truck they're under my control. I take them to my shed, where I have a setup to drain their blood." He smiled at Jenna. "They need to be alive and sometimes they wake but they're too weak to fight."

"Do you drink their blood?" Kane's mouth formed a thin line.

"I'm not a vampire, Deputy Kane." The pastor chuckled. "No, sir, but I take them to a place where they'll be seen by the townsfolk and stake them so they can't rise. I leave them as a warning. I'm not evil or a murderer. I'm doing the community a service."

"Why did you leave Darlene's locket on a pig?" Kane wrinkled his nose. "That was a waste of good meat."

"I found the pig dumped at the landfill. It was a perfect decoy, wasn't it?" The pastor shrugged. "I needed you out of the office, so I could find out if you suspected me." He grinned. "No one told me details, so I needed to find out myself. I waited for Maggie to leave to use the bathroom and then read the witnesses' statements." He stared from one to the other. "Seems to me everyone in town believes in vampires now. My job is done here. I need to move on."

Considering her next question with care, Jenna let the minutes tick by and observed him. His swollen eye where Wolfe had hit him was turning a dark shade of blue and was almost shut but, Rio had informed her, he'd refused to ice it. Maybe it was another ploy for sympathy. Moving into a trigger situation could be dangerous. "When did this obsession with vampires come about? Someone must have told you about them and how to deal with them. It's not something you would come up with on your own. Who was your greatest influencer?"

"That would be my dad." The pastor nodded his head slowly. "He tried to help people as well and ended up dying in prison."

"How so?" Kane's cheek twitched but he remained like a statue. "How old were you when he told you about vampires?"

"Seven." The pastor closed his eyes as if seeing the past. "It was Halloween but he'd often go out at night, and that time I followed him. He had a cabin not far from the house, alongside the river. His fishing cabin he called it. I figured he was going fishing and I went to the door and peeked inside. That's when I saw the vampire. She had blood on her mouth and my dad had marks on his neck, like scratches. He tossed her onto a bench and used his knife for gutting fish to stab her through the heart. She bled all over. I can still smell the blood when I close my eyes."

Jenna swallowed hard. "How did it make you feel?"

"Excited and then frightened when my dad saw me watching. I figured he'd yell at me but he didn't." The pastor smiled. "He took my arm and led me right up to her. He made me kiss her and run my hands through the blood. It was warm and I asked him why he'd killed her. That's when he told me she was already dead and a vampire and he needed to kill her to save us. After that, when he brought them home, he showed me how to drain their blood. He used to be a mortician."

"Why did he drain their blood?" Kane's face was like stone.

"In case the drug wore off and they tried to bite him." The pastor nodded. "It makes them weak. He'd learned his lesson with the one in the cabin. She made so much mess. Draining the blood is easy." He gave Jenna a disgruntled look. "The cops didn't believe him about vampires either."

"How long have you been slaying vampires?" Raven rested his hands on the table. "I gather you participated in all your dad's kills?"

"Yeah, but we decided to bury them deep in the forest." He snorted. "Or in new graves. You know how easy it is to dig down another foot or so and drop in a body and then cover it up. The next day a coffin is placed on top and someone else gets the job of filling in the hole."

Noticing a tremor in the pastor's hand, Jenna wanted to conclude the interview. A triggered psychopath had incredible strength and talking about his kills was triggering him. "Just one more question. Why did you change the system? No one has found your past murders, have they?"

"Like I said before, Sheriff." The pastor gave her a smug smile. "I wanted to warn the town, so why should I hide the bodies? Like I told you, they'd been dead for centuries before I touched them. I released them from purgatory." He met her gaze and held it. "You won't be able to stop me, Sheriff. I'll keep taking down vampires until the day I die. It's my mission in life."

Jenna nodded and stood. "That's all for now. You'll be taken to County. I'll be ordering a psychological profile on you and I would strongly suggest you take the offer of a lawyer." She turned off the recording devices and scanned her card before easing into the hallway. Kane and Raven followed close behind. She looked at them. "Well, that was interesting. I'll send a copy of the interview to the DA. What do you think?" She looked from one to the other.

"He's batshit crazy." Kane rubbed his chin.

"You can say that again." Raven leaned against the wall. "I doubt that ring in the table will hold him if he goes off."

Jenna nodded. "He won't get through the door and we have tranquilizer darts and tasers if necessary to get him into the truck to County." She shook her head slowly, unable to believe what she'd heard. "This is a Halloween story I won't be telling the kids, that's for darn sure."

FORTY-EIGHT

Saturday

Although they'd worked late into the night on Friday, Jenna arrived at the office early on Saturday morning. The background checks she'd ordered on Pastor Dimock and the other stranger, Doug Lowe, had arrived from Kalo. Lowe turned out to be a wrangler out of Wyoming with a clean sheet, but Pastor Dimock wasn't a pastor after all. He lived in town for some months and Father Derry had never laid eyes on him. Jenna shook her head. If this information had arrived earlier, they'd have hauled him in for questioning. She made a note in her files about Lowe, sometime in the future she might need another deputy.

As Wolfe needed to recuse himself from the forensic sweep of the killer's home and vehicle, a team from Helena was arriving at ten. She'd made sure the transcript of the interview with John Dimock and all the forensic evidence Wolfe had logged prior to Julie being kidnapped was in the hands of the DA. At the time Wolfe performed the autopsies and gathered the evidence, there was no conflict of interest. The date stamp when he uploaded the information to the server would prove that Julie was in Helena at the time. From the moment Julie became involved, all of Wolfe's team stood down.

Not having his eagle eye on scene and obtaining firsthand information would be difficult but she'd go along with Kane to execute the warrant. She had no idea if Dimock lived with anyone but doubted it. Most serial killers were loners. Once the Helena team had finished, she would hand everything over to the DA. Months, maybe years, later, the case would come to court and they'd testify. With luck, knowing that this killer and his father had been murdering and burying bodies all over, the local law enforcement departments where young women had gone missing without a trace at least had a starting point and maybe some of the missing women could be located. She hadn't ruled out the possibility that after confessing to previous murders, John Dimock might just divulge where he'd buried them.

Jenna's phone chimed and she was glad to see it was Julie. "Hey, how are you doing?"

"Believe it or not, I'm fine." Julie chuckled. "Although Dad insists that I stay in bed all day. I have a bruise on my cheek and a few scrapes from being thrown onto the ground, but apart from that, I feel good. I'm not mentally damaged in any way. Last night I slept like the dead and then discovered that's perfectly normal after a date rape drug. To be perfectly honest, I can only remember bits and pieces. I recall running out of gas and walking to the roadhouse but after that it gets a little foggy. Dad figures I shouldn't try and remember what happened, but he did ask me why I took a ride with a stranger." She sighed. "I recall buying a can of gas and some guy asking me if I'd like a ride back to my truck. The only thing I can remember is being so tired I could hardly move my legs, but I must have fought like a wildcat from the bruises all over me."

Jenna smiled at Kane, who was listening. "That's good to

know. I'm sure you can remember your trip to Helena. Did you have a good time?"

"Yeah, I did and I met some interesting people." Julie lowered her voice. "I met a student from MU who has the same interests as I do and he's coming to Black Rock Falls in May after he graduates. I'm hoping to show him around. His family lived here when he was a little boy. They died in a plane crash and he was tossed around in the foster system, so now wants to spend his time making sure that kids have good representation. I figure that's the same career path that I want to follow. So, I'm setting my cap toward becoming a children's advocate. I can complete two courses by graduation in May and an internship that will give me extra credits and experience and then I hope to apply for a position at Her Broken Wings Foundation. I'm not asking for any favors, Jenna. I know you are heavily involved with the foundation, but I figure I have the qualifications to work there and so does my friend, Rhett."

Trying to sound serious but grinning broadly, Jenna punched the air. "Well, I don't decide on the hiring and firing. I leave that to people qualified to decide who is best. I just make sure the shelters and foster families never become breeding grounds for abuse." She leaned back in her chair. "Dave, your dad, and I are on the committee to raise extra funds, but the foundation does receive a very generous payment from the government that will ensure we continue to expand."

"Oh, I understand completely." Julie sighed. "I've noticed several positions available, so hopefully they won't have found anyone by May. I'm banking on the fact that no one will want to come to Black Rock Falls in winter and I'll have my application in way before I graduate."

Jenna snorted with laughter. "It didn't stop Dave. I met him on a backroad covered with snow. I was spinning upside down in my cruiser at the time."

"Is Dave there?" Julie's voice sounded very young.

"Yeah, I'm here, Julie. What's up?" Kane moved closer to Jenna's phone.

"I met a nice boy called Rhett. Well not a boy, he's almost twenty-five. He goes to MU and he's very smart. The thing is, he has a snake tattoo up one arm and he rides a Harley. When he comes to town, can you make sure Dad doesn't kill him?"

"I'll do my best." Kane burst out laughing. "I'll tell him not to judge a book by its cover."

"Thanks." Julie cleared her throat. "I'll see you at the ball. I'll be the wallflower wearing a devil's costume. Bye." She disconnected.

Footsteps on the stairs heralded the arrival of Rio waving the search warrants. Jenna stood and held out her hand. "Oh, good."

"The forensic team have arrived. Wolfe's given them his van for the day. They're waiting outside for you." Rio handed Jenna the papers. "Maybe you can show them the way?"

Jenna scanned the documents. "That's brilliant. Thanks." She looked at Kane. "Let's go. I can't wait to see what John Dimock has hidden in his house."

They met the forensic team, led by Don Mandel. He seemed professional and was very quick to insist on the boundaries he required to complete the search. It was nothing unusual for Jenna and Kane, as they were used to wearing gloves and booties during a forensic investigation. Jenna suggested starting with the shed as Dimock had mentioned it during the investigation. What they found inside surprised and disgusted her. Shelves covered three of the walls and on one of them, tall glass bottles of what could only be blood sat as a stark reminder of what the killer had done. On another shelf, clothes had been neatly folded in piles. Beside each one a plastic bag containing personal items, jewelry, earrings, and necklaces, along with driver's licenses. There was no doubt that John Dimock was the killer.

Jenna stood beside Kane as Don Mandel examined a piece of equipment that Wolfe had described in his autopsy notes. It was a two-pronged bloodletting device attached to a plastic hose that dripped into a large glass bottle. The shed had been made ready for the next victim. Realizing how close Julie had become to being the next person strapped to the table made Jenna sick to her stomach, and she needed to step outside for some fresh air. When the forensic crew went inside the house, they found little of interest. It would seem that John Dimock kept his extracurricular activities to the shed, the same as his father. The team searched for trace evidence and collected hair and fibers as well as the bottles of blood and clothes. All these items would prove the case against him. There were no signs that he lived with anyone. The house was a typical bachelor pad.

When they moved to the vehicle, which had been delivered to the premises, they discovered duct tape, rope, hunting knives, and a small bottle of medication, the same type as Raven had discovered during the body search. The vehicle was particularly clean as if he kept it that way to offer a good impression. With the scene processed, the case would be able to proceed. The killer hadn't been on their initial list and knowing he'd been right there under her nose disturbed Jenna. If only she'd done a background check earlier, but before Kane had spoken to him, she really had no cause to doubt his credibility. She climbed into the Beast and they headed back to the office. She glanced at Kane. "How did I miss him? Thinking back, he was over nice, tried to become involved in the case. He wanted to see the first body. I should have been suspicious and run a background check on him earlier."

"I figure his guise as a pastor was a brilliant cover." Kane slid behind the wheel. "Him being interested and wanting to pray over the body didn't send up red flags because in the back of your mind you'd have believed him. This is the art of a psychopathic serial killer's deception. They are very good at making people believe in their character and they adapt to the situation. You needed people to answer phones and he made himself useful, when in fact all he wanted was information. It was a thrill for him watching us trying to catch him. Don't beat yourself up about it. He fooled everyone and had been for years." He smiled at her. "But you took him down. You gotta be happy about that?"

Jenna sighed. "Yeah, he won't be able to kill again." She glanced at the house. "Sometimes I wish we could raze murder houses to the ground."

"It's over, Jenna." Kane headed back to the office. "The DA can take it from here."

When they arrived back at the office, Rio wanted to speak to Jenna and followed them upstairs. She sat behind her desk. "Is there a problem?"

"I'm not sure." Rio sat down in a chair opposite. "We set up trail cams as you ordered and I added one for the horse breeder, Bryce Withers."

Jenna frowned. "I thought we'd all decided he didn't fit the profile." She cleared her throat. "I've never been one hundred percent wrong before. John Dimock's behavior is a lesson to us all."

"I added the camera for a reason and it wasn't because of the murders." Rio leaned forward, his expression earnest. "It's aimed at the road leading to his property, so it doesn't break any laws. The thing is, when we interviewed him we disturbed a shipment of horse pellets. That's not unusual but he had armed guards around the truck, which made me suspicious. I questioned him about the guards and he told me he'd had shipments stolen before." He met Jenna's gaze. "I went back in the files and couldn't find one mention of him calling us about missing horse pellets and he'd need us to make a report for his insurance claim."

"So, you figure something else is happening there?" Kane dropped into a chair and looked at him. "Have you watched any of the footage from his ranch?"

"Yeah, and it's just normal stuff, no big shipments of feed, but I guess he'd receive a delivery only every few weeks. We collected the trail cams today, but I was reluctant to take down the one at the Withers ranch until I'd spoken to you."

Thinking of the possibilities, Jenna tapped on her bottom lip. "You did the right thing leaving the trail cam. He might get a delivery biweekly or monthly. It's a big ranch. Discovering if he is doing something illegal will take time. Check the camera feed and make a note of the time and dates he takes a delivery. If it follows a pattern, we'd be able to use a drone to watch a delivery and if the men are armed again, that might be enough probable cause for a search warrant." She leaned forward on the desk. "Get at it if you believe it's warranted. It might take a couple of months to get a case together, but if Withers is hauling drugs into my county, I want him stopped."

"You got it." Rio stood. "Winter is coming and crime seems to slow down for a time, and we'll have nothing but grunt work to do anyway." He nodded to Kane and left the room.

Jenna smiled as his footsteps sounded down the stairs. "I like it when they think out of the box. It sure makes my job easier."

"You can say that again." Kane smiled.

EPILOGUE

Halloween

The members of the team had parked their trucks outside the sheriff's department and walked in a group along Main. Jenna couldn't believe how hard the townsfolk had worked to recreate a Halloween wonderland for the kids. They'd strung twinkling orange and purple lights across the storefronts. Carved pumpkins sat glowing on porches and all around them kids laughed as they dashed from house to house, or store to store, gathering the treats from people in various costumes with baskets of candy. The horror of the previous week had been forgotten and everyone became involved in the evening. As they walked the motion-sensor automatons sprang into action to surprise the children. Witches cackled from porches, and as they passed an alleyway, they heard a werewolf howling in the shadows.

When they'd dressed in their costumes back at the ranch, and Kane had stepped out as the Grim Reaper wearing a ragged black cape, a skeleton mask, and his shoulder holster, Tauri had doubled up with laughter. Tears ran down his cheeks and he rolled on the floor holding his ribs. Jackson just looked at his father and then tried to pull off Kane's mask. Jenna had to admit that Kane looked the part when he hunched over and walked using a faux scythe, as a staff. Although he'd been hesitant to wear the costume after the horrific murders, the other members of the team insisted that there would be many Grim Reapers wandering the streets and everyone knew that the current serial killer had been locked up. For tonight at least, the town was safe.

As they walked, Tauri and Jaime rushed to each doorway and Kane led Jackson, but soon the little boy grew tired and before they'd walked a hundred yards, he carried the exhausted toddler on his shoulders. Beside him, Carter, dressed as a cowboy, as usual, cracked jokes with the other parents. He carried his own bucket and winked at Jenna every time someone filled it with candy. She shook a finger at him. "You'll make yourself sick."

"Not if I share it with you." Carter grinned and moved back into the crowd. "Look, Tauri, the next place has chocolate. Run, I'm right behind you."

As Tauri, Jaime, and Wolfe's youngest daughter, Anna, took off at a run, vanishing in the swarms of children, Jo came to her side. "I'll stay at the ranch tonight. I've had a long day and I'm beat. I'll watch the kids. I'm sure Raya is exhausted as well."

"Are you sure?" Kane looked at her. "They'll all be asleep before long and Raya usually dozes on the sofa until we get home."

"Yeah, I want to look into John Dimock's files a little more." Jo smiled. "He intrigues me. I'd really like to interview him and see how he ticks."

Jenna bent to pick up a fallen cape and then caught sight of the little girl who'd dropped it. She held it out and the girl ran toward her and allowed her to attach it. "There you go."

"Thank you, Sheriff Alton." The child skipped away swinging her bucket of candy.

"We all need to thank you and Deputy Kane for saving our town once again." A woman, stepped down from the grocery store, smiled at Jenna, and handed her a box of chocolates. "Since you've been our sheriff, I sleep better at night."

Wanting to refuse but seeing Kane's slight shake of the head, she just smiled. "Thank you, that's very kind of you."

By the time they'd reached Aunt Betty's Café, Jackson was starting to fall asleep. His little cheek rested on top of Kane's head and his eyelids drooped. Jenna held up her arms. "He's almost asleep. I think it's time we called it a night." She turned to Raya. "Would you mind taking them home?"

"I can take Jaime." Jo moved closer. "Anna too if it's easier. I have Jenna's SUV."

"Not a problem." Raya and Jo collected the children and they all headed back to the vehicles.

"We have a short time before the ball starts." Kane checked his watch and flicked a glance at Wolfe, who was walking behind him with Norrell. "Coffee at Aunt Betty's?"

"Yeah, sure." Wolfe followed them inside and they took their usual seats.

It seemed suddenly quiet as the noise from the children and displays was muted when the door closed behind them. They all ordered coffee. Jenna stared at Kane, looking lovingly at a man eating a wedge of pie. "There will be plenty of food at the ball."

"The problem is you never know what they're giving you to eat." Kane raised an eyebrow. "Last year they had boiled eggs that looked like eyeballs." He shuddered. "Spaghetti that looked like brains." He stood. "I'm getting pie. Anyone else want some?"

"I'm fine." Carter pushed candy into his mouth. "I have this entire bucket to get through."

"We'll be peeling him off the ceiling before long." Norrell chuckled. "Carter you're too big for a kid."

"You gotta love Halloween." Carter grinned at her. "It's my favorite time of the year, well apart from Christmas, Easter, and Thanksgiving... I guess."

"Jenna." Wolfe had on his serious face. "You know Raven is taking Emily to the ball?"

Jenna nodded. "Yeah, and you've sent Julie along as chaperone." She shook her head. "It's not necessary. Raven is solid. He's a really nice guy and he's respected your wishes and waited until Em passed all her requirements to become an ME before asking her out on a real date."

"I know." Wolfe gripped his coffee cup so tight his knuckles went white. "I like him but what if he wants to marry her and they move away?" He shook his head. "I want her to be happy but I don't want to have the family scattered in the wind."

"I've told you a hundred times, Shane, Raven will never leave the mountains." Norrell squeezed his arm. "I've spoken to him at length about his intentions toward Emily. He doesn't hide anything. He's very honest and straightforward with people. It may never happen. You must allow her to make up her own mind and carve her own future. It's time for you to stand on the sidelines and watch." She pressed a kiss on his cheek. "It's our time now."

"Yeah, y'all are right." Wolfe sipped his coffee. "I'm a meddling old fool." He smiled at Norrell. "Well, not that old. I can still Texas two-step around a ballroom." He looked at Kane. "Eat up. I want to dance with my wife."

The ballroom at the city hall took Jenna's breath away. Doormen greeted them dressed as skeletons, and waiters resembling zombies escorted them to their table. The entire hall had been transformed into a gothic setting. Every table was covered with a black tablecloth and in the center a jack-o'-lantern glowed. Above them, cobwebs draped over the chandeliers held large fat black spiders with red glowing eyes. The band was playing country music but somehow they'd turned them into eerie melodies, and a man sat out front of the band playing the fiddle dressed as Frankenstein.

When Raven arrived with Emily and Julie, for once he seemed a little unsure of himself, constantly adjusting his costume, his attention frequently moving to Wolfe. They drank spiked cider and teased each other about their costumes. Carter was in full flight and joined in the costume contest, playing up his cowboy persona by walking with bandy legs and drawing his revolver and spinning it. He didn't win and returned to the table looking quite sad, and then Wendy from Aunt Betty's Café came over and asked him to dance and suddenly the old Carter was back, toothpick and all.

Jenna and Kane wandered around the buffet. She was pleased to see Kane suitably impressed with the barbecue sliders, pumpkin pies, and caramel apples. He even took a plate from one of the committee members and grinned at Jenna.

"They're not eyeballs." He chuckled.

Before long the dance got into full swing with foot stomping and fiddle playing and even a few slower songs. Jenna watched Emily drag Raven onto the dance floor and when a slow song came on, she could see the smitten expression on his face. She turned to Kane. "If you've finished eating, I wouldn't mind one dance. I promise not to step on your feet."

They shared a slow dance, their first time out alone for the evening since Jackson was born. Jenna placed her arms around his neck. "It's been a tough year."

"It has but we made it." Kane brushed a strand of hair behind her ear and kissed her nose. "Did I ever tell you how much I love you?"

Jenna smiled. "Every day. I love you too."

The song finished and Kane led her out to a balcony. He removed his cape and wrapped it around her shoulders to keep her warm. Jenna stared at her town twinkling all around them and turned to look at everyone inside having a good time. She had Kane, her boys, and the best friends ever. Contentment flowed through her as Kane's arms came around her and his chin rested on her shoulder.

"It looks so pretty, doesn't it?" Kane whispered in her ear.

Jenna nodded. "I'll never leave. I want to grow old here, with you."

"So do I." Kane nuzzled her neck. "It looks like you're stuck with me."

She'd come to Black Rock Falls broken and so had he. Their jobs had thrown them together and constantly placed their lives in peril, but had also granted them this moment of pure joy.

A LETTER FROM D.K. HOOD

Dear Reader,

Thank you so much for choosing my novel and coming with me on Kane and Alton's thrilling Halloween story *Their Haunted Hearts*. If you'd like to keep up to date with all my latest releases, just sign up at the website link below. Your details will never be shared.

www.bookouture.com/dk-hood

Writing about Halloween is a favorite for me. I love the spooky settings and can allow my imagination to run wild. Winter is coming to Black Rock Falls and next time we'll be celebrating the holidays. Snow, ice, and blizzards are forecast, and if that's not bad enough, someone will arrive in town obsessed with sending Jenna and Dave on a roller-coaster ride of madness and mayhem. I hope you'll join me for Book 28.

If you enjoyed *Their Haunted Hearts,* I would be very grateful if you could leave a review and recommend my book to your friends and family. I really enjoy hearing from readers, so feel free to ask me questions at any time. You can get in touch on my Facebook page, X, through my website, or D.K. Hood's Readers' Group on Facebook. Here, we chat about books, have giveaways, and from time to time, I offer members the chance to volunteer to be an extra in one of my upcoming stories. Anyone who appears as an extra receives a special gold seal and an autographed bookplate for their paperback.

Thank you so much for your support. Until next time,

D.K. Hood

www.dkhood.com

facebook.com/dkhoodauthor
x.com/DKHood_Author

ACKNOWLEDGMENTS

To my wonderful, talented editor, Helen, and #TeamBookouture.

PUBLISHING TEAM

Turning a manuscript into a book requires the efforts of many people. The publishing team at Bookouture would like to acknowledge everyone who contributed to this publication.

Audio
Alba Proko
Sinead O'Connor
Melissa Tran

Commercial
Lauren Morrissette
Hannah Richmond
Imogen Allport

Cover design
Blacksheep

Data and analysis
Mark Alder
Mohamed Bussuri

Editorial
Helen Jenner
Ria Clare

Copyeditor
Ian Hodder

Proofreader
Claire Rushbrook

Marketing
Alex Crow
Melanie Price
Occy Carr
Cíara Rosney
Martyna Młynarska

Operations and distribution
Marina Valles
Stephanie Straub
Joe Morris

Production
Hannah Snetsinger
Mandy Kullar
Nadia Michael

Publicity
Kim Nash
Noelle Holten
Jess Readett
Sarah Hardy

Rights and contracts
Peta Nightingale
Richard King
Saidah Graham

Manufactured by Amazon.ca
Bolton, ON